A DESPERATE REMEDY

When Miss Decima Wells sets out in May 1836 to see the astonishing sight of four giraffes walking from London Docks to the newly created Zoological Gardens, she has no idea that her expedition will have such dangerous and far-reaching consequences. Nor does Alexander Peverell, also there to see the spectacle. Newly returned from India, where he has made his fortune, he is concerned only with his father's failing health and his brother Hugh's activities. Matters are not helped by Decima's father, who seeks to entrap Alexander as a husband for his daughter . . .

Books by Elizabeth Hawksley
Published by The House of Ulverscroft:

LYSANDER'S LADY
THE CABOCHON EMERALD
CROSSING THE TAMAR

ELIZABETH HAWKSLEY

A DESPERATE REMEDY

Complete and Unabridged

ULVERSCROFT
Leicester

First published in Great Britain in 2000 by
Robert Hale Limited
London

First Large Print Edition
published 2002
by arrangement with
Robert Hale Limited
London

British Library CIP Data

Hawksley, Elizabeth, 1944 –
A desperate remedy.—Large print ed.—
Ulverscroft large print series: romance
1. England—Social life and customs—19th century
—Fiction 2. Historical fiction 3. Large type books
I. Title
823.9′14 [F]

ISBN 0–7089–4623–2

Published by
F. A. Thorpe (Publishing)
Anstey, Leicestershire

Set by Words & Graphics Ltd.
Anstey, Leicestershire
Printed and bound in Great Britain by
T. J. International Ltd., Padstow, Cornwall

This book is printed on acid-free paper

To Prem
with love

Acknowledgements

My grateful thanks to Prem Beggs, who checked the Indian sections; and to John Olley, who saved me from various architectural errors.

1

Miss Decima Wells, who would be twelve at the end of July, 1827, glowered down at her breakfast plate — she was good at glowering. She kicked her brother Timothy hard on the ankle. He yelped. Serve him right for a tell-tale.

Behind her, in the breakfast parlour in Bloomsbury Square, the two footmen exchanged smirks. Neither of them cared for Master Timothy, who was not above sneaking if one of them nipped out to dally with a nursemaid or have a jar at the local tavern. Miss Decima, the youngest of Mr Wells's ten children, and the only daughter, was known to be a handful.

'Well, Miss?' demanded her father. 'Reading a novel in church? I might have guessed it. Do you have anything to say for yourself?'

'No, Papa.' Decima tossed her head and looked at him as insolently as she dared.

Her father glared at her for a moment and Decima stuck her chin out further. Mr Wells turned to his sister, a faded lady in her fifties, who had brought up Decima after the death of her mother a few years ago, and who now occupied an unhappy position in the household, halfway between guest and indigent relative. 'Ellen, it's your job to see that Decima is brought up as befits a lady. These old Yorkshire ways won't do now, you know. My position in life has altered — altered considerably. The family's new status must command respect and I cannot condone my daughter behaving like a hoyden.'

Ellen flushed painfully and twisted her hands in her lap.

'It's not Aunt Ellen's fault,' protested Decima, 'so don't blame her. And it wasn't a novel. I was reading *The Political Register*.'

Reading a Radical newspaper was guaranteed to infuriate her father, as she well knew. Mr Wells's face turned crimson, he raised his fist and brought it crashing down on the table so that all the china trembled. He tore into her lack of manners and her disobedience.

'At least Timothy knows how to behave like a gentleman's son!'

Behind him, the footmen exchanged sceptical glances: Mr Wells was an upstart if ever there was one! He had made a fortune in cotton and everything in the room, from the brand-new mahogany table to the over-carved backs to the chairs, cried out new money.

Mr Wells dismissed his sister and daughter from the dining-room, Decima swept her father an over-exaggerated curtsey, which trod a fine line between insolence and deference, stuck her tongue out at Timothy and left the room.

They retreated upstairs to the drawing-room — Decima going up the stairs two at a time — where Miss Wells sank down onto a chair and fanned herself.

'Decima, how could you be so wicked? You know what store your pa lays by proper behaviour in church.'

'He only cares because of what people might think,' retorted Decima. But she saw how worried her aunt was and relented. 'I'm sorry, Aunt Ellen. I just cannot bear it when Timothy sneaks on me.' She petted and soothed Ellen back into her usual placidity and then took herself up to her own room, where she locked the door and sat on her bed, staring hopelessly at the carpet.

It was all so unfair and things weren't going to improve as she got older. She was the only daughter and already her father was grooming her for a suitable marriage — by which he meant, if not into the aristocracy, then at least into the gentry. She must be biddable, never express an opinion and grow up to show off her family's new wealth. Only last month, she had been forced into uncomfortably tight stays, whose whalebone dug into her sides.

Furthermore, he had ordered that she spend an hour a day on the backboard to improve her posture.

All she could do to express her defiance was to rebel as much as she dared.

This time, however, she had gone too far. After a week of having to eat her meals up in the old nursery — 'If you behave like a child, then you must be treated like one' — Decima was summoned downstairs to her father's study.

'You are to go to your brother Edmund,' he informed her coldly. 'If your Aunt Ellen cannot bring you up to have the manners of a lady, then Mrs Wells must. She comes from a most superior family . . .'

''One of the Lincolnshire Spaldings','' muttered Decima. She couldn't bear Edmund's wife, Maria, though she was never allowed to call her that, it was always 'Mrs Wells'.

'Edmund has my leave to chastise you severely, if you do not do as you are told. He is sending his coach and Miss Matlock will come down to accompany you on the journey. You will leave on Friday.'

Decima looked at him with shocked eyes, 'Oh no, Papa, please,' she begged. She detested Edmund almost as much as Timothy, and Miss Matlock, a poor relation of Mrs Wells, was a woman of rigid propriety, whose thin lips never opened but to utter some moral platitude.

'You may go, Decima. Close the door behind you.'

It was useless. Miss Matlock arrived to take charge of her. The maids packed up her things. Decima kissed a weeping Ellen and stepped into Edmund's coach as if stepping into a tumbril.

It was not a long journey. Edmund lived in Surrey, near Guildford, and they arrived that evening. Decima was greeted coldly by her brother and sister-in-law and sent at once to the nursery.

The next few weeks were dreadful. Decima was allowed downstairs for dinner if there were no guests, otherwise she had to stay in the nursery with Edmund's spoilt children. Mrs Wells's conversation consisted almost entirely of references to her own exalted social status. 'Your father was right to send you to me,' she informed Decima. 'I believe my tone to be particularly superior. Many have remarked on it. But then, I was a Spalding, you know.'

'What's a Spalding?' asked Decima naughtily. 'It sounds like a sort of apple.'

Mrs Wells looked down her thin nose. 'I hope you are not being impertinent, Decima?

5

I keep a birch rod for use on impertinent girls. The Lincolnshire Spaldings are one of the first families in the country.'

If the Spaldings were that special, thought Decima mutinously, why had she chosen to marry Edmund? He was wealthy, to be sure, but the family was, until very recently, Trade. She remained unimpressed. Nevertheless, Mrs Wells was not averse to using the birch rod and Decima swiftly learnt to button her lip.

The highlight of Mrs Wells's week was meeting Sir George Peverell of Peverell Park after church and hearing him say, 'Good morning, Mrs Wells. Fine hunting weather, eh? Shall you come to the meet on Saturday?'

Later that day, she would be sure to start a sentence with, 'As Sir George said to me only this morning . . . '

Decima, in increasingly rebellious mood, didn't see that Sir George was anything to write home about; a crusty old man, fond of his horses and the bottle. Why should his views be so sought after?

Possibly Mrs Wells realized that Decima was not as deferential as she should be, for relations between them rapidly soured. 'She's so pert,' she complained to her husband. 'And I suspect her of being deep. Let her stay in the nursery and amuse the children.'

Decima became desperate. After the horrors of Mrs Wells's four spoilt children, Timothy's sneaking seemed very minor; at least there was only one of him. After one dreadful day with her nephews and nieces, who pulled her hair, pinched her and threw ink pellets, Decima decided that enough was enough. The next time her niece flicked an ink pellet at her, Decima marched across the room and calmly tipped the whole bottle over Anna-Maria's head.

The resulting row was of Herculean proportions. Decima was soundly whipped and sent home in disgrace, without even Miss Matlock to accompany her. The relief was indescribable. Decima realized that she had found the tactic she wanted. If standing up for herself meant that she didn't have to ape Mrs Wells's depressing gentility or amuse her appalling children, then that's what she'd do.

There had been only one bright spot to the visit, and that was her discovery of the camelopard.

Edmund's copy of *The Times* informed its readers that the Pacha of Egypt, Mohamet Ali, had presented the Emperor of France and the King of England with a camelopard each. Every few days, the progress of these strange creatures was reported. The last she'd heard, before she'd been sent home, was that the English camelopard was in quarantine in Malta.

It was the name which fascinated her. When she was a little girl, her mother used to read her Greek legends with their tales of centaurs and satyrs. According to the reports, the camelopard was half camel and half leopard. The notion that modern creatures could be hybrids, like centaurs and satyrs, struck a chord. Decima felt that she herself was a hybrid; a questing mind in an unsatisfactory female body.

Once she returned home, Decima continued to read her father's copy of *The Times*. She had to wait until it was a day old, for Mr Wells firmly believed that females shouldn't concern themselves with news and commerce, and eagerly scanned it for news of the camelopard. For months there had been nothing, but Decima had become far better informed about current affairs in the process.

At last, her patience was rewarded; the French camelopard had reached Paris. '*It was the most singular sight to see, its elegant head reached to the foliage of the trees; its long neck rose gracefully above the throng; its well-set large black eye was filled with mildness and joy . . . Yesterday, it took its first walk.*'

On the promise of good behaviour, Decima

was once again allowed down into the breakfast-room. She put on a saintly resignation, which infuriated Timothy far more than open defiance and, for her father's benefit, an exaggerated decorum. She was well aware that he was suspicious of it, but there was nothing he could do. At least it meant that she and Aunt Ellen were left alone.

The moment her father and Timothy had left the breakfast-room, Decima reached for *The Times* to see what had become of the camelopard destined for England. Yes, there was news. It was coming, it really was, '*The camelopard, which we now possess, and which has the astonishment and admiration of all which have beheld it, was caught in the environs of Sennaar, in Africa, by the troops of the Pacha of Egypt . . .*'

It was expected within the next fortnight, arriving on the ship *Penelope*. She would see it, she vowed. Even if she had to run away from home, she would see it.

Alas for Decima, the camelopard arrived unheralded. The first she heard of it was in *The Times* of 14 August, which announced that it was now in Windsor Great Park. It had arrived on the 12th and had spent a couple of days in a lofty cellar belonging to a Mr Robertson of the Duchy Wharf in the Savoy, accompanied by two Egyptian cows. They had then been taken to Windsor. When the camelopard died a couple of years later, at about the same time as her Aunt Ellen, Decima cried as much for the camelopard as for her aunt.

As the years passed, Decima found herself thinking that, if only she'd somehow managed to see it, then her life would be different. Of course, that was nonsense, but she couldn't entirely push it away.

In 1834, when Decima was eighteen, another sister-in-law, Mrs Alfred Wells, a lady as anxious for the family's advancement as even Mr Wells could wish, engaged to oversee Decima's come-out and presentation at one of Queen Adelaide's drawing-rooms. Her father's hopes were high. With the lure of a considerable portion, and with Mrs Alfred's push, Decima would capture some gentleman of breeding. 'My daughter, Lady So-and-so,' Mr Wells imagined himself saying.

It didn't happen.

'Why isn't she taking?' demanded Mr Wells of Mrs Alfred. The only men who had asked for his daughter's hand were obvious undesirables, in desperate need of rescue from their creditors.

'Gentlemen don't like ladies who have opinions. Decima has opinions. Besides, she has too much hair and her cheeks are pink. A refined pallor is the thing.' The demure blues and pinks that Mrs Alfred considered suitable for a debutante, did not suit Decima. At five feet eight and a half inches, she was far too tall and her figure too generous for the fashionable ethereal look.

'Takes after her mother,' said Mr Wells grumpily. 'What about that Mr Pownall? Will he come up to scratch?' Pownall was a long way down Mr Wells's list of elegible men, but at least his father was an Honourable.

'Decima has already refused him,' snapped Mrs Alfred.

'What!'

'She says she doesn't wish to marry a man who gambles and who opens and shuts his mouth like a fish.'

Decima, in fact, had been more forthright.

'I don't want to marry at all,' she announced. 'I don't want to be at some man's beck and call and be forever in the straw producing squalling babies.'

'Decima! Such vulgarity!' Mrs Alfred was a firm believer in the unmentionable facts of married life remaining — unmentioned. 'To be married must be every lady's ambition. A lady can only be happy when she is the helpmeet of some proper gentleman. My dear Alfred, for example, is all consideration.'

Decima eyed her sceptically. Mrs Alfred

had given her husband eight pledges of her affection, as she coyly called them, and Alfred showed every sign of demanding that she produce eight more. She had only recently recovered from two miscarriages within six months. If Mrs Alfred had five minutes to call her own, Decima had never heard of it.

'I hate being *out*,' said Decima. 'My clothes have to be seen to be made by the most expensive modiste — and look at them! They are completely overloaded with frills and lace. I feel like a piece of iced cake. I might just as well go around with a label saying 'Money — please apply here!'.'

'Your clothes are exactly what a young girl should be wearing,' said Mrs Alfred stiffly. She had chosen the pale-pink silk herself. 'Your papa wants your value to be known.'

'His value, you mean.'

'Don't be vulgar, Decima.'

Mr Wells did not give up. Every year he pushed Decima into the season under the aegis of one or other of her sisters-in-law, and every year he had the humiliation of seeing her return unwed.

Decima hated every moment. It was like being in a cattle-market, she thought. She came to loathe the young men paraded in front of her with their braying laughs and insufferable airs of superiority. By the time she was twenty, she was feeling desperate. She had very little money of her own — her Aunt Ellen had left £3,000 in trust for her when she was twenty-one. Her father was generous with pin money, but he had threatened to stop it whenever her undutifulness angered him. She certainly couldn't rely on it.

What she wanted was to live her own life — whatever that was. Oh, why couldn't she have been born a boy? Then at least she could go out and make her own way in the world.

The 1836 season began. By May, Decima was struggling, once again, to be interested in clothes and invitations. Mrs Alfred was once again in attendance. But this time, something far more important was claiming Decima's attention.

The camelopards were returning — with a new name. *The Morning Herald* announced that four giraffes, named Mabrouk, Selim, Zaida and Guib Allah, were arriving shortly and would live in the new Zoological Gardens. Their names sounded wonderfully exotic, like something out of the *Arabian Nights*, and this time Decima vowed to see them.

After her father and Mrs Alfred had left the breakfast-room, Decima picked up the discarded copy of *The Morning Herald* and scanned it eagerly. The giraffes would be walking from Blackwall that very afternoon.

To add to the excitement, they would be accompanied by their Nubian and Maltese attendants, in Arab dress, too! They would be coming along High Holborn and she could easily walk there. To hell with the milliner and mantuamaker; she would send a note cancelling them.

She had it all planned in a trice. It never crossed her mind that young ladies out alone and wearing expensive clothes were likely to be accosted, but then, she'd rarely been out by herself. Still less, did she consider pickpockets. She would have only a few shillings in her purse — what else would anybody want to steal? She dismissed any possible unpleasantness from her mind as of no importance, and concentrated instead on the giraffes.

Strange how the idea of seeing Zaida, Mabrouk, Selim and Guib Allah was so appealing. Somehow, they had assumed the status of myth in her mind — they stood for all the opportunities in the outside world which she had never experienced.

After luncheon, she excused herself saying that she had a headache and would lie down quietly for an hour or so. No, she did not want laudanum, only to rest undisturbed. Once alone, she changed into her walking-dress, made sure that the coast was clear and left the house with mixed feelings of guilt and euphoria.

★ ★ ★

In 1836, Alexander Peverell, at twenty-seven the youngest son — though some said no son at all — of Sir George Peverell, returned to England from India where he had amassed a fortune. Society was delighted. He was tall, good-looking with a pale-olive skin and clear grey eyes — and worth at least £8,000 a year.
Then the rumours started.

★ ★ ★

Sir George, then plain Mr Peverell, had gone to India at the end of the eighteenth century with his bride and joined the East India Company. They settled in Calcutta, where Mr Peverell rapidly amassed a fortune. Mrs Peverell had, very properly, presented her husband with two sons in quick succession, but her health collapsed. Her only hope was to go to the hills. The journey to Simla, then a small hill station, took weeks. They travelled by river-boat and bullock cart and finally by *janpan*, when they were carried up precipitous rocky paths amid banks of scarlet rhododendrons. Mrs Peverell nearly died and

15

never recovered her health. She lived quietly with her two sons, Frederick and Hugh, until they reached a suitable age to be sent home.

At eight and ten years old, Hugh and Freddy kissed their mother a tearful goodbye and set off on the long journey back to England. Hugh was particularly distraught. He clung to his mother and would not let go.

'Don't send me away, Mama!' His hot little face, awash with tears, pressed itself into her bodice.

Mrs Peverell was crying too, but there was no help for it. Too many English children died in India and her husband insisted they must be properly educated as gentlemen, in England.

Hugh's fingers were prised open and, sobbing bitterly, he was carried to the *janpan* which was to take them down the precipitous path on the first stage of their journey to England.

Many mothers chose to return with their children, but Mrs Peverell feared that she would not survive the journey. She watched with anguished eyes as her little boys disappeared. She felt desperately lonely.

Two years after her sons' departure, and infrequently visited by her husband, Mrs Peverell suddenly produced Alexander.

Mrs Peverell and her husband were fair

and brown-eyed. Alexander had a pale-olive skin and his eyes were a clear grey. Furthermore, the whispers went, Mrs Peverell had been attended by Sikander, a handsome Pathan . . .

Sir George remembered seeing Alexander for the first time. The baby was about seven months old and was crawling with great determination along the veranda of the bungalow in the hill station. Every now and then he would stop and rest on one elbow, with one leg bent over the other, so that he reclined like some miniature Roman emperor.

Sir George watched him for a long time — a strong-minded baby with an olive skin and clear grey eyes. Not one of his begetting, he felt sure. He could see his wife out of the corner of his eye, chewing her lip, her fingers making a fine mess of her needlework.

'You have a handsome son there, Clara.'

'Indeed, Mr Peverell, and he is a good, strong baby.'

'Good-natured?'

'Oh yes. He hardly ever cries.'

The baby stopped imitating a Roman emperor, crawled towards Sir George, grasped his leg and pulled himself into a sitting position. He smiled up, showing four baby teeth.

'What's his name?'

'Alexander. A — after my brother.'

'Hm. I like him. He'll do.' Sir George had always had a good eye for bloodstock and, possibly, he was still thinking along these lines. The baby would make a fine Peverell.

Later, he met one of the bearers, a man with aquiline features and clear grey eyes. A Pathan, he guessed. Fiercely proud, they had the reputation of being formidable fighters. Sir George looked him over carefully. 'What's your name?'

'Sikander, *sahib*.'

'You've been looking after my wife?'

'The *memsahib* was unhappy.' Sikander spoke quietly, but he looked Sir George straight in the eye and one hand rested lightly on his curved dagger.

'I see.' Sir George drew his own conclusions.

Being a considerate man, he made a point of visiting his wife's bedroom before he left for the plains, and allowed himself to be seen emerging by his wife's maid. But Mrs Peverell bore no more children.

★   ★   ★

Unlike his elder brothers, Alexander stayed in India with his mother. Frederick and Hugh went to live with their uncle and aunt at

Peverell Park in the county of Surrey and in due course went to Eton and Oxford. After the first shock was over, Frederick settled down very happily at Peverell Park. He liked his uncle and aunt and the country life. Hugh became withdrawn. The only person he talked to was one of the housemaids, Dorrie Wimborne, who smuggled him sugar plums. Their letters to their mother grew stilted and infrequent. Frederick usually remembered to send his love to his little brother, whom he had never seen. Hugh never mentioned him.

Alexander grew up a good-looking, self-confident and courageous child. He shot, fished and climbed about the hills with Kumar and Kamal, Sikander's sons. He spoke Hindustani and Punjabi before he spoke English.

'My wild boy,' Mrs Peverell would say, with fond pride. But she insisted that he spoke English correctly and learnt proper manners. He might be the indulged youngest son, but he would not be spoilt and petulant like so many British children.

When Alexander was fifteen his mother died. Two months later, Mr Peverell inherited his brother's title, became Sir George and sailed back to England with his youngest son and settled down at Peverell Park. Alexander was packed off to Eton.

'Well, Hugh,' said Frederick, the evening after Sir George's and Alexander's arrival, 'what do you think of our new brother, eh?'

Hugh was silent for a moment, then spat out, 'The fellow's a blackamoor. I think he's an impostor, that's what I think.'

'You can't mean that!' Frederick was shocked. 'He's been living in India. Of course, he's brown. It'll fade. What do you mean, an impostor? You're not saying Mama played our father false?'

Hugh shrugged. 'All I'm saying is that it's damned smoky. He doesn't even look like one of us. I can't stand him.'

'I like him. He's been very good with Janey.' Frederick had recently married and was the proud father of an eight-month-old daughter. Alexander had been up in the nursery playing with his niece. 'It shows a great deal of good nature in the boy.'

Hugh grunted.

Nobody thought to ask Alexander what he felt about his new home. He loathed it. It was cold, damp, foggy and he didn't fit in. Hugh taunted him and called him 'darky' and the brutality at Eton sickened him.

'Well, my boy,' said Sir George, in 1827 when Alexander was eighteen and leaving Eton. 'Your housemaster tells me that you don't want to go to Oxford.'

'I can't see the point, Papa,' said Alexander. He didn't say that his time at Eton had been one of utter misery. Homesick, grieving for his mother, and hating the fagging and flogging which made up life at Eton, he had merely existed from day to day. An aptitude for sport and an ability to fight back had earned him the respect of his peers, but he was glad to leave.

Sir George frowned. Hugh had come down from Oxford and refused to settle to anything — unless you counted his ridiculous desire to become an architect — hardly a proper career for a baronet's son. All he'd done was run up debts. He didn't want Alexander going the same way. 'What do you want to do, eh?'

'Go back to India. I'd like to do something that will take me round the country. Dealing in indigo or jute maybe. I speak Hindustani, Punjabi and some Urdu. It seems a pity to waste them.'

'Hm.' Dealing in some commodity was acceptable — providing it were in India. 'Would Hugh want to go with you, do you think?'

Alexander laughed. 'I doubt it.' He had never got on with Hugh, who usually referred to him — though never in Sir George's hearing — as 'that bastard'.

Sir George sighed but didn't argue. 'Very

well. I'll give you such letters of introduction as I can and four hundred a year. I hope you can make better use of it than Hugh does.'

'I shan't disgrace the family name.'

'I never thought you would,' said Sir George testily. 'You've turned out a fine Peverell.'

'Thank you, Papa.' Alexander had never asked for information about the rumours concerning his birth and Sir George had never offered any. All the same, Alexander was well aware of them — his brother Hugh had seen to that — and he was determined to make his own way in the world. If England looked at him askance, he would try the land of his birth. He would work hard and make his fortune and then see whether England had anything to offer him and whether he wanted it.

⋆　⋆　⋆

Alexander was in India for eight years. When he finally returned in January 1836, he had made a substantial fortune.

Sir George, older and frailer now, greeted him affectionately and allowed Alexander to kiss him soundly on either cheek, something he would normally condemn as unmanly. 'Well, well, good to see you, m'boy.'

Alexander had turned into a fine man, he thought. He was tall and well-muscled and, in spite of being dressed as befitted an English gentleman, managed to look surprisingly foreign. Sir George had always relished the unusual and he was rather amused by his exotic son.

Frederick, whilst holding out his hand firmly to avoid any embrace, said cheerfully, 'Hello, Alex. Voyage all right?' He clapped his brother on the shoulder. 'I've got a nice bay gelding that might do you. I'll take you down to the stables tomorrow.' Alexander had brought back a number of cashmere shawls and finely embroidered saris for his sister-in-law and nieces, and Frederick felt that his generosity deserved a decent mount.

Hugh only grunted and muttered, 'Impostor.' The moment Alexander arrived, Hugh knew that he hated his dark, exotic good looks, his height and breadth of shoulder and his air of confidence. He was the usurper. He had been the favourite and had stayed in India with their mother.

Hugh tried never to think about his childhood. He could have returned to India once he'd left Eton, or after Oxford, and seen his mother, but he didn't. She had betrayed him. He would never go back. And then she had died and it was too late. Instead, his almost unknown father and interloper brother had returned and Hugh had been forced to see Alexander making himself at home at Peverell Park and sweet-talking Dorrie Wimborne for sugar plums, just as he had done when he was a lonely small boy.

Now Alexander was back, seemingly permanently.

Hugh decided that it would serve his so-called brother right if society learned just how shaky were his claims to be a gentleman.

★ ★ ★

'My dear,' whispered Lady Malton, 'have you heard the rumours about Mr Alexander Peverell? I really don't think he'll do.'

'They say he's worth eight thousand a year at least,' argued her friend, Mrs Coatham. 'I've invited him to Jane's dance. Why should I take my cue from that rackety creature, Hugh Peverell? What sort of man would slander his own mother? Sir George acknowledges Alexander as his son, and he should know.' Mr Peverell was rich, good-looking and had charming manners. She'd be a very poor parent not to make a push for him for Jane.

'Why does he live in Golden Square, then?' objected Lady Malton. 'Hardly an address to

24

inspire confidence.' All the same £8,000 a year was certainly worth considering — if not for her own daughter, then for a niece who could not afford to be so choosy.

A few days later, Mrs Coatham's elegantly engraved invitation to Jane's coming-out dance dropped through the letter-box of Alexander's house in Golden Square.

Alexander opened it, laughed, and tossed it to one side.

Catherine Thompson, who was either Alexander's illegitimate half-sister, or, if you believed Hugh Peverell, no relation at all, sat opposite him at the breakfast-table on this pleasant May morning in 1836. She was the result of an indiscretion between the young George Peverell and a gamekeeper's daughter. Catherine was a faded woman in her mid-forties and she ran Alexander's household for him.

'Shall you go?' she asked wistfully. She had never been to any dance of any kind.

'Mrs Coatham requests the pleasure of my money in supporting her daughter Jane in the manner to which she has become accustomed.'

'But you must marry sometime, and Jane may be very nice.'

Alexander made no comment. He was well aware that in some quarters he was accepted only because of his money, and he resented it.

Life had turned out to be more complicated than he had imagined at eighteen. Then, he thought that an independent fortune would secure his future and, of course, on one level it did. But he wanted to be accepted for who he was, not be forced to pay heavily for rumours about his birth to be ignored.

Alexander discovered that a number of his old schoolfellows from Eton, whilst welcoming his company in their clubs, were chary of introducing him to their sisters. His wealth made him acceptable as a gaming partner, but not always on the ballroom floor.

There were honourable exceptions to this, like his friend, Mr Bertram Camborne, but they were few and Alexander largely withdrew from polite society. He did not see why he should court humiliation.

There had been problems in India too, when he had fallen in love with Rhoda Sadberge. He was wealthy and well-respected and yet Mr Sadberge had refused to sanction an engagement. Alexander had said nothing of this to Catherine, or indeed to anybody, but there were times when he felt both lonely and angry.

'What about these giraffes then, James? Would you like to see them?' He turned to his twelve-year-old nephew, who was eating his toast and simultaneously trying to read a book under the table.

James looked up and nodded. He was a thin boy, just beginning to shoot up and his mother muttered darkly about outgrowing his strength. As a child he had suffered from infantile paralysis and one of his legs was in irons. He managed very well with a stick and hated any reference to his disability.

'Very well,' said Alexander. 'Catherine, you'd like to see the giraffes, wouldn't you? We'll take a cab to High Holborn, so you need not think to be tired.'

Catherine was well aware that the cab was there to spare James the walk — which he would certainly have attempted — and her own inclusion was incidental. She glanced once at the invitation, but did not revert to it. She knew well enough when her brother wanted to turn the subject. In fact, she'd rather not see the giraffes; they sounded too big and she was not reassured by accounts of their gentleness.

'Where would be the best place to see them?' she asked, stifling her fears.

★ ★ ★

Alexander noticed the girl at once. She was standing almost opposite him on the other

27

side of the street and holding on to a lamp-post. She was tall for a woman, which pleased him — he himself was six feet two inches in his stockinged feet. This girl was five feet eight or nine inches and taller than most of the women around her.

Her clothes were of excellent quality, although the colour of her walking dress — an over-bright blue — was appalling. She was a healthy-looking young woman. Her pink, flushed cheeks and round face with its determined chin and mouth too wide for beauty, made her look like a milkmaid out for a spree — except for the clothes, which spoke of wealth, if not taste. Her hair was far too thick, for it pushed up her bonnet in an absurd way. He raised his eye-glass to see her more clearly. Her large hazel eyes, just now widening in astonishment at the spectacle coming down the road, were fringed with dark lashes. No, not a beauty, he decided, but a face of decided character. What was she doing here alone?

Her expression was one of wonder and pleasure. She was smiling and her hands were clasped in front of her as if applauding. As he watched, her mouth opened slightly in an 'Ah!' of satisfaction.

'Now they are something like!' exclaimed James. 'They come from Abyssinia, you know.

I wonder how they were captured?'

'I hope they're safe,' murmured Catherine. She wasn't at all sure about the creatures coming towards them, whose heads were worryingly near the tops of the lamp-posts. She stepped closer to her brother's reassuring bulk.

Alexander forgot the girl. He looked down at Catherine and said, 'They won't harm you, you know. They only eat leaves.'

'Yes, but do *they* know that?' said Catherine.

Alexander laughed.

Decima saw Alexander without realizing that she was the object of his interest. Her gaze passed over him with a slight frown of distaste. He was tall. Her brothers were all tall and, insofar as she noticed him at all, it was as an unpleasant reminder of Edmund, Alfred, Peter, Bartholomew, John, Joseph, Roger, Stephen and Timothy — all of whom she cordially detested.

She was much more interested in the giraffes. She had never even imagined such a creature was possible — *The Morning Herald* had not shown any illustrations. The reality was so startling that she could hardly take it in. She whispered the names Zaida, Mabrouk, Selim and Guib Allah, to herself under her breath.

What on earth did they eat? Did they, could they, sit down? How did they sleep? She had a vision of them leaning against a tree with their eyes shut. Could their markings possibly be real? Or had somebody painted them with those jigsaw patterns? They were walking in an ungainly fashion, and every now and then, the young one skittered on the road and the crowd shrieked in simulated terror. Poor things, she thought. Were they homesick so far from Africa? Perhaps they were comforted by the presence of their attendants, splendidly exotic in their Arab costumes of long flowing robes and brightly coloured tasselled hats.

Long after they had disappeared up the road, the giraffes' long spindly legs and strange sloping shoulders stayed in her mind.

The crowd began to thin and still Decima stayed, one gloved hand on the lamp-post. Her ordinary life was so restricted that her mind was often stuck likewise. It was only occasionally, like today, that she remembered that there was a world outside.

She did not notice a small group of two men and one woman standing just behind her.

They had been eyeing her for some time. Bob, the younger man, wore a cap pulled well down and a much-patched but voluminous jacket. He was a 'dipper', that is he picked pockets, and he had already 'fanned' her skirts and found nothing beyond a knitted purse containing a couple of shillings and a lace handkerchief.

The woman with him gave him a nudge. He shook his head. 'She's a close 'un. Nowt worth bothering with.'

'She has lace on her petticoat, Bob. I saw it. Good stuff. And that gown's silk, if I'm not mistaken. It would fetch a quid or two.'

'Nah! In broad daylight? Come on, Nell.'

'Springer'll deal with her. She ain't with anybody. I wants that gown and the lace.'

The giraffes had gone, the crowd thinned, Decima gave a sigh and turned to go. Suddenly, it happened. Out of nowhere, the hook of an umbrella caught her legs. Someone pushed. She stumbled and fell heavily, she could feel the pavement coming up to meet her. There was a crack and blackness exploded inside her head.

Nell dropped a greasy shawl over her prone figure. Springer surreptitiously pocketed his cosh and, as he went to lift her up, Decima's bonnet fell off.

'Lots of hair, too,' said Nell greedily. She knew places that would buy hair. She watched while Springer slung Decima over his shoulder and reached out to finger the hair, now coming loose from its hairpins. Good thick stuff. She wasted no thoughts on Decima. A girl should look out for herself, that was her view. More fool her if she got nabbed.

Just the other side of High Holborn they entered St Giles. The broad thoroughfare vanished and they were now in a tall, narrow street with a running open gutter down the middle. The smell of dirt, offal, excrement and unwashed bodies was overpowering. Above them, an occasional window had a pole stuck out with washing drying on it — though there was not much chance of it staying clean. A group of children were poking at a dead rat. Springer shifted Decima's inert body and turned down a sidestreet, even dirtier than the one they had just left. Men lounged in doorways and a few shouted words of lewd encouragement. Springer grinned but didn't answer.

Eventually, they reached yet another turning. Here, the houses had once been handsome, with elegant fanlights and well-proportioned frontages, now few of them even had front doors, they had gone for firewood long ago. The treads of the stairs were worn and rotten and piles of excrement stood in corners.

Springer shouldered his way into one of the

dirtiest houses, trod up the stairs, avoiding the rotten treads with the ease of long practice, elbowed his way into a room on the first floor and dropped Decima on to a rusty bed with a stained and split mattress.

'You deal wiv 'er, Nell. I'm off for a jar.'

'You be back?' Nell gestured with a leer towards the unconscious figure.

Springer glanced down, 'Nah. I prefers them alive and kicking. No beauty, is she?' A dark bruise and a large lump were already disfiguring Decima's forehead.

'She banged herself somefink rotten,' said Bob worriedly. 'She be all ri'?'

Springer shuffled uneasily. 'She'll come round. I'm off.' They could hear him running down the stairs.

Nell looked down at the alarmingly pale figure. ' 'Ere, Bob, now don't you scarper. I'll set these off and cut 'er 'air and you can dump 'er in the alley.'

Bob watched as Nell removed Decima's dress and petticoats and then the boots — good leather he could see — and silk stockings.

' 'Ere, hold this.' Nell gave him a hank of hair. She cut off the tresses and folded them neatly. 'Good thick 'air,' she added approvingly.

'Now wot?' said Bob. The girl was lying in

her shift. 'We can't leave 'er outside like that. S'not right.'

'You's a soppy one.' But Nell had a soft spot for Bob and she rummaged around in a couple of filthy trunks at the end of the room and came back with a dirty blouse and a cheap cotton skirt. 'You put 'em on 'er, if you's so keen she's decent.'

'Nah, come on, Nell.'

Nell laughed and quickly and expertly dressed the inert body.

'Look, Nell, let's leave 'er 'ere, ri'? You come and have a bite to eat. I reckon she won't wake for a while. I'll take 'er outside after dark. Better that way, eh?'

Nell nodded. The girl had taken a hard knock, she'd be out for several hours yet. Even if she did wake, she'd be in no state to move. They'd lock her in, she'd be safe enough.

2

Decima drifted in and out of consciousness. She was vaguely aware of the smell of dirt, the stink of old clothes and the persistent odour of urine coming up from the mattress beneath her. When she managed to open her eyes, she took in her surroundings without interest. There were two large dirty sash windows with several panes missing and piles of old clothes on broken chairs, on hooks and spilling out of two old trunks at the end of the room.

Above her head was a fantastically plastered ceiling with a riot of fruit and swags of flowers and medallions of dancing nymphs. The ceiling rose had a chunk missing, revealing split laths. Decima frowned and then winced. Her head was by no means clear, but surely the ceiling belonged in a different sort of room? A stately home, perhaps? Her gaze wandered to a huge marble fireplace. On either side a caryatid held up a heavily carved mantelshelf, above which a handsome coat of arms was supported by snarling leopards. It didn't make sense. She closed her eyes.

When she awoke again, it was dark. There was a single candle at the other end of the room and the shadows of three huddled figures.

'What does this cove want, Springer?'

'What we all wants — more of the ready. His pa won't pay 'is gambling debts no more.' Springer spat onto the floor. 'Gi'us another drink, Nell.'

'Well? You going to do it?'

'Dunno, I don't trust 'im. 'E's the sort wot would get you to nab the silver, then shop you for the reward.'

'What's 'e offering?'

'A couple of ponies.'

'Fifty quid to go to 'is pa's country house, cosh the butler — who could be armed; maybe meet a brawny footman or two — who'd enjoy roughin' you up and 'andin' you to the nearest Justice; open the safe and get the silver? 'E's got to be joking. Wot's 'is name?'

'Peverell.' There was a pause. 'Look. Bob, I don't like it no more'n you do, but it's the dibs, see.'

'You want to dance upon nuffin'? Wot you fink, Nell?'

'Too dangerous. A couple o' 'undred quid, maybe. You needs a good cagsman.'

Springer turned to Bob. 'You interested?'

'Not at fifty quid, mate.'

Decima listened, without much interest, then she fell asleep again.

She didn't remember being lifted up and carried downstairs. Springer had borrowed a handcart from a friend and her inert body was laid on it and covered with an old blanket.

'Where to?' asked Bob. He peered down and was relieved to see that the girl was still breathing. He didn't want a murder hue and cry and it had been obvious from her clothes that she was one of the nobs. She'd have been missed, doubtless.

'Somewhere near one of the theatres. Plenty o'folks there. She'll be picked up by someone and it won't be our problem no more.' He spat onto the cobblestones.

'Behind Drury Lane?'

'That'll do. It's not far.' Springer straightened Decima's body and covered her more carefully. He didn't want nobody asking his business. They'd go nice and quiet — two honest tradesmen off home after an honest day's work.

It was dark. Street lamps sat in small pools of light and the gas hissed faintly. They kept to where it was darkest. Finally, they turned down Brydges Street into Vinegar Yard, which backed onto Drury Lane Theatre, and stopped. Bob looked round cautiously.

A couple of drunks were weaving their way unsteadily across Brydges Street. A few beggars huddled in doorways, but nobody who might be suspicious. He nodded.

Springer picked up Decima and put her down against a door. Then he picked up the blanket, threw it on the handcart and began to wheel it away. Bob, after one last look, followed him.

By and by, a couple of beggars came up. A woman, badly battered by the look of it. Nothing worth nicking, best not to get involved. They drifted away.

* * *

The curtain fell for the last time and the theatre audience began to gather their coats and wraps and leave. Alexander had not cared for the girl his friend Bertie Camborne had invited to amuse him. She had an artificial titter and a habit of squawking 'Oh, reely!' which annoyed him. He shook his head at Bertie as they helped the girls on with their wraps. Bertie and his current chère amie, Belinda, were going on to a 'finish', a tavern where they could drink into the small hours. Alexander saw the other girl into a cab, pressed half a sovereign on her, and left.

38

He turned down behind the theatre, taking several deep breaths to clear the gas fumes from his head. A tedious evening. Alexander was fond of Bertie — he had helped to make Eton bearable and Alexander had spent some happy holidays with the Cambornes — but why did Bertie always go for these half-wits? The night was young yet, not much after half-past eleven. He'd walk home, the fresh air would do him good. He turned in the direction of Covent Garden and nearly tripped over the body.

The woman was trying to get up. She had edged nearer the gas lamp and was reaching for it to steady herself. Drunk, Alexander thought in distaste, it was not uncommon to see drunken women in the gutter.

Then he saw the bump and the bruise. Coshed. She raised her head painfully and opened her eyes, trying to focus.

Alexander's gaze became intent. It was the girl he'd seen earlier looking at the giraffes, he was sure of it. He had a good memory for faces and he remembered those hazel eyes and that determined chin. But why was she wearing that filthy blouse and skirt and why was her hair sticking out as if she'd been shorn like a sheep?

'I'm afraid you're hurt, ma'am. May I help you?'

Decima looked up. 'Thank you, I don't seem to know . . . '

It must be her. She certainly didn't sound like a street girl. He reached out his hand and helped her to her feet. Yes, it must be the same woman. She was tall, as he remembered. She clutched the lamp-post and whispered, 'I'm sorry, I feel most dreadfully sick.' She turned away and vomited helplessly into the gutter.

Alexander gave her his handkerchief. She'd taken quite a knock, he could see the beads of sweat standing out on her forehead. He waited until she had recovered.

'If you will tell me where you live, ma'am, I'll engage to see you home. Your family will be worried.'

'I . . . I'm sorry, sir. I'm afraid I do not know.' The hazel eyes looked up at him and her face was flushed with shame. 'I . . . I cannot recall.'

The devil, thought Alexander, now what? He could hardly leave her here. He'd have to take her back to Golden Square and God knows what Catherine would think. Still, there was no help for it. 'I believe some loss of memory is inevitable with such a bang. If you will allow me, I'll take you to my house and my sister will look after you.'

He had expected some demur, but the girl

40

only frowned a little and winced. She allowed him to guide her towards Russell Street and the nearest cab stand.

Once inside the cab, Alexander leaned back against the squabs and watched the girl. She was sitting huddled into a corner and, in the glow of the occasional gas-light, he could see that her face was taut with pain and anxiety. Once she put up her hand and gingerly felt the bump on her forehead.

The cab swung round into Golden Square and stopped. The cabby let down the steps and Alexander helped Decima to alight. She stood quietly on the pavement in her bare feet and, though he could see gooseflesh standing up on her bare arms, she appeared not to notice. She has dignity, he thought. He paid the cabby and the horse and cab trotted off into the night.

Alexander never expected either his staff or Catherine to wait up for him, so he let himself in and locked the door behind them. As he did so, he heard somebody come down the stairs. It was his valet, Wilmot.

'Ooh, Mr Peverell,' Wilmot exclaimed, when he saw Decima. 'Whatever have you done, sir?' Wilmot had long fingernails on thin white hands and he waved them about agitatedly.

'Been playing Sir Galahad,' said Alexander,

wryly. 'You'll have to wake my sister and one of the maids. This poor lady needs help.' He turned to Decima and indicated one of the hall chairs. 'Sit down, ma'am, my sister will be down shortly to help you.'

Wilmot raised his eyes to the ceiling. '*What a to-do!*' he exclaimed.

'Don't just stand there,' said Alexander.

For the next half-hour all was bustle. The unusual noise woke the cook, who appeared in an astonishing frilled night cap and a voluminous purple dressing-gown. The two housemaids tiptoed downstairs, followed by the kitchen maids, Catherine and one of the footmen.

The atmosphere became one of gaiety and giggles. The footman enjoyed seeing the girls in nightdresses and dressing-gowns and pinched the bottom of the younger kitchen maid as she reached up to get the bath tub off its hook.

'Ger off, you,' she said, with a playful swipe.

'You poor thing!' exclaimed Catherine. The situation had been explained to her several times, but she had difficulty in taking it in. Still, once she understood that he had not brought home some fly-by-night, she was perfectly prepared to be sympathetic. 'Come upstairs, and get out of those dreadful clothes. Oh dear, I wonder what would be best?'

'Shall Meg and me bring up the bath, Mrs Thompson? And we could make up the bed in the Pink Room,' said Georgie, one of the housemaids. She was used to Catherine's indecision.

Eventually, Decima was clean and dry, her wound anointed and the old clothes taken away to be burned. Catherine lent her a nightdress.

Catherine watched as Georgie ran the warming pan over the bedsheet. 'You have your sleep out and I'm sure you'll feel more the thing in the morning.'

Decima obediently climbed into bed.

'I'm afraid I don't know your name, my dear.'

'Neither do I,' said Decima bleakly.

'It really doesn't matter,' said Catherine quickly, seeing tears in her guest's eyes. 'I am Mrs Thompson and you are in the household of my brother, Mr Peverell. Pray, do not worry.' She left the room, closing the door gently and went to tap on her brother's bedroom door.

It opened at once. 'Did she tell you her name?'

Catherine shook her head. 'She didn't know.'

'Names,' said Alexander. 'Who are we, Catherine? How far are we defined by our names? Perhaps it will be a rest for our guest not to remember who she is, who knows?'

Catherine smiled uncertainly. She had suffered a lifetime of slurs and innuendo about her illegitimate status. The main reason she had agreed to marry the late Mr Thompson was that at last she would have a name which was hers by right.

'You'll have to look after her for a day or so,' said Alexander. 'I've promised to go to Peverell Park, if you remember.'

★　★　★

Sir George Peverell was sitting in a wing armchair under a large cedar on the lawn at Peverell Park, looking out towards the lake created by Capability Brown for the second baronet, beyond which he could see a small herd of fallow deer. To the right was the house, elegant in its Queen Anne red brick, where his two elder sons, Frederick and Hugh, were doubtless talking about his will. Hugh would be hoping for something large enough to pay off his gambling debts, and Frederick would be trying to reason with him. Freddy, thought his father, would make a perfectly adequate Sir Frederick in due course. He was solid, unimaginative perhaps, but a good husband and father. He had married a bossy young woman with a very respectable dowry and was the father of three daughters. That was his only fault. He should now do his duty and sire an heir.

The Peverell lawyer had been with Sir George all morning and would stay until his youngest son, Alexander, arrived later that afternoon.

A couple of days ago, Sir George had taken Frederick over to the stables to see his mare, Coral, and her new colt. The walk was too much for him and a couple of footmen had had to carry him back. Stupid! He had known it, of course, but chosen to ignore his doctor's advice.

'Your heart is very delicate, Sir George,' Dr Lane had said. 'I do beg you not to subject it to the slightest strain.'

'Pooh! What's the point of living, if I may not do what I want?'

Sir George continued to eat the things he liked and to enjoy his wine. He knew he'd put on weight, his glass told him so. He was frequently short of breath and had chest pains. But what else did he have to live for?

But his recent collapse had sobered him. He was now sixty-six, a goodish age for one whose health had been undermined in India.

He knew, quite as well as his doctor, that time might well be running out. Sir George was determined to leave everything tidy for Frederick. He certainly didn't want any quarrels about his will after his death. If any of his sons didn't like what he'd done, they could say so to his face and have done with it.

He scowled at the fallow deer. What would happen to Hugh? He was thirty-seven now, a wastrel and a gambler. What the devil had gone wrong? He'd had the same upbringing as Frederick; a devoted ayah in India, a decent nursemaid in England, Eton, university, and then what? He'd wanted to work with that damned architect fellow, Soane, but that was not to be thought of. Why the devil couldn't Hugh be content with the army or navy, or even the church, as befitted a gentleman? All he'd done was get into debt. He was just enough in awe of his father to control his debts now, but what would happen when Freddy took over? Would his eldest son succumb to pressure and pay out?

Lastly Alexander. He had been right there; Alexander had made a splendid Peverell — a tall, attractive young man, intelligent and with good business acumen. He would leave him £10,000, the same as Hugh. And the six small Moghul paintings which he knew Alexander admired.

If Frederick's wife produced only daughters, and Hugh didn't marry, which seemed likely, then the baronetcy would eventually go to Alexander — the cuckoo in the nest. It wouldn't be the first family where such things happened and now, at the end of his life, Sir George found that he didn't care. Alexander was a Peverell because he had acknowledged him as such. He would make sure that his will emphasized that.

★ ★ ★

Alexander arrived later than he meant to. Catherine was in one of her twitters about their unexpected guest and had to be reassured. Then one of his horses had thrown a shoe. By the time he reached Peverell Park, it was six o'clock. The butler opened the door as the carriage drew up at the entrance. Wilmot got out, let down the steps and then tweaked his hair into shape as a footman emerged from the house to take Alexander's bags.

Alexander climbed out and nodded to his coachman to take the carriage round to the stable block, then turned to the butler. 'Ah, Timson. Good to see you. My father all right?'

'Sir George has retired to bed, Mr Alexander.'

'Where are my brothers?'

'In the drawing-room, sir.'

Alexander nodded. 'Wilmot, stop preening and lay out my evening clothes. I'll be up shortly.'

The place was just the same, a curious mixture of the traditional English house with additions from Sir George's Indian background; tables heavily inlaid with ivory, some very fine rugs and a Buddha sitting at the end of the hall.

Alexander went upstairs to the drawing-room.

'Alex!' Frederick rose and came over to shake hands, clapping his brother heartily on the shoulder.

'Sorry, I'm later than I meant to be. A horse threw a shoe. How are you, Freddy?'

'Tol-lol. The girls have been asking after you.' Frederick was fond of his brother and, if he had any doubts about his paternity, he never voiced them. Alex was generous to his three daughters and always remembered their birthdays and he never asked Frederick for money.

Alexander turned, 'Hello, Hugh.'

Hugh Peverell sat moodily sipping brandy and didn't answer. He reached out and kicked at a small footstool, which fell over. 'Alex,' he nodded curtly.

Frederick looked at Hugh and shrugged. 'Dinner's in twenty minutes, Alex.'

'Then, if you'll excuse me, I'll go and change.' He left the room.

'Really, Hugh,' said Frederick crossly, 'You might be more civil.'

'Oh, go to hell,' said Hugh.

★　★　★

The following morning, Hugh's mood had not improved. He watched sourly whilst Alexander greeted his father at breakfast, kissing him soundly on both cheeks.

'How are you, m'boy?'

'Well, Papa. I'm sorry to see you in such poor health.'

'Anno domini. Mustn't grumble.'

Hugh banged down his coffee cup. 'Brought that mincing valet of yours with you?'

'Wilmot? Of course.'

'Damned Miss Molly.' His tone suggested that Alexander doubtless shared Wilmot's inclinations.

Alexander raised an eyebrow, but remained silent. He helped himself to kedgeree from the hot plate and allowed Frederick's wife, Alethea, to pour him a cup of coffee.

Alethea disliked Hugh. He kept trying to bully money out of her husband and harassed

49

the maids if he got a chance. She always heaved a sigh of relief when he left. Alex was worth ten of him. The only time that Hugh had made one of his insinuations about Alexander's parentage in her hearing, she had slapped him down. 'You are insulting your mother,' she'd said coldly, and Hugh had mumbled an apology. She smiled now at Alexander and informed him that his nieces were longing to see him.

Breakfast over, Alethea excused herself and the gentlemen moved through to the library, where the lawyer was waiting. Sir George, leaning heavily on his stick, moved slowly and wheezily to a leather armchair and sank down, gesturing to Frederick to fetch his footstool.

The lawyer cleared his throat. 'Your father has asked me to explain his will to you all now to avoid any arguments after his death.'

Most of what Sir George proposed was straightforward. Frederick, as eldest son, would inherit the estate. There were various annuities to retired servants and a couple of elderly cousins. Hugh and Alexander would get £10,000 each. Alexander was free to do what he would with his, but Hugh would have only the income, the money to be held in trust, with Frederick and Alexander as joint trustees.

'What!' Hugh leaped to his feet. 'This is outrageous!'

'Not at all,' said the lawyer, with a grim smile. 'Common in many families. It ensures that you will always have an income, come what may.' And you won't be able to waste the capital, he thought sourly. He had several times been called upon to raise money for Hugh's Oxford debts until Sir George had finally called a halt.

'I won't stand for it!' shouted Hugh. 'It's a damned insult.' He spun round and pointed at Alexander. 'I suppose you're privy to all this?'

'Hardly.' Nor was it an arrangement Alexander wanted. It would involve him and Frederick in endless trouble. He could also see why he was made trustee with his brother. Freddy was a conscientious fellow, but he was no match for Hugh in one of his moods. He, Alexander, would never allow himself to be pushed into allowing Hugh to get his hands on the capital, and their father must know that.

Hugh turned to Sir George. 'At least let it be just Frederick.' He could handle Frederick.

Sir George didn't answer.

'Why should Alexander get anything? We all know he's as rich as Midas.' Even Hugh didn't dare query Alexander's paternity in front of his father, but the question hovered in the air.

'Alexander gets his fair share because he is my youngest son,' said Sir George, thinking that it was a pity Clara hadn't played him false over Hugh; he could then have repudiated him and saved them all a lot of trouble. He turned to Alexander. 'Do you agree to being a trustee?'

Alexander shrugged. 'If you wish it, Papa.'

'Is there anything else?'

'Yes,' Alexander spoke. 'What about Catherine?'

'Catherine?' Sir George looked puzzled.

'Mrs Thompson. Your daughter by the keeper's girl, I forget her name.'

'I gave her five hundred pounds on her marriage.'

'She is now a widow with a son. Mr Thompson left her very poorly provided for.'

'A bastard daughter,' muttered Hugh. 'That's rich, coming from you.'

'What do you suggest?'

'That you take some of the money you're leaving me and leave it to Catherine. I have no need for it and a few thousands will make all the difference to her.'

'I have no idea where she is now.'

'She is living in Golden Square as my housekeeper — and very bad she is at it, too!

I offered to give her an annuity, but she didn't want to be beholden to me.'

'Another one of your misfits,' said Hugh savagely. 'That deformed maid of yours and your nan-boy valet. Why don't you start a freak show?'

'That's good of you, Alex,' said Frederick. 'Why didn't you come to me?'

'You have your three girls. Besides, you will be supporting Cousin Jane and Cousin Maud,' grinned Alexander.

'Hm,' said Sir George. 'What do you want?'

'Leave Catherine three thousand pounds and a thousand for young James when he's twenty-one. Then she may be independent and I can get another housekeeper without hurting her feelings.'

'Three thousand for a by-blow,' muttered Hugh. His debts were well over that amount; if Alex didn't want his money, why didn't he give it to Hugh, who was at least legitimate?

'I'm leaving you the Moghul paintings, Alex,' added Sir George. 'I know you've always liked them.'

'Thank you, Papa.'

'I'm also dividing up the silver. It's all labelled in the safe. Hugh will doubtless sell his, so I've left him your mother's pieces which are more marketable.' No one spoke. 'Well, I think that's all. It can be signed and

53

witnessed this afternoon when the clerks get here. Hugh, ring the bell for my man. I'm tired and need to lie down.'

Later, Alexander and Frederick wandered out to the stables.

'Freddy, where is the safe key?'

'Papa has it.'

'Is there a duplicate?'

'Not as far as I know. Why?' There was a pause. 'You're not suggesting that Hugh . . . ?'

'Five hundred a year is not going to keep Hugh's head above water. That safe holds a lot of silver, as well as the Peverell jewellery — the good stuff. I daresay Mama's emeralds are there, and the rubies Papa brought back from India.'

'You wrong him. Alex, Hugh's unfairness to you makes you think worse of him than he deserves. I don't deny that he's a wastrel, but he is not a thief.' Frederick spoke sternly. He would soon be head of the family and its honour must be upheld.

★ ★ ★

Alexander left the following morning. He was glad to go. Frederick was still upset about the aspersions on the family honour and his goodbye was cool. Hugh had not bothered to

54

'I hope Mr Peverell won't object to seeing my ankles. Mrs Thompson's dress is far too short.'

Georgie gave her an old-fashioned look. 'I daresay he's seen many females' ankles, Miss.'

'Oh dear,' said Decima in dismay. 'One of those.'

'Oh no, Miss. He's quite the gentleman.'

'Aren't they all,' said Decima drily.

Georgie giggled.

Decima spent a peaceful day alternately dozing and reclining on the sofa. Her head ached too much for her to read, but she was content to sit quietly and watch Catherine sew. She tried to allow her mind to rest. There was no point in worrying about the morrow. Somewhere at the back of her mind was the knowledge of some anxiety, but she did not have the energy to deal with it.

It was after one doze that she woke up remembering the giraffes. She lay back and smiled. So that was why she'd been out. Of course. And they were wonderful, everything she could have hoped for. Creatures of myth come alive; Zaida, Mabrouk, Selim and Guib Allah.

'I've remembered the giraffes!' she said, smiling.

Catherine shuddered. 'They frightened me.

They were so big.'

'But so gentle. I loved that strange way they walked. And the pattern on their coats. I went out especially to see them.'

★ ★ ★

Alexander returned to London the following afternoon. He did not see Decima, who was resting, but Catherine reported that her memory was slowly returning. Her name was Decima. She had a sister-in-law she was concerned about and she lived in one of the big London squares.

'Decima? Unusual. It makes it easier to track down her family. I'd better get off to Bow Street at once.'

Alexander anticipated no problems and, in fact, he was relieved to have something else to think about than the state of his father's health and the niggling worry about Hugh. Miss Decima's family must be anxious about her; there was bound to be some message at Bow Street.

However, when he got there, the officer he spoke to looked grave.

'Yes, sir. A Mr Wells came in on Thursday evening, an angry old gentleman he was, to be sure. He left a message.' He consulted his book. *As Miss Decima Wells has left her home without the permission of her father, she can henceforth look after herself and be damned to her.*

Alexander frowned. 'Can he be serious?'

'He was purple with rage, sir. Gobbling like a turkey cock.'

'Good God! Miss Wells only went out to see the giraffes — foolish of her to go unaccompanied, perhaps, but hardly a hanging matter. You'd better give me his address.'

The officer did so. 'I hope the young lady will be restored to her home, though it sounds as if she'll be in for a rare trimming, if not worse.'

Alexander took the piece of paper and left. It was not far to Bloomsbury Square and he stopped for a moment and stood outside the house. The door was a shiny black, the stucco was a fresh white and the doorknob and knocker were newly polished brass. Houses in Bloomsbury Square did not come cheap; Mr Wells was plainly a man of substance. Alexander braced his shoulders and trod up the steps. A footman opened the door.

'Pray ask if Mr Wells is at liberty to see me. It concerns his daughter.' Alexander handed him his card.

The footman looked dubious. 'I'll ask sir, but it would be best if you spoke with Mrs Alfred Wells first.'

That must be Miss Decima's sister-in-law. 'Very well.'

'If you'll just wait a moment, sir.' He made as if to close the door.

Alexander had no intention of being treated like a tradesman. He stepped inside. The footman glanced over his shoulder as if expecting a wrathful Mr Wells to emerge from his room, and then went upstairs. Alexander looked around, and didn't care for what he saw. Everything looked as though it had just come from the furniture showrooms that morning; the backs of the hall chairs bore an improbably elaborate coat of arms in inlaid wood; a carved ebony Negress held her hand out for calling cards. New money, thought Alexander. But why not? He was hardly in a position to carp. No, he did not object to that, rather it was the uncompromising hostility of Mr Wells's message at Bow Street.

A few moments later, a lady in an over-trimmed gown and lace cap tiptoed down the stairs, her finger to her lips, and beckoned Alexander upstairs. Suppressing a smile, he followed her.

'Oh, Mr Peverell, I have been so worried!' she said, the moment they were in her sitting-room and the door was closed. 'Mr Wells is so unforgiving. What has happened to my poor sister-in-law?'

Alexander told her.

Mrs Alfred wrung her hands agitatedly. 'I fear Mr Wells will never . . . but Miss Wells has plenty of brothers. One of them must offer her a home. Indeed, I have written to my husband this very morning.' She didn't dare add that at least two of Decima's brothers would almost certainly decline to have her: Edmund had never forgiven her childish behaviour in pouring ink over his daughter's head, and she didn't think Timothy would take her in either. Her own husband would not be best pleased. The trouble was, Decima was so uncompromising and held such unladylike views. They would never be able to marry her off. 'It is a great imposition, I know, but would you and your wife mind having Miss Wells for a short while? Things will take a little time to arrange.'

'I am not married.'

'Not married! Oh dear, then that would never do.' Trust Decima, she thought crossly.

'If you are concerned about propriety, my widowed sister and her son live with me, I can assure — '

There was a thump and a furious banging of a stick. The door shot open and an elderly man, his heavy jowls crimson with rage, stumped in. He raised his stick at Alexander.

'Out! How dare you, sir?'

Alexander took a step back, 'Mr Wells . . . '

'I don't want to know.' He seized Alexander's card from his daughter-in-law's grasp and tore it into pieces. 'I don't allow blackamoors into my house. If you have my daughter, you may keep her. Good day to you!'

Alexander's lips whitened. He turned and bowed to Mrs Alfred, 'Goodbye, ma'am. Pray rest assured that my sister and I will do what we can for your sister-in-law.'

'Out!'

Alexander left. Behind him, he could hear the angry voice rise to a crescendo and then wails from the unfortunate Mrs Alfred. The footman was waiting by the open door.

'Tell Mrs Wells to send round Miss Decima's clothes, would you?' He handed him half a guinea together with another card. 'Quite a tartar you have there.'

The footman gave a grin and hastily pocketed the coin and card.

★ ★ ★

Decima spent the morning quietly; it was a strange household and no mistake. The cook, if she weren't mistaken, drank. Poor Mrs Thompson was obviously quite unused to giving orders and could only plead. She reminded Decima of Aunt Ellen. Their luncheon, when it came, comprised the remains of a ham, looking as though somebody had hacked off the best bits, some wilting lettuce, a wrinkled cucumber and a stale loaf.

'Mrs Salter has problems,' said Catherine despairingly. 'I can't . . . I don't . . . '

'Never mind,' said Decima, 'I'm not really hungry.' Gradually, over the morning, she had remembered her name and why she had left Bloomsbury Square and the resulting anxiety about her father's wrath had taken away what little appetite she had. A hollow dread settled in the pit of her stomach. She knew that her father had cast off her brother John. Her father would never say what John had done, but Decima had suspected some financial impropriety. It now crossed her mind that her small rebellion might result in a similar fate. She tried to scold herself into tranquillity. There would be a tremendous scold and then everything would be as it was before. She picked at a bit of cucumber and pushed a sliver of ham around her plate.

After luncheon, Decima retired to her room and fell into an uneasy doze. She was lying on an uncomfortable, prickly mattress and looking up at some elaborate plasterwork on a ceiling and a huge ornamental fireplace. Where was that? Was it a dream? Or was it where she had been? People had been talking. What about? It hovered at the edges of her memory.

When she awoke and returned to the drawing-room, Alexander had come back and was talking to his sister. Decima entered the room quietly and, at first, neither of them saw her. It was the first time she had seen Alexander properly and, for a moment, she was struck dumb. He looked like something out of the Arabian Nights. He had an olive skin, a strong, almost hooked nose, dark wavy hair and brilliant grey eyes. He was extraordinarily good-looking in an exotic kind of way. This was enhanced by the banyan he was wearing, a loose morning coat in a crimson richly-figured Indian silk over his fawn Gambroon trousers.

All at once, she felt what a fright she must look, with a skirt that was several inches too short, cropped hair and a large bump on her forehead. She took a quick step backwards to leave the room.

Catherine looked up. 'Ah, there you are, my dear.'

Alexander rose and came forward. 'I am Mr Peverell. You won't remember me, I daresay.'

66

Decima found that her voice had deserted her. She shook his hand automatically and tried to mumble something, but she had no idea what. She sank down in the nearest chair, tucked her ankles underneath her skirts, and tried desperately to gather her wits together. What the devil was the matter with her? Had the bang on her head addled her brain?

She straightened her back and cleared her throat, 'I must thank you for rescuing me, sir,' she said formally, ignoring the quaver in her voice. 'I understand from your sister that you have been making enquiries on my behalf at Bow Street.'

Alexander exchanged a glance with Catherine.

'You have seen my father,' stated Decima. 'W . . . was he very cross?'

'I'm afraid so.'

Decima took a deep breath. 'H . . . has he cast me off?'

'My dear Miss Wells,' broke in Catherine, 'I don't doubt that your papa will come round. In the meantime, my brother and I hope that you will honour us with your presence for a few days. We trust that your good sister-in-law will be sending your clothes.'

'My sister is right,' said Alexander. 'He will doubtless think better of it when his wrath has cooled.'

Decima swallowed. 'I beg your pardon, but you do not know him and I do. He will never have me back. He threw out my brother John and never mentioned him again. I . . . I shall have to get used to the change in my circumstances.'

She was pale, Alexander saw, but she had neither dissolved into tears nor hysterics. How old was she? Eighteen? Nineteen? Would he have coped with similar dignity at her age?

'Pray, try not to worry.' He spoke reassuringly, but he was not hopeful. He hadn't liked that red-faced vulgarian, but there was no point in alarming Miss Wells unnecessarily.

'I shall have three thousand pounds of my own when I am twenty-one in July,' said Decima. She tried to smile. 'I am going to need it!'

'But Miss Wells,' expostulated Catherine. 'You cannot set up on your own!'

'What else should I do?'

'I understand that you have brothers . . . '

Decima shuddered, 'Nine of them. All detestable.' At least she'd never have to see Edmund, Alfred, Peter, Bartholomew, John, Joseph, Roger, Stephen or Timothy ever again. Particularly Timothy.

'But your chances of marriage, my dear . . . '

'Marriage? Ha!'

'You don't want to get married?' Alexander looked at her curiously.

'No, I do not.' She shuddered. Every time she stayed with one of her brothers, she remembered anew why she didn't want to marry. Her poor sisters-in-law were harassed and neglected by their lords in about equal measure. The only freedom they had was to produce as many children as possible, preferably sons. 'Oh, if only I were a man!'

'Why would you like to be a man?' asked Alexander.

'Men who are not married can have a much more amusing time than women. Besides, they can go out and earn a living, make a fortune, even.'

Catherine was now looking horrified. 'My dear Miss Wells, you really must not say such things!'

Decima smiled for the first time. 'I know. It's most unladylike, but I really am sick and tired of buttoning my lip because of what some m — I mean other people, might think.' Perhaps, after all, there could be some advantages to being cast off.

'You will need a man to arrange about your fortune,' said Alexander drily. 'Preferably some relation. Do you have a godfather, for example, if you'd rather not ask one of your brothers?'

'My godfather is dead. Unfortunately, in my family, females are seen as superfluous to requirements; every one of my male relations would be happy to get their hands on my money.'

'I know the feeling,' murmured Alexander.

Decima looked at him. 'You do?'

'I have a brother . . . still, never mind that. Tell me, Miss Wells, why were you watching the giraffes?'

'I've always wanted to see a centaur, giraffes are the nearest I could get. When I was a child, they were called camelopards — half camel, half leopard — and I suppose that's what gave me the idea that they were like centaurs — you know, half man, half horse. What I really like,' said Decima seriously, 'is metaphor. The giraffes are a metaphor for other possibilities.

'I wondered how they sleep — it doesn't seem possible that they can sit or lie down. How could they fold themselves up? And why are they speckled in that extraordinary way? They stand for other ways of being. They don't fit in to our normal assumptions, or rather, what we, here, call normal. But in Africa, they are the norm and we are the curiosities. I like that.'

She stopped suddenly. Both of them were looking at her, Catherine with concern.

'Of course you think in this odd way after the dreadful blow you have suffered,' said Catherine soothingly.

Decima laughed, 'I'm afraid I think like this all the time, Mrs Thompson. I am the despair of my family. I usually try to keep it to myself.'

3

The ornate room in Jones Court was full of smoke. The caryatids supporting the marble mantelpiece looked down sternly as Nell grilled three bloaters over a sluggish fire. Fish oil spat onto the wood which gave off an acrid reek. There was a loaf of bread on the table, three chipped plates, a piece of fly-blown cheese and a jug of beer.

Nell turned the bloaters one last time, grunted approvingly, tipped them onto some newspaper and carried them to the table.

Bob and Springer were poring over a rough map and barely looked up when Nell slapped the bloaters one on each plate and pulled up her stool.

'Well?' she demanded.

Springer hacked off a hunk of bread and said, 'I been telling Bob that Peverell Park ain't an easy place to break into. There's a five-mile drive, a mortal lot o' outdoor servants and more inside.'

'Bloody swells!' Nell tore her bloater apart with her fingers.

'And there's a ruddy great lake to go wiv it.'

'Don't tease 'er, Springer,' said Bob, winking at Nell. ''E's found a way.'

'A back road, leads up to the stables. Could be all ri', if . . . '

'If?'

'There's a stable lad, name o' Collins, who's willin' to 'elp — for a fiver. Gettin' the stuff away's a problem. Collins 'as some mates in the Old Grey Mare in Guildford wot can 'elp, he says.'

'Where's the stuff kept?' asked Bob.

'A wall safe in the butler's pantry. 'E sleeps in a cubby hole just off of it.'

'Armed?' Bob knew that butlers guarding the silver often were.

Springer nodded, though Collins didn't believe he knew how to use a gun. The poor old buffer was well over seventy.

'Reckon it's worth it?'

'Collins says there's a mortal lot o' silver. The old man brought some good stuff back from India — and the family jewellery. 'E's seen some of it. Rubies near as big as bantam's eggs. Gold plate too. It's got to be worth it.'

Nell belched sourly, it sounded too good to be true. 'Wot about this Peverell bloke wot wants it?'

Springer picked up the bloater bones and flung them into the fire where they set up a spatter of fish oil. 'We've a choice. Either we do it wiv Peverell — 'e'll get the key so as we can take an impression — that'd be easier, or . . . '

'Or?' Nell leaned forward eagerly.

'Or, we dispense wiv his services and get in a cracksman. More expensive, but the stuff's ours.'

''E'll know who's to blame.'

'Aye. 'E'll have to be silenced.'

'No,' put in Bob. 'I ain't having no killing.'

'Who said anyfink about killing?' Springer grinned, showing chipped yellow teeth. 'There's other ways. 'E gambles more than is good for 'im, 'is pa's 'ad to pull 'im out of the River Tick more'n once. 'Ates 'is younger bruvver. A spot of blackmail might do it. I fink a bit o' research is called for.'

Bob was worrying at a bit of fish bone which was stuck between his teeth. He grunted.

Springer jerked his head at him. 'That's your part, Bob. You's good at nosin' fings out. Maybe we could use the bruvver somehow. Get crackin' on the Peverells.'

★ ★ ★

A couple of days after Alexander's visit to Mr Wells's house, a wooden crate arrived in

74

Golden Square on the back of an old cart, it contained most of Decima's clothes and an agitated note from Mrs Alfred.

Your father won't let me pack up your things, so this is the best I can do. Oh, Decima, what have you done? He's so angry with you. He threatens to cross your name out of the family Bible. Alfred writes that it is all my fault; Edmund is furious; he and Timothy have been summoned; Peter, Joseph and Roger are away and Bartholomew washes his hands of you. Stephen will come down later . . . .The writing trailed away. There were a couple of tear blots and a scrawled *Theresa Wells* at the bottom.

Inside the crate, Decima's clothes had been hurled in anyhow, as if Mrs Alfred had had only a few moments to do it. Stays, gowns, petticoats, stockings and shoes were dumped indiscriminately together. A set of pearls and a gold bracelet that had been Decima's mother's were hidden in the toe of a stocking and Mrs Alfred's own purse, which contained ten pounds in loose change.

Decima had never particularly liked Mrs Alfred, but this evidence of her agitation and concern touched her. She tidied away her clothes with a heavy heart. She realized that what she had seen as a mild escapade, was viewed by her father as outright rebellion.

Was this what had happened to her brother John, she wondered? It was never talked about. She had no way of knowing whether his 'crime' had been as trivial as her own. Would her father ever change his mind? Her offence had been minor, but he was an autocrat where his children were concerned — and he had had matrimonial ambitions for her.

Could she manage on the money Aunt Ellen had left her? It would be £150 a year, barely the cost of a few gowns for the season. Yet, many working families lived on a pound a week, it would be wealth to them. Somehow, the reality of her situation refused to sink in. How could she imagine it when here she was in Golden Square, living in ease and luxury? Yet the ten pounds which Mrs Alfred had sent her was all the money she had in the world.

In many ways, her situation was improved. Her bruises were healing as they ought. Nobody shouted at her; she liked Catherine, who reminded her of Aunt Ellen, and she was astonished at James. She had never seen a boy so unassuming and quiet. Timothy at twelve had been obnoxious, always bossing her about, when he wasn't being sanctimonious. It was a pleasure to talk to James who actually listened to what she had to say!

'He's a delightful boy,' she told Catherine. 'So quiet! You'd hardly know he was there.'

Catherine blushed, pleased. She felt diffident and awkward in so many areas of her life, that this praise was balm to her timid soul. She had done her best with James, helping him to find ways of coping with his disability and encouraging him to be self-reliant.

'He knows he mustn't annoy his uncle. We are both only here because of my brother's kindness. I do what I can to help run the household in return, but I find it . . . I was not brought up to it . . . and Cook can be so . . . I'm afraid I can be such a mouse sometimes.' Catherine hardly dared say so, even to herself, but grateful though she was to Alexander, she found the running of a household this size a burden which often gave her sleepless nights. A cook, four maids, a footman, a boot boy and a groom — it was too much.

'I could help, perhaps, with Mrs Salter,' suggested Decima. She didn't want to humiliate Catherine further, but really, their luncheon was almost inedible and dinner not much better. Mrs Salter took Catherine's diffident orders with a smile of barely concealed contempt. Decima was outraged for her.

Catherine was touchingly grateful at the suggestion. She had mentioned only that she was a widow, left in sadly reduced circumstances and skated over her exact relationship to the family; Decima hadn't liked to probe.

When Decima went downstairs to order luncheon, Mrs Salter enlightened her — with relish.

'She's a by-blow of Sir George's.' It was ten in the morning and the smell of gin in the kitchen was overpowering.

'Poor thing,' said Decima. 'Not an easy position for her.'

'It's all very well for some of us,' said Mrs Salter belligerently, 'but we ain't all had silver spoons in our mouths and I don't take kindly to her coming the lady over me. My parents were properly married, even if my pa battered my ma something terrible.' She wished Decima would go. She wanted a drink.

Decima sat down at the kitchen table. 'You must have had a hard time.'

'I was the eldest of seven, Miss Wells, and my pa sloped off when I was about ten. My ma took in washing to make ends meet. Three of the little 'uns died of fever that Christmas.'

'I'm sorry,' said Decima. 'Is your mother still alive?'

'Nah. She took up with a cheapjack down Shoreditch way. Another no-gooder he was.

He weren't interested in my ma, he just wanted to get his filthy hands on Liza, my youngest sister.'

'Men!' said Decima.

Mrs Salter looked up startled. She'd hoped to shock her unwelcome visitor. She had heard rumours that Miss Wells had been thrown out by her father, but it was obvious, just to look at her gown, that she wasn't short of a penny. She didn't want Miss Wells coming down and trying any Lady Muck stuff on her. 'You suffered from the same thing, Miss?' she asked curiously.

Decima shook her head. 'I daresay your Liza's pretty; I'm not.'

'You've landed on your feet here, Miss,' said Mrs Salter sourly.

Decima was used to supervising a large household and she was not standing for insolence. She raised an eyebrow.

'Mrs Thompson has asked me to help her with running the house while I'm here. I came down to see about luncheon.'

Uppity madam, thought Mrs Salter. Only a slip of a girl, too. She had Mrs Thompson where she wanted her, under her thumb and she didn't want Miss Wells interfering. 'I only takes my orders from Mrs Thompson.'

'Yes, but you don't. The luncheons are inedible. Today we would like some cold meat and salad. Nothing fussy, but I know there are cucumbers and lettuces in the market just now and, if we can't do better than that old ham, we'll have some cold chicken. Thank you, Cook.'

'Mr Peverell will have something to say about this,' declared Mrs Salter, hands on hips.

'Indeed he will,' returned Decima. 'I shall talk to him myself. In the meantime, there will be no more drinking during the day. If you want to be under the table when your work's done, that's up to you, but not during the day.' She inclined her head and left the room.

The moment she'd gone, Mrs Salter turned to the boot boy, who was grinning in a corner, and boxed his ears.

★   ★   ★

In no time at all, Decima had settled down in Golden Square and, if Mrs Salter were still fighting a rearguard action against her, Catherine and Georgie were firmly on her side. Decima was enjoying her new freedom to speak her mind and Catherine, while protesting, found her outspokenness a revelation.

'It's not your fault that your parents

weren't married,' said Decima robustly, when Catherine had finally dared to confide this information. 'If Sir George has settled something on you, it's only what he ought to have done. Personally, I think he could have done more. Five hundred pounds is not a lot of money.'

'He expected my husband to support me.' Catherine sighed. Mr Thompson had seen her as a source of income and was aggrieved that only £500 had been forthcoming and that settled on his wife.

'Money,' said Decima, sighing in her turn. 'Why is it that women are usually so poor? It's as if money itself is masculine. I suppose it's because men control it.' She hoped that there would not be a problem when her twenty-first birthday arrived in getting control of hers.

'But men can deal with it so much better, my dear Miss Wells. Look at my brother. He had four hundred a year from his father, went out to India, and now he is a wealthy man, worth twenty times that. I wouldn't know where to start.'

'What does he do?' Decima asked curiously.

'He imports goods from India; silks, cotton, jute, anything really.'

Decima didn't pursue the subject. She

found Alexander extraordinarily difficult to cope with. Her brothers all ignored or belittled her. If they did listen to her, it was only to dismiss what she had to say as of no importance or interest.

Alexander was unfailingly courteous and, not only listened, but responded. Decima found it most unnerving. They only met in the evenings, but though each day she vowed to be conciliatory and polite, as befitted a guest, every evening she found herself on a collision course.

The very evening after she had first tackled Mrs Salter was typical.

They had enjoyed an unexceptionable dinner for once. The roast loin of veal and spinach had been tender, the lemon pudding light and tangy. The difference was marked.

'Mr Peverell, why do you allow Cook to drink?' Decima asked before she could stop herself. 'She was almost under the table this morning. And I'm sure she sells the candles when they're barely used. And the beef dripping. She must be making a fortune.'

Alexander raised an eyebrow. He was not used to being interrogated on his domestic arrangements, 'What do you suggest I do?'

'Sack her. Cook's perquisites are one thing; incompetence and theft is another.'

'She has produced a good meal this

evening. Exceptional, in fact.' Alexander had been surprised.

'That's because Miss Wells has spoken to her,' said Catherine hastily. 'You know how silly I am about taking her to task.'

'Have you taken over my household then, Miss Wells?'

Decima felt herself colouring. 'I know it's none of my business,' she began, 'but the luncheons have been inedible.'

'Really?' Alexander sounded sceptical. 'My sister has never mentioned it.'

'She wouldn't, would she?' murmured Decima.

Alexander glanced at Catherine, who was looking appalled. 'Is this true, Catherine?'

'Oh, Alex, I don't want to complain . . . Miss Wells exaggerates . . . and I don't eat much during the day.'

James looked up. 'They are awful, Mama, you know they are,' he said with finality.

Alexander turned to Decima and raised a quizzical eyebrow. 'I'm beginning to feel a certain sympathy for your papa!' But he smiled.

Decima could understand men who shouted, but not one who seemed amused. She looked down at her plate and then, because she couldn't help it, up at Alexander to catch a quizzical look from those clear grey eyes. She wished that he weren't so very good-looking; it confused her.

In an effort to control her awkwardness she said firmly, 'If you could tell Mrs Salter to take her orders from me, the food will stay improved. But what I can't understand is why you've been letting her get away with purloining so much.'

'I happen to know that she sends money to her sister's family. A bit of beef dripping seems a small price to pay to stop another family from starving.'

'Perhaps I should visit,' said Decima.

'I think not,' Alexander was firm.

'Why not? Surely you're not against ladies' charitable work?'

'Too often it can be interference. Ladies usually expect objects of their charity to be humble and grateful.'

'Why should you assume that I am one of them?' demanded Decima.

'Wouldn't you be?'

'I'd like to see for myself what their situation is. There are a number of practical things which could help without the recipient having to be humble and grateful. I assure you, I've lived all my life having to be of a meek and lowly disposition — '

'Not noticeably!' put in Alexander.

'No, I prefer fighting,' acknowledged

Decima, smiling at him in spite of herself.

'Oh, Miss Wells! Are you sure that visiting would be wise?' put in Catherine. 'I believe Liza lives in Bermondsey. Such a very unsalubrious area.'

'I'll survive,' said Decima shortly. It could hardly be more unsalubrious than that squalid, stinking room she'd been held in. Maybe it was time she led a less sheltered existence.

'Very well. You may have the curricle,' said Alexander. 'That way you'll be safe. We can't have you being kidnapped for a second time.'

'Thank you. Though now they've got my hair and my lace petticoats, I can't see why anyone would want to bother.'

Catherine gave a faint shriek. 'My dear Miss Wells,' she whispered, 'you shouldn't, you really shouldn't.'

'Shouldn't what?'

'The p-word. One doesn't mention such intimate garments in front of a gentleman.'

Decima looked at Alexander. He was looking suspiciously bland. 'I simply cannot believe that Mr Peverell does not know about such things.' A man in his late twenties, rich, good-looking — he could not possibly be ignorant of female underwear.

Catherine was pink with embarrassment. 'One pretends, my dear.'

'Ah, pretence,' said Decima drily. How hypocritical, she thought. She'd been dealing with pretence all her life.

Catherine relaxed. 'I knew you'd understand.'

Decima reached out and patted her hand. She was well aware how unladylike she'd been and it wasn't fair on poor Mrs Thompson to tease her so. She looked across at Alexander. He was turning his wine glass idly. He caught her eye and raised his glass in silent toast.

Decima, to her fury, found herself blushing.

★　★　★

Liza's family, Decima discovered, comprised four people; Liza, her husband, who was a stevedore, when he could get the work, and two children, aged five and two. Liza was expecting a third shortly. They lived in a room in Thomas Lane, respectable enough, and it had the advantage of a pump stand nearby. Bermondsey was not yet too built up, and there were market gardens and timber yards to the south, but there were also a number of tanneries whose smell pervaded everything.

It was a hot afternoon when Decima, accompanied on Alexander's insistence by

Georgie, paid her visit. Two of Decima's brothers were in holy orders, and she was used to these sort of visits. She knew that there would be dirt and smells and distressing sights, but she had never understood how her brothers' habit of praying loudly for temperance, continence, or whatever virtue they believed suitable for the occasion, could be of any benefit to the recipients. She'd often thought that if she'd had to live in such miserable circumstances as some of the wretches she'd visited, then she, too, would take to drink.

Liza's room had the minimum of furniture. A large bed stood in one corner, a table with one leg propped up on a brick, stood by the window and there were two chairs on either side of a rag rug by the fireplace. Otherwise the room was bare. But Decima noted that it was swept. A broom stood in one corner, attesting to Liza's industry. The children, though thin, were clean and tidy. She turned her attention to Liza.

'Please sit down,' she said gently.

Liza was showing her pregnancy and did not look well. Her face was taut and she kept pressing her hand to the small of her back. Decima sat in the other chair and uncovered her basket. She handed each child a gingerbread man and then, with a smile, offered Liza one, too. Liza tucked it into her pocket; doubtless it would be shared between the children later.

'Is your husband working at the moment?'

Liza shook her head. 'Times is 'ard, Miss. 'E got a day's work last week, but I dunno when 'e'll get more work. 'E's . . . out just now, looking.'

For what? Decima wondered. She noted that there was a tract propped up on the mantelpiece. So Liza had another visitor. Decima hoped that whoever it was had left more than a tract behind. Bit by bit, Liza's story came out. She was being circumspect, but it became obvious that she'd married her Joe as a means of escaping from the unwanted attentions of her stepfather.

''E's a good man, is Joe,' Liza finished. ''E don't bother me much.' She glanced at Decima and added sullenly, 'But a man has 'is needs and I 'ave to do me duty.'

It took a minute or so for Decima to realize what Liza meant. Disgusting, she thought.

'Does he drink?' she asked.

'Sometimes.'

'What about the landlord?'

''E's fair enough. We owes him six or seven shillings, but 'e ain't dunning us. 'E knows I pay when I can.'

'Do you have a secret place where you put

money? I mean so that it doesn't go on drink?'

Liza looked astonished, but nodded. This wasn't at all what she was used to. She'd been expecting an exhortation to sobriety.

Decima gave her five shillings. 'For the rent.' She reached down into the basket. 'I've brought you some food. Bread, cheese, apples, some lamb chops and a couple of bottles of beer. Oh yes, and a large pork pie. Mrs Salter made it especially. Now Liza, this is for you as well, you need to build up your strength for the baby.'

She glanced at the tract, *Mollie's Drunken Father. A Story for Children.* What good was that supposed to do? She hoped Liza would use it for firelighters.

Liza glanced at her children who were absorbed in looking out of the window. She went over to the fireplace, eased up a loose floor tile and pushed the five shillings underneath. She was just straightening up, when there were footsteps. The door crashed open and two men lurched in, bringing with them a smell of beer. The children rushed over.

''Ere, Liza. Got visitors, eh?'

'This is my 'usband Joe, Miss, and 'is friend, Bob.'

Joe patted his daughter on the head and

tossed his son up in the air a couple of times. Then he caught sight of the food on the table, picked up a bottle of beer and looked suspiciously at it.

'For you,' said Decima.

Joe remembered his manners. 'I take it kindly, Miss. We's more used to prayers than beer from visiting ladies like yourself.'

'I daresay. But I'm sure the beer is more welcome.'

'I won't say it ain't.' What the devil did she want? Bob, he saw, was staring at her as though he'd seen a ghost.

'I hope you will make sure that your wife gets her fair share of the food,' said Decima.

'She ain't 'ungry much. She says so.'

'Of course, she says that,' said Decima impatiently, 'but it's up to you to see that she eats enough.' She stood up. 'Come, Georgie, we must go. Goodbye, Liza.' She smiled at the children and nodded to Georgie to pick up the empty basket.

The moment they'd gone, Bob rushed to the window.

'Wot's up?' Joe opened the beer bottle with his teeth.

''Er. I seen 'er somewhere before.'

'Maybe she visits Nell!'

Bob laughed, 'That'd be the day!'

'Where she from, Liza?' Joe tipped up the

bottle and drank, wiping his mouth with the back of his hand.

'From me sister's.'

'Oh, Peverell's.' Joe lost interest. He took out his knife and hacked off a hunk of cheese. The children watched him with round, hungry eyes. He broke off two small pieces. ''Ere, you two.'

'Peverell?' said Bob sharply. 'Where's 'e 'ang out, then?'

★　★　★

It was a relief for Decima to have Liza and her family to think about, it saved her from fruitless worry about her own concerns. She didn't think Joe was a bad husband. Thoughtless, maybe, but not violent in the way that some were. The children hadn't cowered as she'd done when she was little, when her father was in one of his rages.

All the same, he came first. He'd have his pick of the food and the rest of them could take the leavings. If she gave Liza anything sellable, like a comfortable rocking chair, Joe would probably take it to the pawnshop. What was really needed was to get Joe a permanent job — which was impossible. Liza usually sold lavender, but she was so near her time that that was impracticable.

What about the children? The elder child, little Joey, looked as though he were of an age to go to school, but she doubted whether he did. Most schools would charge a penny or twopence a week, and Joe and Liza would have better uses for a penny. A penny would buy a small loaf of bread or some sprats.

All the same, if the boy could be got to school and perhaps have a decent meal while he was there, that would make a difference. A lad who could read and write must be better equipped for life than one who couldn't.

'You're very silent, Miss Wells,' said Alexander over dinner. 'How did you get on with Liza?'

Decima told them and ended with her wish to find a school for little Joey.

'It's so difficult to know whether it's a Christian household,' said Catherine worriedly.

'Frankly, I don't think it matters,' said Decima.

'Not matter! But my dear Miss Wells, some of these people are little more than pagans!'

'Even pagans love their children,' argued Decima. She looked across at Alexander. 'You have lived in India, Mr Peverell, don't you agree?'

'Yes, but I'm surprised that you do. Most people in this country are content to condemn other religions.'

Catherine was looking distressed. 'But Alex, surely you must agree that one must be careful to whom one gives charity?'

'Yes, but not because of religion.'

'But how else can one judge?'

'What does Miss Wells think?'

'I want to do what will be of practical benefit,' said Decima. 'If Joey can be properly educated and, in due course, apprenticed, then that will surely help the whole family? I shall need your help, Mr Peverell. Until I am twenty-one, I shall have very little money.'

'What will you do?' asked Catherine, awed and alarmed by her young guest's competence.

'I shall speak to the local vicar and find out about schools in the parish; if Mr Peverell will pay for Joey's schooling and a good meal while he is there, then I think that Liza will see that he attends regularly. It may be all that we can do.'

'But what about Joe's nasty drunkenness?'

'I cannot see Joe giving up drinking for me,' said Decima drily. 'The important thing is to get those children fed.'

'But if Joe stopped spending money on drink, there'd be more money for the children,' argued Catherine. Surely it was wrong to stand by while a man took the bread out of his children's mouths?

'Mrs Thompson,' stated Decima, 'if you can stop any man doing what he has set his mind on, you must be unique. In my experience, exhortation, begging, or even reason, has no effect whatsoever.'

Catherine was silenced. She had begged her husband to work, at least for the sake of his son, but to no avail. He had slowly and steadily frittered away his business. He had claimed the quarterly income her £500 brought in, and his debts had gradually used up the small amount of money her mother had left her. Her tears and pleadings had had no effect.

'You have an extraordinarily low opinion of men,' observed Alexander.

'Yes,' said Decima baldly.

Alexander smiled suddenly. 'Then I must obviously uphold the honour of my sex and pay for whatever school you decide is suitable for Joey.'

★ ★ ★

Decima had taken very little notice of Bob. He had not taken part in the conversation in Thomas Lane and he had stood outside her line of vision. But Georgie had noticed him. He was a slight young man, about twenty years of age, with straight fair hair and shrewd blue-grey eyes. He'd winked at her and she'd blushed. Of course, her good side was towards him and he wouldn't have seen her birthmark, but she liked the attention.

She'd accompanied Decima to Liza's several more times. Decima found a suitable school, which for sixpence a week gave the children milk and a bun on arrival and a good plate of stew with plenty of extra bread at midday. Alexander agreed to pay. Joey was not of an age to care much about the education, Decima thought, but at least he'd get fed. She impressed on him that he'd have to work hard. 'If you're not learning anything, they'll throw you out,' she said. 'There'll be other children who are waiting for a chance.'

'I'll work, Miss, honest,' said Joey. Miss Wells had given his mum some money for boots. Joey was used to going barefoot, but it made him feel grown-up to have boots like his dad. He hoped his pa wouldn't pawn them.

On the way back, Decima happened to glance over the back seat of the curricle. Georgie, do you recognize that young man?' The man was walking, sometimes running along the pavement and looked as though he were following them.

'I . . . think it's Bob, who came with Joe that first day, Miss.'

'Surely he's not following us?' They always went in Alexander's curricle and the coachman could be trusted to see off anybody who meant trouble.

'I don't know, Miss,' said Georgie, blushing.

Decima looked at her. The silly chit was pink.

Georgie said nothing more, but every now and then she turned round and looked at Bob.

★ ★ ★

Decima had been at Golden Square for a couple of weeks and was beginning to feel at home. She almost forgot that she was a guest under the most peculiar circumstances. Alexander told her that he was having talks with the Wells lawyer about her money and didn't anticipate any problems. Her Aunt Ellen had been efficient and the money, now increased by compound interest to just over £4,000, would be Decima's on her twenty-first birthday.

'Thank you, I am obliged to you,' Decima spoke stiffly. She was unused to being grateful to any man.

'Not at all. In turn, I must thank you for keeping my sister company. Not to mention

96

the improvement in the meals!'

Decima couldn't help feeling that Alexander was amusing himself at her expense. She glowered at him, dropped a brief curtsey and retreated upstairs to where she and Catherine were sewing. Alexander went back to his study and closed the door.

When, half an hour later, Decima and Catherine heard visitors who were shown into the study, neither of them thought it worthy of comment. Alexander did most of his business from home. His clerk, Mr Upshawe, came in every morning to deal with the correspondence. If Alexander went out to see some business colleagues in the City, then Mr Upshawe was at Golden Square to hold the fort. Decima picked up one of Alexander's shirts and began to sew on a button.

Some ten minutes later they heard a door open downstairs and footsteps coming up. Alexander came in. He looked grim.

'Miss Wells, two of your brothers are here, would you come downstairs for a moment, please?' He spoke tersely and Decima could see that, underneath his usual courtesy, he was furious.

Oh God, she thought, what had they been saying? Which of her brothers were they? Please God, don't let it be Timothy! Alexander said nothing further, only stood aside for Decima to precede him. She swallowed once or twice, wiped her hands on her skirt, and went downstairs on legs that trembled.

Alfred and Timothy were standing by the window, conferring. They turned round.

Alfred came forward and kissed her cheek. 'You have caused us all a great deal of worry, Decima.'

Going to see the giraffes hardly constituted a major crime, thought Decima. She stared coldly at him.

'I pass over your undutiful behaviour towards our father, but your placing yourself in the house of a man unrelated to you is another matter.'

'Why? I was concussed when Mr Peverell brought me here. When he learned who I was and tried to take me home, Papa wouldn't have me. What else was I supposed to do?'

Alfred looked taken aback. 'Are you lost to all vestiges of feminine delicacy?'

Decima sighed. Why did she even bother to answer him? It would be of no use. It never had been of any use. Out of the corner of her eye, she could see Timothy bowed in prayer over his clasped hands.

'Has it come to this?' went on Alfred, as Decima said nothing. 'Speak, girl!'

'I am here as the guest of Mrs Thompson,'

said Decima wearily. 'I really cannot see what you are in such a twitter about.'

'You are not!' retorted Alfred, with a triumphant glance at his brother. 'You are in the house of an unmarried man and your reputation is at stake.'

'Nonsense.'

'I have informed Mr Peverell that there is only one way that reparation can be made. I am shocked and saddened that I had to point out his duty to him. You must marry at once!'

'Marry!' echoed Decima, with a horrified glance at Alexander, who was leaning against the door jamb, his arms folded. 'Are you seriously suggesting, Alfred, that Mr Peverell be coerced into marrying me?'

'It is his duty as a gentleman.'

'Humbug!'

Timothy came forward. 'Indeed, it is not.' He attempted to take Decima's hand and she pulled it away sharply. 'Our father has looked into Mr Peverell's circumstances and he is well able to support a wife. You would be most fortunately placed and I know that, in the event of your marriage, Papa would be pleased to forgive you.'

'Yes, I daresay,' said Decima bitterly. She spun round to face Alexander. 'You cannot possibly have agreed to this ridiculous idea?'

'No, I have not.'

Decima turned back and confronted her brothers. 'This has nothing to do with Mr Peverell's reputation as a gentleman and everything to do with your greed . . . you . . . you schemers! I daresay you earmarked a suitably large settlement for yourselves. You are despicable!' She took a deep breath and turned back to Alexander. 'Please tell them to go, or I shall not be responsible for my actions. I can only apologize for their insulting suggestion.'

Alexander opened the door. 'If you please, gentlemen.'

'But Decima,' cried Timothy, moved inexorably towards the door, 'you are throwing away the chance of a splendid match. Peverell is very rich, you know.'

'I have no intention of marrying any man. Ever. And certainly not one who has to be frog-marched to the altar.'

'I shall pray for you.'

'Doubtless,' said Decima, unmoved. For her brothers, the Almighty was a superior member of the Wells family.

The moment the front door closed behind them, Decima sank nervelessly into a chair and put her head in her hands.

4

Hugh looked around him uneasily. He'd been led down so many twisting lanes and, on one occasion, through some evil-smelling cellar, that he no longer had any idea where he was. He must be somewhere in the St Giles's Rookery, but beyond that, he didn't know.

He was in a large room which had once seen better days, that was clear. He looked curiously at the fireplace and admired the round breasts of the marble caryatids. They were the only bits which looked polished — doubtless by countless male hands over the years. Otherwise, the room was dirty, and it smelt.

The setting did not reassure him, even though he'd come here voluntarily. Springer and Bob, the two men in the room with him, who on previous meetings had seemed so friendly and obliging, were now menacing and unsmiling.

'The doocid fifty you's offerin' ain't enough,' said Springer. 'There's the bleedin' butler for a start, afore we gets to the safe. The stuff 'as to be got away quiet-like, and the silver'll 'ave to be christened . . . ' He snorted at Hugh's incomprehension. 'Given a new name, guv. It'll 'ave your family crest on it, belike? So it's traceable. That'll need a silversmith wot deals with such things, and it's 'ot property till then.'

'You won't have to break into the safe,' said Hugh irritably. His conscience was niggling at him and he didn't like it. 'I know where my father keeps the key. I can hire Bob here as my new valet and he can take a wax impression. The butler can be dealt with — he likes a drink.'

'They'll never believe I'm your bleedin' valet,' said Bob scornfully.

'Well, groom then, stable boy,' said Hugh, 'I usually drive down with somebody. I daresay you can handle a horse?'

'Daresay I can.' Bob grinned and spat. 'But why would you be goin' down at all? You ain't so keen on your brothers, I 'ear.'

'How did you hear?' Hugh felt another twinge of anxiety.

Bob shrugged. 'Common knowledge.'

'I'll be going down to see my father. Family duty — he's an ill man.' Hugh hated Alexander, and Freddy was a dull dog, but he was not going to discuss them with this riff-raff.

'All ri',' said Springer. 'Bob'll go down wiv you and make the impression. That'll 'elp.

But the rest you leave to us. And it'll cost you. It's a dangerous job and an 'anging matter.'

'One hundred.'

'Two-fifty.'

'Two-fifty! What makes you think I have two-fifty to spare? I'll have to go to a bloodsucker to raise the wind as it is.'

'Then raise it a bit more.'

There was a pause. Bob stood with his back to the door. Springer was leaning against the windowsill, idly cleaning his nails with a knife. Neither man was overtly threatening, but Hugh was acutely aware that the knife was sharp and that Bob was blocking the exit. In some other part of the house he could hear a woman screaming and a man shouting. Nobody took any notice.

He forced himself to relax. He leaned back in his chair, spread out his legs and studied the cornice. The palmette design was unusual, but it set off the noble proportions of the room. The ceiling had what was once very fine plasterwork with medallions depicting dancing nymphs, and satyrs blowing pan pipes. Hugh was not interested in architecture for nothing: Bob and Springer might have led him down umpteen alleyways to confuse him, he thought suddenly, but this room was hardly anonymous. The coat of arms above the mantelpiece was traceable, for a start. It should be possible to identify the house and where it was.

He straightened up. 'Very well, two-fifty it is. But what guarantees do I have that you won't scarper with the lot?'

Bob laughed. 'You can squeal with the rest of 'em, I daresay? You knows us and can identify us. The esclops would be 'appy to stretch our necks.' He glanced across at Springer, who was smiling slightly; it was not a pleasant smile.

'But I employed Bob here.'

'You was done, wasn't you? They'll believe you, a gentleman. You can collect any reward your pa puts up. Whichever way you look at it, you can't lose.'

I'm trapped, thought Hugh. They'll never let me out unless I go along with this. He had no option.

'I agree.' And if they attempted to double-cross him, they'd find that this house wasn't so hidden as they believed.

The atmosphere lightened.

'Now there's a gentleman I likes to do business wiv,' said Springer. 'Bob, fetch some porter. You'll join us, sir?'

Hugh nodded and wiped his face with his

handkerchief. He wished he'd never got himself into this.

Decima had been half-expecting some repercussion following her brothers' visit, but there was silence, Alexander didn't refer to it and neither of them had mentioned anything to Catherine. The whole bizarre episode was as if it had never been.

Instead of being reassured, Decima found this state of affairs unnerving in the extreme. For the first time, she began to feel an awkwardness in being in Golden Square. The idea of Alexander as a potential husband hovered in the air and she couldn't banish it. It would have been so much easier if she'd been able to discuss it with Catherine, or anyone. Then it could have assumed its proper proportion, become of negligible interest. As it was, she found herself thinking about it more than she liked. What on earth had Alexander thought? Had he been disgusted? He must have been. Certainly with her brothers. But with her?

Of course she did not want to marry. God forbid that she should ever put herself in the position of any of her sisters-in-law; bullied, ignored and confined. It would be like being buried alive.

Alexander continued to treat her with the same courtesy, but every now and then she caught him looking at her speculatively, and she couldn't help but wonder if similar thoughts were going through his head.

It was Alexander who brought up the question of marriage a few days later. It was a Saturday afternoon. Mr Upshawe had gone home and they were in the drawing-room. They were alone for once, Catherine and James had gone to the park and were not yet returned. Alexander was telling her of his progress with the Wells lawyer. 'You should have your money in July,' he said. 'Everything seems to be in order.'

'I am grateful to you,' said Decima.

'You don't seem very interested.'

'I'm thankful to have the prospect of an income, however modest. But I've always tried to seek contentment elsewhere.'

'With your giraffes?'

She laughed. 'If you like. I was so pleased to have seen them. It was wonderful when that memory returned. It would have been awful to have gone through what I did and not remember them.'

'I am surprised that your personal fortune isn't larger,' observed Alexander, after a pause. 'I understand, from your brothers, that your father made his money in cotton and is now investing in the railways. He must be a wealthy man.' It was the first time he'd mentioned her brothers, and Decima felt her colour rise.

'Papa prefers to use his money as a bargaining counter,' she said awkwardly.

'You mean that your dowry would reflect your husband's income?'

'Something like that.' She could feel her cheeks burning.

'And you're not interested in marriage?'

'I'm certainly not interested in blackmail.'

'But otherwise?' Alexander persisted.

Why is he cross-questioning me, wondered Decima. She wished he'd stop. Where were Mrs Thompson and James?

'I have nine examples of marriage in front of me, and I don't care for any of them.'

'But would yours have to be the same?'

'How else could it be?' snapped Decima. Voices were heard in the hall, then slow footsteps as James made his way upstairs. 'Oh! Mrs Thompson and James are returned!' she cried with relief.

★ ★ ★

One evening shortly after dusk, Georgie, her head shrouded in a shawl, slipped out of the house and hurried out of the square. The nightwatchman was in his box at the Lower John Street exit and he nodded sourly at her. She'd told him earlier that she was going to see her cousin. Cousin indeed! The night-watchman didn't believe a word of it, but Georgie was well known to him and had worked for Mr Peverell for a number of years. It was no business of his to ask awkward questions.

Georgie was meeting Bob at the Golden Cock in Brewer Street. They'd have a drink and maybe a bit of kiss and cuddle.

She'd spoken to him several times at Liza's and liked the merry twinkle in his eyes. Catherine discouraged followers and she knew that Cook and the footmen would only make unkind remarks about her having to see him in the dark. It seemed best to confide only in Meg. God knows, she'd covered for Meg often enough.

Bob preferred to keep things quiet, too.

'I ain't that respectable, Georgie,' he said. 'Can't afford to be. But I'd never do anyfink really wrong.'

Georgie believed him.

She hurried along, ignoring the importuni-ties of various men who thought that any girl out on her own was fair game. Bob, as he had promised, was waiting for her. He took her arm, elbowed open the door of the Golden Cock, and steered her into a small room lit by an oil lamp swinging from a hook in the ceiling. It was dark and shadowy and Bob led her to a table in the corner.

'Sit there, Georgie, and I'll get us a beer. Shan't be a mo.' He left. When he returned, he snuggled up to her on the settle and took her hand.

'That's better.' He gave it a squeeze, 'Miss Wells is a nice lady, I'm sure, but I can't talk to you proper when she's there.'

Georgie gave a sigh and shyly laced her fingers in his. Several beers and cuddles later, Bob whispered, ''Ow does Miss Wells come to be in the 'ouse, then?'

'Mr Peverell brought her home one evening. It was ever so exciting. She'd been battered about, had a bump ever so big on her head and couldn't remember a thing, who she was, nor nothing.'

'But 'er memory's come back, belike?'

'Most of it. Though she don't talk about it much. She ain't a gabblemonger.'

'And the older lady?'

Bit by bit, Bob coaxed the information he wanted out of Georgie.

'What you want to know for?' she asked curiously.

'Just interested. To see if they treats you right.' He nuzzled her neck and Georgie giggled.

The settle was a good place for a bit of kiss and cuddle, but Georgie was a sensible girl, whenever Bob's hand strayed too far, she slapped it down. 'Geroff! I'm a respectable girl.'

'I know, Georgie, honest.'

'Well, it don't seem like it!'

'Can't help it.'

'I ain't running the risk of getting a high apron with you, Bob, so don't you think it.'

Bob subsided. In fact, he'd found out what he wanted to know and it was a relief that Miss Wells hadn't recognized him.

'Know much about Mr Hugh Peverell?' he asked next.

'I ain't hardly seen him. He don't get on with his brother, that I do know. Why?'

'There's a chance I might get a job wiv 'im. Wiv 'is 'orses.'

'Oh Bob!' Georgie clasped her hands together. Visions of Bob in some respectable job in the stables and herself in neat print frock as his wife flashed through her mind. 'How did you hear of it?'

'I often 'angs round stables, see. I heard

from a mate that Mr Hugh Peverell was looking for a likely lad, so I applied,' said Bob vaguely.

There was no way that he'd settle for a steady job. A stable boy would earn barely twelve pounds a year, though there'd be tips as well. Too slow by half. Bob preferred life on the shady side of the law and often had sovereigns to jingle in his pocket, though you'd best not enquire too closely where they came from.

'What a pity our Mr Peverells don't get on,' said Georgie sadly. 'Otherwise we could meet.'

Bob heaved an inward sigh of relief. It would be bad enough evading Sir George and the elder son and his brood at Peverell Park, he didn't want Mr Alexander Peverell and his household as well, especially if Georgie were mooning around after him.

★ ★ ★

Sir George Peverell took his breakfast in bed. It allowed him to eat his kedgeree without having to make conversation and to read his correspondence in peace and quiet. On this particular morning, he was glad of the privacy, for a most unwelcome letter had arrived.

Dear Sir George

I am writing to bring to your notice a most serious matter concerning my only sister and your youngest son, Mr Alexander Peverell. My sister, who is not yet twenty-one and foolish, as young girls often are, left the protection of her home and is now residing in your son's house in Golden Square, to the infinite distress of her family.

Two of my brothers, Mr Alfred and the Rev. Timothy Wells, visited Mr Peverell to urge him to consider our sister's reputation, but he was obdurate. It is incumbent on me to urge you, as head of the family, to persuade Mr Peverell to offer my sister the protection of his name, the only honourable course for a gentleman to take.

In the event of her marriage and suitable settlements by your son as recompense for the injury to our sister's reputation, our father, a most forgiving man, will settle a portion of £12,000 on her and receive her

112

once more into the family.

Believe me, Sir George, your most humble and obedient servant,
E. Wells

The letter disturbed Sir George so much that his appetite vanished. He pushed his tray away and left the kedgeree congealing on his plate. What the devil was Alex up to now? He had mentioned nothing of all this when he came up only a week or so ago.

Sir George was well aware that his son had had his amorous adventures. Friends in India had written to tell him of a Pushtu girl who had been his mistress. Doubtless there had been others. Then there was Miss Rhoda Sadberge. Alex had said nothing to his father about her, but Sir George's correspondent wrote that he had been very much in love. Nothing had come of it, however, to Sir George's relief. He had never cared for Miss Sadberge's father, a man of dubious financial probity.

Miss Wells was a more serious matter. Her family was one of what Sir George called 'the mushroom fraternity' — they had sprung up overnight, but they were wealthy and respectable. Mr Edmund Wells, the author of the letter he was now holding, lived scarcely five miles away and the family, if not on visiting terms, were certainly acknowledged by Sir George. Mr Wells would probably choose not to publicize his sister's situation, but any rumours concerning Alex's behaviour were bound to be damaging.

Sir George cursed his enfeebled state. Once, he would have gone post haste up to London and had it out with his son, now he could no longer do that. Nor did he want to talk to Frederick about it. Freddy was a good son, but a trifle starchy in his notions. He would be horrified at the idea that Alex had seduced the daughter of a gentleman. But see Alex he must.

He rang the bell for his valet and told him to remove the tray.

'But you've hardly touched it, Sir George. Are you all right, sir? Would you like me to send the groom for the doctor?'

'Doctor? Nonsense. No, I need time to think. Make my excuses to Mrs Peverell and say that I shall not be down to luncheon. And, for heaven's sake, don't let her come up here bothering me.'

'Very well, Sir George.' After another concerned look, the valet took the tray and left.

Half an hour later, a solution occurred to Sir George: Catherine and that son of hers. Have them both up for a visit. Catherine's mother had been a lively wench, they'd had a

114

lot of fun together making love in all those haystacks, he was sorry when it came to an end with his marriage and he'd sailed to India.

He picked up the letter again and reread it. There was a whiff of blackmail there, too, in the 'suitable settlements by your son as recompense for the injury to our sister's reputation'. If Alex didn't take care, he would find himself paying out heavily to be leg shackled to a female he could neither love nor respect.

He hauled himself out of bed and hobbled over to the davenport in the corner of the room, sat down and pulled a piece of paper towards him.

My dear Alexander
I am enclosing a letter from Mr E. Wells. You know your own business best, but it must be sorted out and, if possible, the girl returned to her family — I take it you don't want to marry her. If you wish, bring her and Catherine and the boy to Peverell Park and things can be done quietly from here.
Your affectionate father
G. Peverell

P.S. I have said nothing of this to Freddy. I shall tell him that I have invited Catherine and her son and he will be satisfied.

Hugh Peverell had rooms in Piccadilly above a tobacconist's shop and it was there, one afternoon, that he sat in his smoking-jacket, with a Turkish cap on his head and a large glass of brandy in his hand. Beside him, on a small table, were a sketch book and pencil and about twenty guineas in change. It was all he had in the world until quarter day.

Last week, he'd been playing bezique at the Cocoa Tree Club in Pall Mall and had won several hundred guineas. But most of that had gone in paying off his most pressing creditors. He had owed his landlady several months' rent and she'd become increasingly unpleasant. His tailor had refused to extend his credit and his bootmaker had pointed out that he was owed something over sixty pounds and he'd appreciate being paid before Mr Peverell ordered another pair of boots. His subscription to White's was overdue and a polite but firm reminder had made it clear that he risked losing his membership.

Hugh regarded paying off creditors as a waste of money but, on this occasion, he had had no choice. However, there was no denying that a smiling landlady sending up some devilled chops and a slice of her homemade apple pie was some compensation. Hugh liked his food and one of the reasons he had chosen this lodging was that

Mrs Hart was a notable cook.

He picked up the sketch book and flicked through it: in it were a number of sketches of Springer and Bob's room in St Giles's. Such elaborate plasterwork suggested a house of some pretensions to grandeur — at least when it was built, however much it had come down in the world later. Perhaps he should get dressed and wander round to White's. The library there had a number of books of architectural interest. Maybe he could get some clue to the house's whereabouts. If he were fortunate in his search, he might risk some of his remaining guineas at the faro tables.

Several hours later, Hugh pushed back his chair in the Great Subscription Room at White's, growled goodnight to his fellow players and made to leave. He'd been careful not to risk more than ten guineas, but now they were gone. It was not even as if he'd learnt much from the library either, except that the building was probably near Great Queen Street and may have been part of Sir Kenelm Digby's development in the seventeenth century.

He made his way out of the Great Subscription Room towards the stairs.

'Hugh!'

It was Alexander.

Hugh made to brush past. Alexander took his arm.

'You look cut up. Out of luck, eh? Come and have some supper with me.'

'Damned nabob,' Hugh muttered, but he was hungry and he needed a drink. He allowed himself to be led into the dining-room.

They decided on whitebait, followed by roast fillet of veal, and Alexander plied him with wine, port and brandy. Hugh grew talkative and embarked on a long rambling diatribe against two men with whom he'd had business dealings. What the devil is he up to now, Alexander wondered? He made no comment, only refilled Hugh's glass. Shady types, went on Hugh, slurring his words, who'd thought to get the better of him, but he wasn't one of your green uns. No, they'd soon learn to regret any fast and loose they thought to play with him.

'Badly dipped, Hugh?'

'What if I am?'

'You should try working. Go to India. There's money to be made there.'

'India?' Hugh shouted so loudly that several members turned round and stared. 'I wouldn't go back to that stinking hell-hole if you paid me. Revolting place. Disgusting, dirty people.'

'You didn't always think so,' said Alexander, frowning. 'Our ayah told me how much you loved it. Don't you remember Sikander teaching you to ride? He certainly remembered you.'

'Filthy Pathan. And the ayah was horrible.' Hugh's face was twitching with suppressed passion. He seized the brandy bottle and filled his glass with an unsteady hand. 'I never think about those times.'

There's something very wrong here, thought Alexander, watching his brother.

Hugh drained the glass and poured himself another, hiccuped and then said, 'Going down to Peverell. Worried about m'father. Think I should see him.'

'Oh yes?'

'Take my new man. Says he can handle the reins. We'll see. Good chap. Good with horses.'

'When are you going?'

'Dammit, what's that to you?' shouted Hugh belligerently. 'I don't have to explain my movements to you, you damned bastard.'

Several men raised their heads and looked across. One, Mr Bertram Camborne, half rose from his chair. Alexander caught his eye and shook his head. Bertie sat down again.

'Come on, Hugh,' said Alexander quietly. 'Time you were in bed.' He hauled Hugh to his feet and gestured to a waiter. 'Tell Robert to get a cab for Mr Peverell.'

'Certainly, sir.'

Alexander saw Hugh into a cab, gave the jarvey the direction and a couple of shillings. 'See him safely in, will you?'

He watched the cab out of sight and walked slowly up St James's Street towards Piccadilly and Golden Square. He had stumbled on something, he was sure. But what? Hugh was surely up to no good and if he were going to Peverell Park, then he, Alexander, would do well to go too. God forgive him, but he didn't trust his brother.

★ ★ ★

There was no doubt in Decima's mind that life was considerably more interesting in Golden Square than it had ever been at home. She had reached a state of armed truce with Mrs Salter: Decima didn't enquire too closely where the beef dripping went and Mrs Salter sobered up enough to provide edible meals.

She and Georgie discussed ways to deal with her unruly hair, which was far too thick and still too short to put into any recognizably fashionable style.

'I always hated having ringlets round my

ears,' Decima confessed. 'It emphasizes my round face so.'

'You should try it smoothed down and caught up in a knot on top, Miss,' said Georgie.

Decima sighed. 'It's too short. I'll have to wear a cap.'

'Caps can be very pretty, Miss.'

'But so spinsterish.'

Georgie grinned. For somebody who insisted she didn't want to get married, this was an odd statement. But then, Georgie had never quite believed her.

Seeing what she could do for Liza and her family gave Decima a feeling that she was of some use in the world. Joey was enjoying himself at school and, back home, would impress his little sister by sitting in a corner, practising his letters on an old piece of slate. Occasionally, he would save a piece of bread for her. Joe had found some temporary work. If Liza came safely through her confinement and, in due course, returned to her lavender selling, then things would be easier for them all.

There was one thing, though, which niggled at Decima. Often, while they were there, Bob came in. At first she had taken little notice of him — it was Joe and Liza who concerned her. Then she realized he might be interested in Georgie. Certainly, Georgie herself seemed to think so. That, Decima decided, was no business of hers and Georgie was a sensible girl.

But there was something about Bob which was tantalizingly familiar and she couldn't pin it down. He was wary of her, too, she noticed. He rarely stayed in the room when she was there — he would coax Georgie outside to talk, almost as if he didn't want to be seen too closely.

Decima said nothing to either Liza or Georgie, but she thought about it from time to time.

Then, with the aid of Catherine and Wilmot, Decima tackled her wardrobe.

Ladies' fashion for the 1830s was for exaggerated width of the shoulder line, huge balloon sleeves, tightly laced waist, full skirt and tiers and tiers of decoration, none of which suited Decima at all. Coupled with the blues and pinks that Mrs Alfred thought suitable for a debutante, Decima felt that she looked like a huge iced cake. It might be fashionable, but it was scarcely becoming.

When Decima mentioned it to Catherine, she exclaimed at once, 'Oh, I can help you there. You must ask Wilmot's advice.'

'Wilmot?' echoed Decima in surprise.

'Why, yes. His taste is impeccable. I don't

know how it comes about, but he is really interested in fashion. My brother tells me that whenever he goes to Peverell Park, Mrs Peverell always seeks his advice.'

'I don't know what he could suggest,' said Decima dubiously. 'I have no money to buy new clothes.'

'But, my dear Miss Wells; I have drawers and drawers full of silks. Alexander brings me lengths whenever there's a shipment from India and I really don't know what to do with them all.'

'Oh no, I couldn't,' stammered Decima. The thought of wearing something Alexander might recognize as of his provenance was too embarrassing to contemplate.

'I understand your scruples, my dear,' said Catherine earnestly. 'Of course, you could not accept anything from my brother, that would be impossible, but I am sure that *I* may offer you something. Indeed, I shall be thankful to see them used.'

Without waiting for Decima's agreement, Catherine rang the bell for Wilmot and explained the situation.

Wilmot's eyes lit up. 'Oo, Miss Wells!' he exclaimed. 'What a privilege! Do let me help.'

Meg and Georgie were summoned and in no time the drawing-room chairs were covered with bales of silks, chintzes and

Indienne calico. Faced with every material the feminine heart could desire, it was impossible for Decima to refuse. Besides, she could see that Catherine spoke the truth when she said that Alexander would never remember the half of what he had given her.

Wilmot draped lengths around her and hummed and hawed. 'If I may say so, Miss, soft autumnal colours would suit you better; greens, browns and oyster.'

'Quite true, my dear,' said Catherine, who had been watching while Meg and Georgie scurried to and fro at Wilmot's bidding. 'You have lovely hazel eyes. Blue and pink do not really show them off to advantage.'

'Yes, I can see that,' said Decima. 'But what can be done about my height? These huge sleeves are so ridiculous and make me look as wide as I am tall.'

'They're ever so fashionable, Miss,' said Meg, who stuffed hers with odd scraps of material to get the required balloon shape.

'The Bishop sleeve is coming in, Miss,' said Wilmot. 'Tight-fitting at the top with the fullness lower down. And if I may suggest fewer flounces.' He eyed the frills on Decima's skirts with disfavour. 'Simplicity should be your keynote.'

'Wilmot hath spoken,' giggled Georgie.

Wilmot pursed his lips. '*Mr* Wilmot to you.'

'He's quite right,' said Decima reprovingly. She looked at him and smiled, 'Thank you. I'm very grateful.'

A selection was made and Decima and Catherine set to work, helped by Meg and Georgie, who were promised Decima's old clothes as perquisites when her new wardrobe should be finished.

For the first time in her life, Decima enjoyed thinking about what she was going to wear. The beige chintz day dress with its sage green sprigs was far more becoming to her than any of Mrs Alfred's hyacinth blues or rose pinks had been. Her new moss-green silk walking dress was a delight.

And though Alexander smiled when he first saw her in a new gown, he did not embarrass her by making any comment, but she felt that he approved of what he saw. In fact, Catherine had primed him strictly not to say a word.

'The poor girl is so self-conscious about her height,' she said. 'I was sure that you would have no objection to my giving her a few of the silks you bring me.'

'None at all,' said Alexander. 'So, Miss Wells has had the Wilmot treatment, has she?

A great improvement. She's really a very striking girl.'

But both ladies' thoughts were soon to turn from clothes, for the next morning Catherine received a letter.

The only people who ever wrote to Catherine were an old friend from her schooldays, now a farmer's wife, who wrote at Christmas, and Alexander, if he were away on some business trip and wrote to tell her of his return. The arrival, therefore, of a letter in an unknown hand, startled her considerably. *Mrs Samuel Thompson*, read the inscription in a firm, rather old-fashioned script. Catherine picked it up gingerly and turned it over.

'Oh dear,' she said worriedly, 'I do hope nothing has happened to Eleanor.' She took the paperknife Alexander offered her and broke the seal.

My dear Catherine
I am now an old man and my time is running out. I should like to further my acquaintance with you and meet your son before it is too late. I have asked Alexander to bring you both to Peverell Park for a visit.

I hope that you will agree to gratify the wishes of your affectionate father,
G. Peverell

P.S. I understand that you have a young friend staying and my invitation, of course, extends to her.

When Catherine looked up, her eyes were misty. Alexander smiled at her.

James, looking from one to the other, said, 'What is it, Mama?'

'Your grandfather wishes to meet you.'

James turned this over in his mind. 'About time, too.'

Decima said nothing. If they were all going to Peverell Park then what would happen to her?

'My father wrote to me a day or so ago about this,' said Alexander, turning to her. 'He does not wish to disrupt my domestic arrangements. You are invited as well.'

'That's very kind of him,' said Decima suspiciously. She was sure that there was more to this than met the eye, but it was impossible to say so. Catherine and James were so excited and pleased, that it would be churlish to say anything which would put a damper on their pleasure.

Alexander was more worried than he liked to admit about his father's letter. There was no doubt that Mr Wells could make life very unpleasant both for himself and the family, if he chose to do so. The only thing holding him back was that any talk would ruin Miss Wells and adversely affect the Wells's social pretensions.

Alexander could see, quite as well as his father, the threat of blackmail implicit in the letter. The settlement they expected him to make would be substantial — and he doubted whether much of it would be settled on Decima. She had been quite right when she accused her brothers of greed.

Part of him cursed the moment he had come across Decima's battered figure on the pavement behind Drury Lane, but, of course, he could never have left her there. Perhaps he should have not attempted to restore her to her family — but again, how could he not?

What was done was done. The small silver lining was that he now had an unexceptionable excuse to go to Peverell Park. At least he could keep an eye on whatever Hugh might be up to.

There were other members of the household who were interested in the news; Georgie was ecstatic, Mr Peverell had told her that she was to accompany them as maid to Catherine and Decima. It was a promotion, if only temporary, for Catherine did not normally have a personal maid. What thrilled Georgie was that there might be a chance to see more of Bob.

He'd mentioned that he'd been taken on by Mr Hugh Peverell and would soon be accompanying his master to Peverell Park. She could hardly wait to tell him. The next time she went with Miss Wells to Bermondsey, she'd leave a message with Joe.

Bob was not pleased to get it.

'That girl o' yours, she 'as summat to tell 'ee,' Joe smirked. 'I 'ope it's summat 'ee want to hear!' He mimed a rounded stomach suggestively.

'Nuffink like that,' said Bob. He had had all the information he wanted from Georgie and now hoped to drop the acquaintance. She was a decent girl, far too decent to his way of thinking, but he didn't want to upset her. 'Tell her, usual place Tuesday evening. If she can't make it, Wednesday.' It had better be worth it, he thought.

Georgie slipped out of the house on Tuesday evening when Mrs Salter was snoring in front of the fire, a half-empty bottle of gin beside her. Meg had promised to cover for her. She hadn't seen Bob for a week or so and he'd been evasive about his movements. Georgie told herself that she wasn't worried exactly, but nevertheless, she was pleased at the excuse to see him.

He greeted her affectionately enough. When they were seated once again on the settle, Georgie told him her news.

'All of you!' exclaimed Bob. 'You're all going to Peverell Park? When?'

'On Friday. Oh, Bob, just think, we can see each other more easily there — especially if your Mr Hugh comes down as you said he might.'

Bob stared down at his beer with a frown on his face.

'You . . . are pleased about it, aren't you?' pleaded Georgie.

He roused himself. ' 'Course I am.'

'It's a promotion for me, Bob. Another shilling a week while I'm there.'

He could see her looking anxiously at him. 'You deserve it, Georgie. And thanks for telling me.' He gave her a perfunctory kiss and Georgie tried to be content.

Dang and blast, he thought, now what?

5

Alexander's curricle was for town use, or for short journeys, but it would only seat two, so Sir George sent his own travelling carriage to fetch the Golden Square party to Peverell Park, accompanied by the under-coachman and two postilions. Footpads were not unknown on Wimbledon Common and the postilions were armed.

It was twenty-eight miles to Peverell Park, nearly a full day's journey.

'We'll break at Esher,' said Alexander. 'We can change horses and lunch at the Bear.'

Catherine was shaking with nerves. She came into Decima's room before they set out and confessed that she had scarcely swallowed a mouthful of breakfast.

'I've never stayed in a big house before,' she confided. 'You'll think me very silly, I know, but I shall feel so out of place.' She didn't add that her mother had taken her there one cold winter's day when the hunt was meeting in the grounds. Sir George, plain Mr Peverell then, had been in India, and Catherine had clung to her mother's skirts and looked at the huge house and the ladies and gentlemen on their horses as if they were from another planet.

'You're an invited guest,' said Decima reassuringly. 'I'm sure they'll make you welcome.'

Catherine said nothing. If Mrs Salter could make her feel all the awkwardness of her illegitimacy, however would it be with a grand housekeeper, butler and all at Peverell Park?

'My dear Decima,' she said hesitantly, 'won't you call me Catherine? We are supposed to be friends, you know, and I need a friend during this visit.'

'I'd be delighted, but I'm sure you are worrying overmuch.' She, too, needed a friend, she thought. Peverell Park was too near her brother Edmund's house for comfort and she couldn't banish the thought that that had had something to do with her own invitation.

Sir George's travelling carriage pulled up at the front door and Decima, Catherine, Georgie and James climbed in. The luggage was strapped on top. Wilmot climbed up to sit beside the coachman. The postilions jumped up, and they set off. Alexander had elected to ride beside the carriage.

James, who was initially excited, gradually subsided into his corner of the carriage, one hand pressed to his mouth. Decima looked at him. He was looking green about the gills.

'Are you feeling sick, James?'

He nodded.

She pulled down the window sash and called to Alexander. The carriage stopped and James got out gratefully. 'It sways so,' he said, 'I'm sorry, Uncle Alex.'

'My brother Timothy was often carriage sick,' said Decima. 'But he was all right if he sat with the driver.'

'Wilmot,' said Alexander, 'you'd better swap with Master James.'

The journey continued without further mishap. Georgie, who was sitting on one of the forward seats, was plainly wrapped up in her own thoughts. Though she smiled faintly, she was transparently not taking anything in.

James had recovered by the time they reached the Bear in Esher and was able to make a good luncheon. Alexander was obviously well known there, for he greeted the landlady with a 'Hello, Mrs Plumpton. How are you keeping?'

'Why, it's Mr Peverell!' She dropped a curtsey and beamed. 'I hope this doesn't mean bad news from Peverell Park?'

Alexander shook his head, 'Sir George is as well as can be expected at his age. Can you do us a private room and some luncheon? And I daresay Mrs Thompson and Miss Wells would like to tidy themselves.'

A maid was summoned to show the ladies upstairs and Mrs Plumpton provided a generous enough spread of pies and cold meats to satisfy everyone.

It was all very different, Decima reflected, from when she travelled with any of her brothers, who seemed to think that their status depended on being rude to waiters, offensive to the landlady and complaining as much as possible. She had always felt embarrassed in their company.

They had made good time and, while Catherine chose to lie down for a while, Decima and Alexander sat quietly under the apple trees in the inn garden.

'Poor Catherine is very nervous,' observed Alexander as he poured out a cup of coffee and handed it to her.

'It is inevitable, I suppose,' replied Decima. 'She doesn't know her father at all. She even asked me what he looked like.'

'Have you met my father then?' Alexander looked surprised.

'I'm sure he doesn't remember me,' said Decima cheerfully. 'I was only twelve at the time and staying with my brother Edmund at Merrow. My sister-in-law introduced me after church.'

Alexander frowned. Wellses as acquaintances of the family would make things doubly difficult. He was not concerned for his own reputation, Hugh's malicious gossip had undermined that long ago, he was more worried about Freddy and Alethea and his three little nieces.

'You probably haven't met my brother and his wife,' Decima continued. 'Our families are not on visiting terms. Though my sister-in-law feels she should be! She was a Spalding 'one of the Lincolnshire Spaldings' and she cannot help wondering why your father isn't more impressed! So your reputation is quite safe,' she added mischievously.

'My reputation! My dear Miss Wells, my reputation as far as Society goes is almost non-existent.'

'Good God. Why?' Decima was intrigued. 'Do you lead an immoral life?' She wouldn't have thought it. He did not come home drunk. It was true that occasionally he was not there in the mornings but, whatever he did, he was discreet about it.

'Let us say that Society harbours certain queries about my background.'

'I'm sorry. I don't understand.'

'Catherine would say that it is not suitable for a young lady's ears.' Alexander wondered how far this unconventional young lady would go.

'I daresay,' retorted Decima. 'If you don't want to tell me, of course I shan't press you, but pray don't worry about my ears.'

'I'm rather surprised that you've heard nothing downstairs.'

Decima shook her head, 'I've led a very sheltered life, Mr Peverell. They may have dropped any number of hints. I probably missed them. It really is most annoying. I've always *longed* to be more worldly!'

Alexander laughed. 'Very well, then. There are rumours that I am not the son of Sir George Peverell at all — though he acknowledges me.' He was well aware that the topic should be unmentionable, but somehow he did not doubt her discretion.

Decima thought about it. 'How do they know?'

'I don't look like the rest of the family.' He hesitated and then added, 'I look foreign.'

Decima turned and considered him carefully. It was true he was slightly darker than most people she knew and there was something about the shape of his eyes . . .

'Does that matter?' she asked curiously. 'I'm hardly in a position to judge, my experience is so limited, but I still can't see the point of these rumours.'

'Ah, but rumour has it that my father is a Pathan, an Indian from Kashmir.'

'Really!' Decima's eyes lit up. 'How exotic.'

'Almost like a giraffe in fact?'

Decima nearly said, 'But I'm very fond of giraffes' and only just stopped herself in time. She blushed.

'Society demands pure-blooded Englishmen,' Alexander finished.

'Humbug,' retorted Decima. 'The king is hardly English! Queen Adelaide comes from Saxe-Meiningen, wherever that is. You really should not take so much notice.'

Alexander drained his coffee cup, put it down on the tray and said deliberately, 'But the rumours are true.'

'You mean your father really is an Indian?'

'Yes.'

'How do you know?'

'I've always known. He was my mother's bearer. Sikander was his name. My own name, Alexander, is simply the English for Sikander.'

Decima was suddenly aware that Alexander had just told her something very private. Her experience of men confiding things was non-existent, but both Aunt Ellen and Catherine had shared secrets with her. She hoped she knew the rules.

'What sort of person was he?' she asked.

Alexander considered. 'Courageous, though he could be as gentle as a lamb with a sick child; upright — his code of honour was everything to him; and loving. I think he taught me everything worth knowing.'

'You are fortunate to have had such a father,' said Decima quietly. 'I cannot say the same about mine, pure-bred English though he be.'

It explained something of Alexander's isolation, she thought. Invitations came for him, but he rarely accepted. If he went to his club, he never invited people home. Decima had supposed that this was due to the horrors of the cooking, but she now began to wonder whether Mrs Salter's role wasn't to make it impossible for Alexander to invite anybody back. Would anything change, now that the meals were edible?

That men could be vulnerable was a new idea to her. Why should they be? They had all the power. She had certainly never heard any of her brothers, or her father, express any doubts whatsoever. She had never expected to feel sympathy for a man and was disconcerted to find that she felt pity for Alexander's position. She thought of the giraffes; they, too, came from a strange land, but at least there were four of them — they could be company for each other.

There was a sound behind them and Catherine and James came down through the trees.

'Thank you for listening to me,' said Alexander formally. 'I don't usually talk about it. Ah, here comes Catherine. It's time we made a move.'

'I shall respect your confidence,' replied Decima. She stood up, shook out her skirts and called, 'Have you had a pleasant rest, Catherine?'

★ ★ ★

Bob and Hugh had driven down to Peverell Park the previous day. Hugh had a smart Stanhope which a friend stabled for him in his mews and he hired a horse whenever he needed it. As a small boy in India, Hugh had been a timid child and terrified of horses. It was Sikander who had helped him overcome his fear so that, in the end, Hugh was one of the most confident of riders. Since talking to Alexander, Sikander had come into his mind several times. Hugh pushed the memory away and flicked irritably at the horse's rump with his whip. What the devil was some dirty Pathan to him?

He and Bob discussed their plans. Bob wanted to look at the layout of the place for himself and to meet Collins, one of the stable boys, who would be working with them. He didn't tell Hugh, but Springer was staying in Guildford at The Old Grey Mare, an alehouse with an unsavoury reputation. This was a major robbery, if they could pull it off. They would make money — lots of it.

Hugh's job was to make a wax impression of the key to the safe. Bob had shown him how it was done: you took a ball of softened wax and pressed one side of the key on one side of the wax and then the other on the other side. Springer would then take the wax up to London and get the key made.

'It's a damn nuisance, my brother coming up,' said Hugh for the twentieth time. 'Why the devil does my father want to see his by-blow now?' She must be well over forty, he thought. If he'd wanted to make her acquaintance, he should have done so years ago.

'Look at it this way, sir,' said Bob. 'They'll keep your pa occupied.'

Hugh grunted. 'All the same, it's a damned queer start.'

Now the plan was underway, Hugh was having cold feet. He couldn't help feeling that Bob was with him partly to keep him up to the mark. If only the dibs had been in tune. If only he hadn't gone to that disastrous race-meeting and lost nearly a thousand. Sometimes he thought he hated gambling, but he supposed it was in his blood. It was all too late.

Bob and Springer had confided only a small part of their plans to Hugh. Bob was worried about Miss Wells recognizing him.

'She ain't seen much of me, I've taken care of that, and she's mentioned nuffin' to Georgie; all the same I don't like being in the same 'ouse . . . '

'You won't be in the 'ouse,' Springer pointed out. 'You'll be in the stables. But I reckon as we could get rid o' Miss Wells. Maybe we could plant sumfink on 'er. A bit of jewellery, perhaps? The family ain't acquainted wiv 'er. She'd be a prime suspect.'

'Come off it, Springer. Wot about the rest o' the silver and all?' That was the trouble with Springer, he thought. He was never satisfied.

'Who cares? It don't matter if they drops the charges later. We'll be away by then.'

Bob felt uneasy about doing over Miss Wells. She'd been good to his mate Joe. Besides, he had hopes of Georgie, which he hadn't mentioned to Springer. He didn't want to upset her. If he played his cards right, he might get a lot further with her than she'd allowed him so far.

Bob and Hugh arrived at Peverell Park. Hugh got out and one of the footmen brought in his luggage. Bob was directed round to the stables.

'I shan't want you again this evening,' said Hugh dismissively.

'Very well, sir,' said Bob, touching his cap. Bastard, he thought.

Bob drove the Stanhope round to the stables and made himself known to Simmonds, who was in charge. Then he would have a word with this Collins. Springer had said that he was a likely lad, but Bob preferred to see for himself. It was a big haul. The arrangements had to work like clockwork. Collins would be in charge of the cart which would take them and the stuff to the carriage. He would then return the cart and pony to the stables and, if he did his job properly, nobody would be a penny the wiser. Collins would be five pounds richer for one night's work. He should be satisfied.

The stable block was behind the house and out of sight behind a small apple orchard and a high wall. In the centre of the stable block was a small clock tower which struck each quarter-hour.

'You soon gets used to it,' said Collins, a restless young man with a nervy look about him. 'I don't notice it no more.'

There were carriage houses, stalls, loose-boxes and the saddle room and above them storage space for hay and straw bales and the stable-hands' rooms. Collins would be sharing a room with Bob: Simmonds had a couple of rooms up a flight of stairs at the back of the stable block. The stable staff ate in the kitchen, though, apart from Simmonds, they were served at a different table from the Peverell Park housekeeper, butler and Mrs Peverell's lady's maid. However lax they might be upstairs, precedence was strictly observed downstairs. Georgie, Bob learned, would be eating with the housekeeper as befitted her temporary status. He was relieved.

'I needs to know the layout 'ere,' said Bob to Collins, when he'd unpacked his bag. 'Can you show me round?'

But Simmonds had work for Collins, so Bob set off on his own. All the domestic offices were at the back of the house and gave out onto a walled yard, he discovered. By peering through windows he found the dairy, the coal hole, the men's and women's privies and the laundry. All these had direct access to the back yard, but not to the house. The back door to the house was separate and gave onto a corridor, off which were the kitchen, scullery, butler's

143

pantry, housekeeper's room and the like.

The yard had two exits; a large gateway, which led directly down to the stables — and was fully visible from the house, unlike an arch in the wall to the left, which led to a laundry drying area outside and beyond that, a wood. There was also a path beside the drying area wide enough, Bob reckoned, for a small cart. It went down past the stable block and through a paddock to the back lane which led to the main road.

That would be the one to use for transporting the goods to the carriage. It was concealed from the house and passed the blind side of the stable block. The horse's hooves could be muffled and the cart's wheels tied with sacking to deaden any sound. Smuggling ways, thought Bob, grinning to himself.

A little bit of poking about this evening after dinner, and he could find out the exact layout of the inside as well.

This was going to work — he knew it!

★   ★   ★

Sir George had an eighteenth-century attitude towards his illegitimate offspring. He had no time for modern reticence in such matters. Catherine was his natural daughter and be damned to anybody who was offended. Accordingly, when his travelling carriage drew up, he was there to greet them in the hall.

A footman came down the stairs to let down the carriage steps and Alexander dismounted and handed his horse to a stable boy. He saw Decima, Catherine and James out of the carriage, smiled reasuringly at Catherine and ran up the steps to greet Sir George.

'You're looking better, Papa.' Then he turned, 'This is Catherine and James.'

Catherine clutched at her cloak and stepped forward nervously.

'Let me look at you,' said Sir George. He took hold of her arms and turned her towards the light. 'Hm, you favour me too much to be a beauty. Welcome, my dear.' He kissed her on both cheeks and turned to James. 'So you're James, eh?' The bushy eyebrows went up alarmingly. They shook hands. 'Now, what do you like, m'boy? Do you fish? Shoot?'

'No, sir,' said James. 'I like books and drawing.'

Sir George looked nonplussed for a moment. 'You'd better meet your Uncle Hugh, then. He's a bookish sort of fellow.'

Alexander led Decima forward. 'And this is Miss Wells, a friend of Catherine's who has been staying with us.'

Sir George shot her a searching look. 'Welcome, Miss Wells. I see your brother and sister-in-law sometimes in church. But you must introduce me properly.'

'Yes, sir,' said Decima without enthusiasm.

There was a small stampede behind them on the stairs and three little girls, curls bobbing wildly, charged across the marble floor and flung themselves at Alexander with cries of 'Uncle Alex!' He bent down to hug and kiss them all, finally standing up with little Frederica still clinging to him.

'Hey! You're strangling me.' He unwound her arms, put her down and turned to greet Alethea and introduce Catherine and Decima.

Alethea came forward and kissed Catherine. 'I've been so looking forward to meeting you, Mrs Thompson,' she said. 'I hope you're not too tired after your journey.' She shook hands with Decima and shepherded them both towards the stairs.

'But James?' said Catherine.

'Alexander will look after James,' said Alethea firmly. 'I have put him in the nursery wing with the girls.'

Catherine did not dare say anything more. Mrs Peverell was so very fashionable, she thought, with her wasp waist and hair done in plaits encircling her ears. She found her tall elegance rather intimidating.

Alethea did not altogether approve of her father-in-law inviting his by-blow to stay, but she knew what was due to the head of the family and she was fond of Alexander. But why was Miss Wells here? Sir George had said she was a sister of the man with the pushy wife they saw in church. However, her first duty was to be pleasant and welcoming. Her second duty was to see that everything ran smoothly. Hugh called her bossy, but Alethea saw herself simply as a good manager.

She ushered the ladies to their rooms, told them that dinner was at half past six and a maid would be sent up at twenty past to show them to the drawing-room.

'I shall send your maid up with hot water,' she promised. 'You will want to wash before changing for dinner.' She smiled and left them.

Catherine's room was next to Decima's, both were newly decorated and comfortable and neither of them a small, poky room fit only for the governess as Catherine had feared.

'Mrs Peverell is very affable, don't you think, Decima?'

'Yes,' replied Decima doubtfully. She had detected a note of disapproval. 'But we obviously have to do as we're told!'

'I don't mind that, at least I know what's expected of me.' She paused and then added, 'I do hope James is all right with those wild little girls.'

In due course, two footmen came up to Decima's room with her trunk and then Georgie appeared.

'It's ever so grand, isn't it, Miss?' said Georgie, indicating the large room and the view of the lawn going down to an ornamental lake.

'I hope you're being treated well downstairs, Georgie.'

'Yes, thank you, Miss. I have a little room all to myself, on account of my being a lady's maid!' She bustled about, shaking the tissue paper out of Decima's clothes. 'Wilmot is first oars here, I can tell you,' she confided. 'Everyone wants to know the latest fashions from him. Mrs Peverell says she won't even think of ordering her winter wardrobe until she's spoken to him. It just goes to show, doesn't it, Miss?'

'It does indeed.'

'Everyone's very curious to see Mrs Thompson and Master James. Mrs Wimborne, the housekeeper, says that those born on the wrong side of the blanket can be just as good as those on the right. Look at Mr

148

Alexander, she says.'

'Georgie! This is just gossip. If Sir George acknowledges him, there's no call for you to question his birth.' She thought of that conversation under the apple trees at the Bear. Mr Peverell could not escape the rumours even here.

'Sorry, Miss,' said Georgie, unabashed. She started to hum. Mr Hugh had arrived and that meant that Bob would be here too. She'd see him down in the kitchen at dinner, though she'd be at the upper table — wouldn't Bob just stare to see her there!

Decima couldn't help wondering what the rumours were surrounding her own arrival. Would anybody have connected her with the Wells family they saw in church? And whatever would Edmund say when he saw her?

She dressed for dinner in a mood of some anxiety. She had no faith in Georgie's discretion and God knows how the Peverells would react to her own arrival if they knew the truth. Would they be as censorious as her brothers had been?

Fortunately, Decima soon realized that she herself was of minor interest — a sideshow as it were, to the main attraction. It was Catherine and James (who was allowed down for the occasion) who were the focus of all the attention in the dining-room.

Seeing them together, thought Decima, it was obvious that Catherine was related, at least to Frederick and Hugh. They had the same brown eyes and the shape of their faces was remarkably similar. Catherine's paternity, at least, could never be in doubt.

Catherine could be shy in company, but with a new evening gown (designed by Wilmot) and basking in unexpected approval, her timidity only showed as a pleasing modesty. James was his usual well-mannered, confident self and chatted away quite unselfconsciously.

'James says he likes drawing.' Sir George spoke as if this were a regrettable minor handicap. 'That's more your department, Hugh.'

'What sort of drawing?' Hugh looked at James curiously.

'Palladio,' said James promptly, 'I like buildings.'

Hugh's eyebrows shot up.

'Good God!' cried Sir George. 'Another of them! You'd better get your uncle to show you his temple.'

'What temple?' asked James.

'I wanted to be an architect,' said Hugh shortly. 'I wasn't allowed — not a gentleman's profession, you see. But, as a sop, I was allowed to design and build a small temple on the island in the lake. If you're interested, I'll row you over.'

James began to question him eagerly.

Sir George decided that Catherine would do and he was pleased that James was a grandson he could like, but he had never been very close to any of his children. Frederick and Hugh had left India when they were small and he'd seen them only a couple of times on trips home. Even Alexander, who'd stayed in India, had been visited perhaps once or twice a year.

He liked Alexander the best of all his sons and felt the most protective towards him. He had done his best to scotch the rumours surrounding his birth by coming up to London every couple of months and taking him to dine at his club. The world should see that his father had no doubts about his parentage. Sir George might believe privately that Alexander was unlikely to be of his begetting, but he thoroughly resented Society's impertinence in coming to the same conclusion.

It was only now, in his old age, that Sir George appreciated the benefits of a family. He liked seeing his granddaughters scampering about, but he was not the sort of grandfather to have them on his knee and tell them stories.

However, it was Decima who interested him this evening. Alexander had written to correct Mr Wells's assertion that she had been seduced. Sir George didn't care for the stable she came from, as he put it, but it was obvious that she was a respectable girl, not the brassy female of his imagination. She was pretty — he was rather taken with her fluffy hair — and held herself well, and he approved of the pale-green silk evening gown she wore, which brought out her remarkable hazel eyes.

She had good manners, too, responding pleasantly when spoken to, but allowing Catherine and James to be the centre of attention. He liked the fact that she treated Alexander with ordinary courtesy — he'd seen some ladies withdraw their skirts in a fashion that was only just short of insulting.

He turned to her and asked if she rode; there were some very pleasant rides here-abouts.

Decima shook her head. 'I've always wanted to ride, but there was no opportunity.' Her brothers rode, she thought resentfully, but it was considered unnecessary for girls. 'I haven't often visited the country. I was thinking as we came here that I didn't even know the names of the birds or trees.'

'Alex,' said Sir George, 'Miss Wells claims

she's ignorant of birds' and trees' names. You must teach her.'

'It's no use asking me, Papa. I can tell a mynah or a gul-mohur, but both are rather thin on the ground here.' He smiled at Decima, who smiled back briefly.

Hugh had been looking at Decima and decided that he liked what he saw. He wasn't at all clear why she was here, but that didn't concern him. He preferred women with a proper figure and Miss Wells had a generous bust and pretty arms. For some reason her hair was short — had she been ill? The way it fluffed up round her head was most attractive. She was not, he saw, struck by Alexander's so-called charms, though his brother plainly liked her.

It would probably annoy Alexander if he, Hugh, made up to pretty Miss Wells. Good. He would enjoy doing that.

It would take his mind off what was to come. The moment he thought of it, of Bob somewhere in the stables and the unspeakable Springer probably nearby, the food turned to ashes in his mouth.

The meal came to an end. Alethea rose and Decima and Catherine with her. The ladies, and James, left the room and the men settled back to their port. Sir George looked at his sons.

Frederick, who took his moral responsibilities as eldest son seriously, said, 'The less said about Mrs Thompson's birth, the better.' He disapproved of his father's candour on the matter. 'However, that is not her fault. A very pleasant woman. Nice boy, too.'

'Don't be so preachy, Freddy,' put in Hugh, who always enjoyed stirring things up. 'We all remember that little actress of yours.'

'Don't worry about taking James to the temple, Hugh,' said his father. 'One of the stable boys can row him over, if he really wants to see it.' Sir George's tone said very clearly that he thought it unlikely.

Hugh's mouth tightened. He had enjoyed building that temple, but his family had never taken his interest in architecture seriously. Maybe James was the same, just being polite to an uncle. As always, resentment surged up in him. If his father lost his silver, too bad. He, Hugh, had been cheated out of his chance of doing something he was good at. Dammit, he was *owed* that money.

Alexander was pleased that Catherine and James were accepted, but he was well aware that, as far as his father was concerned, the main plot lay with Decima. Had his father had any further communication with Mr Wells? Would things become unpleasant when Decima was returned, as she must be, to her

154

unspeakable brothers? She had come to Peverell Park under false pretences, and Alexander felt suddenly that he was betraying her.

★ ★ ★

Decima had much to think about when she retired to bed that night. She had been expecting something similar to the atmosphere in Bloomsbury Square when the family were staying. Her father would be at the head of the table with Mrs Edmund Wells, as eldest daughter-in-law, at the foot, and the others arranged in strict order of precedence. Meals were a nerve-racking affair. Conversation was stilted, inaugurated entirely by her father and with only his sons contributing. The ladies of the family remained largely silent unless addressed and then they were expected to support their husbands.

The meal at Peverell Park was far more relaxed. Conversation flowed easily, even though Hugh occasionally sniped at one or other of his brothers, usually Alexander. Sir George, whilst not interested in architecture, at least allowed the subject to be discussed. Catherine was made to feel welcome and James listened to. Even Decima herself was accorded the proper courtesies. It was all very new and strange.

The following morning, Catherine and Decima went up to the nursery to see James. He had been put under the care of the girls' nurse and, from now on, would be expected to take his meals in the nursery. Catherine was worried as to how he was managing.

They had just finished nursery breakfast. James was still sitting at the table. To Decima's surprise, Alexander was also there, sitting cross-legged on the floor with Clara beside him. He was reading to her. He rose to his feet as Catherine and Decima came in. As always, he moved with extraordinary grace. Decima had noticed it before and, for the first time, she found herself wondering if that were part of his Indian heritage.

Janey was eyeing James with an air of possession.

'Do you ride?' she asked him.

'No.'

'Why not?'

'I can't, with this leg.'

'Oh,' Janey considered. 'Would you like to?'

'If it were possible.'

They stared at each other. Janey was looking serious. She was the eldest daughter and, like her mother, expected to get her own way. James was thinking that to see the world from the top of a horse would be something.

'Uncle Alex, I don't see why James shouldn't learn to ride if he wants to. Simmonds could help him up and he could have Brandy, she's a quiet old thing.'

Alexander looked at Catherine. 'What do you think?'

Catherine swallowed. She had always tried to encourage James to be as independent as possible. 'If he were taught by somebody responsible,' she said hesitantly. If he fell, she thought. What would happen if he fell?'

'What about you, Miss Wells?' asked Alexander. 'Would you like to learn to ride?'

'Very much.' Why had her brothers made it so difficult, she wondered?

Alexander glanced at the nursery clock. 'Time for lessons. James, you'd better see Miss Price while you're here. She can help you with your Latin.'

James looked sceptical. He'd outgrown his mother's small ability to teach him years ago and, in London, relied on a visiting tutor. 'A woman!' he said disgustedly. 'Has it come to this?'

Janey tossed her ringlets, 'So?' she said.

'I don't suppose she can teach me much.'

Clara looked from one to the other. 'Miss Price reads Latin for *fun*,' she offered.

Alexander laughed. 'Miss Price is a lady of

157

most superior attainments. I daresay she'll give you a run for your money.' He opened the door for Catherine and Decima and they left the room.

'I suspect that both Janey and Miss Price are about to enlarge James's horizons,' observed Decima, as they went downstairs. Female subservience did not hold too much sway at Peverell Park, she noted.

'I think it will be good for him,' said Catherine composedly. James had been too much alone — as she had been as a child. He would learn to cope.

★ ★ ★

Hugh was not pleased to learn that his father had arranged to see Alexander in the library at eleven. The library was where Sir George kept the safe key. Hugh had relied on his father visiting the stables, as he usually did in the morning, to look at his new colt. It would be a good time for Hugh to take the wax impressions of the key. Now it would have to wait. He should have done it last night, but somehow he had let the opportunity slide. The whole evening had been more of a strain than he had thought.

It was meeting James, his lame nephew who was interested in Palladio. Somehow, all the frustration of not being allowed to follow his inclinations came back with renewed force. He must look out his old architectural drawings for the boy. But possibly James had forgotten all about it by now. There would be all the excitement of learning to ride, and his interest in the temple would evaporate.

Hugh was surprised at how much he minded.

★   ★   ★

'Well, Papa,' said Alexander, sitting down opposite his father. 'What have you done about the Wellses?'

'Acknowledged his letter. Said I'd be in touch when I'd heard from you. Anyway. I wanted to see Miss Wells for myself.'

Alexander raised an eyebrow.

Sir George smiled grimly. 'Come now, you must allow me some natural curiosity. I had two such very different stories from you and Mr Wells.'

'And which did you believe?'

'Now don't poker up. Yours, of course. But you're in a damned mess, Alex. You might have been playing knight errant, but unfortunately, Miss Wells's family are in a different game.'

'Blackmail — or extortion.' Alexander

laughed suddenly and told his father of Decima's rout of Mr Alfred and Mr Timothy Wells. 'I must say I enjoyed it,' he ended. 'She certainly didn't mince her words.'

'This is all very well, but what the devil is going to happen to the girl? Like it or not, she is now in some sense your responsibility. I wish to God you'd never found her that evening.'

Alexander shook his head, 'I've thought that, but I did and, whatever happens in the future, I could never have left her there. I . . . well, I liked the way she looked at those giraffes.' He smiled, remembering that look of awed pleasure which had touched him.

Sir George considered him for a moment, then said, 'I suggest we let Mr Wells make the first move. Doubtless he'll be in church tomorrow. I shall allow Miss Wells to introduce him.' He chuckled, 'If I were Mr Wells, you're a fish I'd want to play very carefully. You're a catch well worth landing. The Wellses have far more to lose than you do. If any rumours get out, Miss Wells, however unfairly, will be labelled a lightskirt, and that will be that.'

'I don't want to be landed by Mr Wells,' objected Alexander, with a touch of hauteur.

'Of course not. They may be content with having our acquaintance. A bore, but better than some hole-in-the-corner marriage which you don't want.'

'Miss Wells doesn't want it either. She has made that perfectly clear.'

Sir George looked at him sceptically, but said no more.

★   ★   ★

Decima enjoyed her first riding lesson, though she suspected that she'd be sore for a week. Alethea lent her a riding habit and Simmonds mounted her on Coral, a quiet chestnut mare, fit, he assured her, for a lady. At first it seemed desperately unsafe, seated sidesaddle, one leg hooked over the pommel, but Coral ambled along patiently and Decima relaxed and began to enjoy herself. She tried not to look at the ground, which seemed a long way down, and concentrated instead on holding the reins the way Simmonds taught her and keeping her back straight.

In fact, she realized, sidesaddle was probably safer than astride — not that any lady would ride astride and risk a man seeing her ankles. The arm of the pommel held one leg securely and her other foot was firmly in the stirrup.

'That's the way, Miss,' said Simmonds encouragingly.

They were going round the paddock, Simmonds holding the leading rein and when they eventually turned back towards the stable, Decima saw Alexander, leaning over the paddock gate, watching them.

'How did it go?' he asked her, smiling.

'Wonderful! Though I daresay I shall need a mustard bath tonight.' She stopped, suddenly aware that Catherine would probably say that the word 'bath' should not be mentioned in a gentleman's hearing. She flushed slightly and concentrated on her posture.

Alexander opened the paddock gate for them and followed them round to the stable block. They had just entered the stable yard when Bob came out of a loose box.

Decima gave a start and clutched at the mane as the mare threw up her head. By the time she'd regained her balance, Bob had disappeared.

She patted Coral's neck. 'Sorry, Coral. My fault.' She looked at Alexander. Should she say anything? If so, what? That a man she had seen at Joe and Liza's, who appeared to be sweet on Georgie, had suddenly appeared at Peverell Park? He would think she was mad. Was it Bob? Perhaps she had been mistaken.

'Come, Miss Wells,' said Alexander. 'We must get you down.'

Decima looked at the ground. How on earth did one descend without falling off?

'Take that leg out of the stirrup, that's right. Now unhook the other from the pommel and slide down.'

'Slide down!'

'I'll catch you. Put your hands on my shoulders.'

'Are you sure?' asked Decima, a trifle breathlessly. She wasn't at all convinced that to fall practically into a man's arms could possibly be the right thing to do.

'Come on, be brave.' He could see perfectly well what was worrying her and was quietly amused.

Oh well, she thought. Here goes. She put her hands on his shoulders and slid off. Alexander caught her round the waist and put her gently on the ground. Decima barely had time to register his strength before she was released.

'See,' he said. 'Simple.'

'Thank you.' Decima was grateful that he had not taken advantage of his position. On the other hand, perversely, she half-wished that he had. Or, at least, that he might have wanted to.

Alexander left them to go and look at his father's new colt and Decima turned to thank Simmonds, who had been watching with a broad grin on his face.

'How did I do?'

'Shaping up well, Miss. You've a natural seat on a horse.'

'I hope I shall be able to kneel in church tomorrow!'

Simmonds chuckled, 'Best take a cushion, Miss. The pews in St Mary's are very hard, not even a bit of carpet to sit on.'

She walked slowly back to the house, partly because she was discovering muscles she hadn't known she had, and partly to allow herself time to think. She hadn't worried when Simmonds had helped her into the saddle, she scolded herself; it would be foolish to think any more about Alexander lifting her off. She turned her thoughts resolutely to Bob. Presumably, his presence here was why Georgie looked so excited. But how did he know Mr Hugh? Should she tackle Georgie? Why did she keep feeling that she was missing something?

★　★　★

Georgie had assured Decima that everybody downstairs was being kind to her, but the truth was rather different. Céline, Alethea's lady's maid, had swiftly realized that Georgie was little more than a jumped-up housemaid and made her disdain clear by being coolly indifferent. Then, Georgie had overheard several remarks about her face looking as though she had had a pot of paint flung at it. She was used to comments about her birthmark, but they hurt all the same. The housemaids had decided that she was above herself and let her know it.

'Take no notice,' whispered Wilmot, when they met at the breakfast-table. 'Rise above it, dear.'

Georgie smiled, but it was with an effort. Bob was sitting with the lower servants and was plainly enjoying himself amid a gaggle of giggling girls. Even he had deserted her. She finshed her lunch with an effort and waited for Mrs Wimborne to indicate that she might leave the table. The housekeeper had made it perfectly clear that, whilst Georgie might be allowed to eat at the upper table, she would not be asked to drink tea in the housekeeper's room.

Mrs Wimborne nodded. Georgie rose and, head held high, walked towards the door.

She had to pass Bob, who was standing chatting to Dorothy, one of the chamber-maids. He didn't even smile at her. Georgie's cup of humiliation ran over. She turned her head aside so that he should not see her tears and then felt something slipped into her skirt pocket. Miraculously, her mood changed. She could hardly wait to get to the privacy of her room.

I ain't hardly seen you. I'll cum up to the kitchin tonite at mid-nite. Let me in. XXX

There was no signature, but Georgie hugged the note to her heart.

6

That night, Decima found it difficult to sleep. Her muscles were aching, she was trying not to think about Alexander, who had somehow infiltrated her thoughts more than she found comfortable, and she was worried about Bob. If that weren't enough, the following day was Sunday. Church. And Edmund would be sure to be there.

Whatever would he say when he saw her? Appalling thoughts of Edmund denouncing her as a harlot in front of the congregation went round and round her head. He was quite capable of it. Mrs Wells, too, would surely be furious that Decima had been invited to stay at Peverell Park, when she herself was barely acknowledged by Sir George.

There were the usual night-time noises; wood cracked and a mouse scuttled. She could hear the hall clock chime the hours and, further off, the faint sound of the stable clock. Then there was the creak of footsteps outside her room. She sat up and listened intently. The hall clock had just struck midnight. Whoever was up at this hour?

Decima's room was in the guest wing at the side of the house, near the back stairs that the servants used.

The sudden, awful thought flashed through her mind that it was Georgie. Her spirits had been suspiciously high when she had helped Decima change for dinner that evening. Surely she wouldn't dare have an assignation with Bob at this time of night? Decima shuddered to think of the consequences if Timson — who slept in a small room off the butler's pantry — discovered her.

She slipped out of bed, put on her dressing-gown and tiptoed to the door, just in time to see Georgie's head descending the turn of the stair. She was about to follow her, when she heard another sound, this time from the front stairwell at the other end of the corridor. She crept across and peered down. The library door was open and somebody was holding a light, for she could see the shadow. Heart thudding, Decima crouched down at the top of the stairs, out of sight but within hearing.

Hugh and Bob came out of the library.

'That's done then.' Hugh was speaking. 'Are you satisfied with the impressions?'

'They're good 'uns. I'll get 'em to Springer.'

'How long will it take?'

'A day or so, it depends.'

'Where is he?'

'Nowhere you need to worry about.'

'Where, dammit? If he's in the village, there'll be gossip.'

''E ain't. 'E's nearby. Wiv a cove 'e knows wot runs a stable. I'm not saying no more. If you don't know you can't tell, can you — sir.'

'Oh God, if anything should go wrong.'

'It won't. I'd better be off.'

A click and Hugh unlocked the front door. 'Go on the grass, that way you won't crunch on the gravel.'

Bob's shadow vanished. Hugh shut the door and locked it, then sighed. He stood for a few moments irresolutely in the hall, then he sat down on one of the hall chairs, put the lamp on the floor and sank his head in his hands.

Decima's unease grew. Something was up, she was sure of it. But what could she do? Hugh was a son of the house, she had no right to interfere.

Eventually, Hugh raised his head, stood up and turned to come up the stairs. He moved slowly, as if weighed down, and his lamp cast moving shadows up the walls. Decima backed into her own room and stood with the door ajar. With the same slow tread, Hugh turned down the other corridor to his own room and she heard his door close.

Cautiously, Decima opened her door again. Where was Georgie? She had not heard her come up the back stairs. Decima waited for perhaps ten minutes. Nothing. Then she decided. She must make a push to stop Georgie from being imprudent.

She pulled her door gently to and crept down the back stairs. She could hear voices. Two people were whispering, there were smothered giggles and the sound of kissing. As Decima went lower, she could feel a draught coming from the back door. Someone, probably Georgie, had opened it and Bob must be in the kitchen with her.

The kitchen door was open. A lighted candle stood on the table and lit two figures, closely entwined.

An unaccustomed pang of envy shot through Decima. She began to turn away, unwilling to interrupt their privacy. Then she heard Georgie.

'No, Bob, don't.'

'Come on, Georgie. You like it, don't you?'

'Yes, but no more. No, Bob, I mean it.' A pause. 'No, please stop.' Georgie's voice was rising.

Decima moved silently to the kitchen door. To her right, just inside the door was a dresser. On it was a bowl. She reached out and gave it a push.

There was a crash as the bowl fell and broke on the stone floor.

In a flash, Bob was out of the back door and Georgie was running up the back stairs, her nightdress, buttons undone, brushing against Decima as she passed.

Decima waited in the darkness until all was silent and then tiptoed into the kitchen, took the candle and locked the back door. Whatever Bob was up to, there would be no second attempt tonight.

★ ★ ★

The vicar of St Mary's was gratified to see that the two Peverell pews were fully occupied on this fine June morning. Even Sir George was there, leaning heavily on his stick. There were Mr Peverell and his lady, their three children, the nurse and the governess, Miss Price. That was only to be expected. He was surprised to see Mr Hugh and Mr Alexander, neither of them regular worshippers. Then there were two other ladies in the party and a lame boy.

The Wells family, too, were out in force: Mr and Mrs Wells and their fine family and one of his brothers and his wife.

The organ swelled, the congregation rose

and the service began.

When Decima saw that her brother Peter and his wife were with Edmund, her heart sank. Like Timothy, Peter was in holy orders; doubtless he had some moral exhortation prepared. Whatever could she say? She was too tired to think clearly. After the alarms of the previous night, she had not slept well.

She sang, knelt and sat automatically, without the faintest idea of what she was doing.

The service was over and the congregation made their way outside. Sir George turned and beckoned to Decima. Edmund and Peter were hovering nearby. There was no escape.

'Now, my dear,' said Sir George, 'you must introduce me to your brothers.'

Decima took a deep breath, 'Edmund! Peter! How delightful to see you. Sir George, pray allow me to introduce my brothers to you. Mr Wells, Mrs Wells. The Reverend Peter Wells and Mrs Peter Wells.'

Bows and curtseys were exchanged. Sir George introduced his sons and Alethea and Catherine. Decima could see Edmund's wife glancing round to make sure that their introduction was noted by the rest of the congregation.

Edmund scowled at Alexander, but said nothing. The conversation was the platitudes of such occasions.

Peter came up to Decima. 'You have caused us all a great deal of anxiety.'

'For that you must blame Papa,' said Decima coldly.

'You must not seek to cast your wrongdoing on his shoulders. This whole sorry business must be rectified, and soon.'

Decima said nothing.

'Edmund and I will call at Peverell Park and speak to this Mr Alexander Peverell in the presence of his father. A man of Sir George's position in the world will see that his son behaves as a gentleman should.'

Out of the corner of her eye Decima could see Edmund in earnest conversation with Sir George. Finally, he looked up and gave Peter a brief nod. Neither brother looked at Alexander.

At luncheon, Decima lost her appetite. She picked at her food and barely touched her wine. For the first time, she regretted her exploit. She knew that Sir George had been ill; neither he nor Alexander deserved the trouble she had inadvertently brought upon them.

Under cover of the general conversation, Sir George leaned towards Decima and said, 'Miss Wells, your brothers wish to have a word with you. They will be coming at three o'clock. Would you come to the library then, please?' He saw that her face was white with anxiety and added, 'My son has told me the real story.' He smiled, but said nothing more.

★ ★ ★

Five people were in the library. Sir George was sitting in his leather wing armchair, his glass of medicine at his elbow, taking no part in the conversation, but watching all the participants. Decima was sitting bolt upright by the window and Edmund, Peter and Alexander were standing.

'My sister's reputation is in your hands, sir,' Edmund was saying. 'Do I have to demand that you behave like a gentleman?'

'She has been living with you, in a bachelor household, without even the vestige of a chaperon,' put in Peter. 'A lady! I venture to think that my authority as one in holy orders will carry some weight.'

'But perhaps we wrong you, Mr Peverell,' continued Edmund smoothly. 'Could it be why you have brought my sister here to meet your father? Should we be congratulating you?'

Decima stood up jerkily, 'I have heard enough,' she declared. 'You ought to be ashamed of yourselves, both of you.'

'This has nothing to do with you,' stated Edmund. 'This is between men.'

'Humbug. It has everything to do with your social ambition and nothing to do with Mr Peverell here, who only did what any Christian should do and rescued me when I was lying badly beaten in the gutter.'

Edmund gave an indulgent laugh, 'I daresay that is your story, Decima, but I am not so green as to believe it. No, you sneaked out to meet him, do not deny it.'

'I went out to see the giraffes!' cried Decima indignantly.

Peter and Edmund both laughed. Even Alexander and Sir George smiled.

Decima stamped her foot. 'Very well, then.' She turned to Alexander. 'Mr Peverell, would you mind proposing to me and we'll end this nonsense.'

There was a startled pause. Sir George's hand whitened as it gripped his stick. Decima looked at Alexander expectantly. His lips twitched.

'As you wish. Miss Wells, would you do me the very great honour of accepting my hand in marriage?'

'May the Lord be praised!' cried Peter. 'The sinner has returned to the Path of Righteousness.'

'I am pleased to see that we were not

mistaken in you,' added Edmund.

'No,' said Decima.

Edmund spun round. 'What did you say?'

'I said no. Mr Peverell, I am greatly honoured, but I cannot believe that a marriage forced on us both would be for the happiness of either.' She turned to her brothers. 'I hope you are satisfied,' she cried angrily. 'I despise your trickery and your distortion of the truth, which has led to the hounding of an honourable man. He has done what you wanted — before witnesses — and I have answered him and let that be the end of it. I want nothing to do with either of you, ever again, and if Papa wishes to cross my name out of the family Bible, so be it.'

'Do you have no care for your reputation?' demanded Edmund, as much put out as his conceit allowed him to be.

'Yes I do. I care for my integrity, which is more than you and Peter do for yours.' She turned to Sir George. 'I am sorry, Sir George, that you have seen this. I am ashamed of how my family must appear.'

'It has been most instructive,' replied Sir George. 'If you wish to retire, my dear, I think my son and I can finish this without you.'

Decima dropped him a curtsey, bowed to Alexander and left the room.

Edmund chewed his lip. Peter clasped his

hands in prayer and communed silently with the carpet.

Sir George took a sip of his medicine and said, 'What you both must consider carefully is this: whose family is going to be most hurt by any rumours that you put about? Believe me, they will not be coming from this house. Miss Wells, as a friend of my daughter Mrs Thompson, is a guest here. I have allowed her to introduce you and your wives. I suggest that you think about it.

'Alex, see these gentlemen to their carriage, please.'

'Certainly, Papa.' Alexander moved to the door and opened it.

When he returned to the library, Sir George was looking thoughtful.

'A spirited young woman, Miss Wells,' he remarked.

'Yes, indeed,' Alexander smiled. 'I am not used to having my reputation defended by a tigress!'

'All the same, she is in a difficult position. She cannot stay here for ever and you can hardly take her back to London with you. What is to become of her?'

'I know, Papa. She has this idea that she will set up on her own. She will have about two hundred a year.'

'Impossible. She is far too young.'

Alexander sighed, 'She is a resourceful girl but, in some ways, alarmingly naïve. I dread to think what would happen to her in some lodging-house on her own.'

'What do you suggest?' It crossed Sir George's mind that his son was surprisingly protective towards his young guest.

Alexander hesitated. His main concern in coming to Peverell Park had not been Decima, but keeping an eye on whatever Hugh had in mind. And for that he needed to stay.

'Could we leave it for a week or so? Miss Wells will be twenty-one on July 5th. I have Catherine and James to think of as well. Perhaps things will sort themselves out. It may be that the appalling Mr Wells will see a way to welcoming his sister back into the family fold.' As he spoke he thought, no, it would be like shutting her up in a box.

'You were a brave man, proposing like that,' observed Sir George. 'It was a risky thing to do.'

'I was almost certain she'd refuse.'

'And if she hadn't?'

Alexander didn't reply, only fiddled with the acorn on the window blind.

★ ★ ★

Decima left the library in a mood of righteous indignation. She ran up the stairs to the landing window and, not ten minutes later, had the satisfaction of seeing her brothers climb into the carriage and drive away. The mood did not last long. She began to feel depressed and uneasy. In a few weeks' time she would be twenty-one with an independent fortune. The income from that, some £200 a year, would enable her to rent a small cottage and have a maid, possibly two. Oh, the blessed peace of it.

She tried to summon up her usual daydream of a neat parlour and herself with a cat on her lap, a cosy fire in the grate, and a cup of tea by her side. The main thing had always been the absence of men; no father to berate her for not ordering muffins, or demand that she be quiet, or forbid her to read the newspaper.

Now she realized that there would be other omissions, too. No Catherine to chat with, no Liza to visit and help, no Wilmot to advise on her clothes, no Alexander to . . .

She tried to scold herself back into some sort of normality. There were other families, apart from Liza's, she might help. She might make other female friends. As for men, she didn't need them.

She sighed, rose, and went to the

drawing-room. Only Alethea, Catherine and James were there. James was sitting at a round table by the window and painstakingly copying some architectural drawings in the way that Hugh had taught him. She moved across.

'Uncle Hugh is awfully good at drawing,' he said. 'Look! He sketches interesting buildings and keeps notes. That's what I mean to do. He says it's the best way to get to know a building.' He pushed one of Hugh's sketch books in her direction.

Decima sat down and began to leaf through it. Hugh's taste was eclectic; he didn't just concentrate on grand country houses. Much smaller buildings also held his interest: a gatehouse, a cottage *ornée*, some ornamental gates.

She turned over a page idly and, suddenly, her heart lurched. There was a room she recognized; the elaborate ceiling, the marble caryatids and the coat of arms above the fireplace. Hugh had not drawn any figures in the room, but Decima could instantly name one of them. Bob. That's where she had seen him. And there had been two others with him, another man and a woman.

Suddenly, everything came back, the smells, the feel of the lumpy mattress under her back, Bob and his two companions. And then scraps of conversation. The name Peverell had been mentioned, she was sure. And something about silver.

She pulled herself together, closed the sketch book and turned her attention to James as he explained about *cyma reversa* and *cyma recta* and the difference between Doric, Ionic and Corinthian orders. All the time she was thinking that Alexander must be told about this.

They dined at half-past six, and at six the ladies went upstairs to dress. Just as Decima was going to her room she caught sight of Wilmot. He was obviously going to Alexander's room, for he carried a freshly ironed shirt. Nobody else was about, so she gestured to him.

'Wilmot, I must speak with Mr Peverell urgently and in private. I have discovered something of the first importance.'

Wilmot didn't bat an eyelid. 'I shall tell Mr Peverell, Miss Wells.'

Decima gave him a nervous smile, slipped inside her own room and tried to concentrate on changing for dinner. She could get dressed perfectly well on her own, what she could not manage was her hair. It had grown a fraction, but not nearly enough to put up and it stuck up round her head like a fluffy halo. Georgie was very good at coaxing it into some sort of shape.

When Georgie came in, she brushed and pinned, and then threaded Decima's string of moonstones through the curls.

'It looks as though it's meant, Miss,' she said encouragingly.

Decima made a face in the glass and smoothed the bodice of her new, sage-green evening-dress. She still thought she was too tall, but at least, thanks to some decent clothes, she looked elegant rather than overgrown.

'You look like a queen, Miss,' breathed Georgie, patting Decima's sleeves into shape and arranging her shawl.

'Yes, Boadicea,' sighed Decima.

Georgie smiled. Miss Wells was a lovely lady, she thought. She had noticed Mr Hugh looking at her. Things could get interesting if he set up a flirtation. Mr Alexander wouldn't like it one bit.

Decima picked up her fan, checked the back of her skirt in the cheval glass and left the room.

Downstairs in the drawing-room the family was assembling for dinner. The gentlemen were already there, Sir George and Frederick in black evening jackets, Hugh in dark green and Alexander in claret, which set off his exotic looks. Decima frowned. She wished he weren't so very good-looking, it made it quite difficult to concentrate sometimes. He caught sight of her and came across, stopping for a brief word with Frederick on the way.

'I understand you wish to speak with me, Miss Wells,' he said in a low tone.

'Yes, but privately.' Decima cast an agonized glance in Hugh's direction.

'Is that not a little rash?'

'Rash?'

'My father will think you are playing fast and loose with me!'

Decima looked up at him uncertainly. Her colour rose.

Across the room, Alethea watched them, a frown on her face. Whatever was Alex about to be singling out Miss Wells? It would not do, it really would not do. She had nothing against Miss Wells personally, a charming girl, but Alex must not be allowed to develop a *tendre* for her.

At that moment the gong went.

Alexander held out his arm to Decima. 'I'm sorry,' he said, 'I couldn't resist teasing you a little. You colour up so delightfully.'

'This is serious, sir.'

'Oh?'

Decima lowered her voice. 'To do with Mr Hugh.'

Alexander ushered Decima to her chair

and pulled it out for her. 'After dinner,' he said.

★ ★ ★

Hugh felt more and more as though he were living in a nightmare. Bob wouldn't tell him where Springer was staying, only that he now had the wax impressions and had gone up to London to get the key made. He would return either tomorrow or Tuesday with a counterfeit key and the whole plan would be put in motion. Far from feeling relief that his financial problems would soon be over, he felt nothing but an increasing unease and all the horrors of a tormented conscience.

Several times he thought of going to his father and confessing the whole, but shame held him back. Then there was Alexander. He couldn't help feeling that his brother knew something. Damn him, why had he chosen to come down now? Hugh felt a renewed surge of irritation, which had not been soothed by an incident that morning before church.

Hugh enjoyed fondling any of the maids he caught in a corner, but he was well aware that they avoided him, though — the little sluts — they put themselves in Alexander's way if they could. He had overheard two of the housemaids chatting as his brother went past.

184

'I wouldn't mind making his bed — unmaking it rather,' giggled Dorothy.

The other flicked at her with her duster. 'For shame, now!'

'Come on, Suke, you was the one who wanted to take his hot water up this morning.'

Sukey grinned. 'He's ever so handsome in his nightshirt.'

'I bet he's even better without it!'

'Oops, here's Mr Hugh!' Both girls picked up their dustpans and brushes and ran down the back stairs.

Hugh felt the sour taste of envy in his throat. For one awful moment he was a small boy again, hearing of his baby brother's birth, *I hope you will love him*, his mother had written. Love his supplanter? Like hell he would.

Then there was James. Hugh liked James and found, to his surprise, that he enjoyed passing on his architectural knowledge to a fellow devotee. And James was living with Alexander. It had been Alexander, not Hugh, who had rescued James and his mother from poverty.

That afternoon, when Hugh and James had been discussing the architectural orders, Hugh had thought of dropping a few words into James's ear about his precious Uncle

Alex. He couldn't do it. He couldn't bring himself to destroy the child's trust. Instead, he had suggested that, if James were still interested, he would row him across to the island in the lake to view his Roman temple. James's enthusiasm was ample reward.

As Georgie had suspected, Hugh was also interested in Decima. Hugh was a bosom man — a woman should look womanly, in his view — and Decima's figure appealed to him. She'd make a marvellously voluptuous caryatid, he thought. Like James, she accepted Hugh's preference for architecture over hunting, shooting and fishing as perfectly legitimate, and Hugh appreciated not having to apologize for so outlandish an interest.

She was sitting next to him at dinner and Hugh, ignoring Alethea's claims on him, talked mainly to Decima. He hoped she wasn't feeling sore after her riding lesson the previous day. Alexander, hearing Hugh's solicitous enquiry, frowned. It was unlike Hugh to notice anybody's concerns other than his own. He wasn't sure that he liked this development.

Decima made a face and laughed. Then she said, 'James has been explaining to me about the different orders of architecture. I hope I've got the term right.'

'He's really interested,' replied Hugh. 'I've said I'll take him over to the island tomorrow to see my temple, if the weather holds. If it would interest you, Miss Wells, I'd be happy to include you in our little expedition.'

'I'd like to come, but . . . ' said Decima doubtfully. She cast an agonized look at Catherine across the table. For some reason, she wanted a proper chaperon.

Alexander had been listening. 'Catherine,' he said. 'You'd like to see Hugh's temple, wouldn't you? Hugh, if you take the bigger boat, you and I can row and the two ladies and James can be comfortable. I'd like to see your temple again.'

Damn him, thought Hugh, but there was nothing for it but polite acceptance.

'Is your temple dedicated to anybody?' asked Decima, suddenly feeling much happier about the excursion. 'Temples usually are, I believe. Diana, perhaps?'

'Bellona,' said Hugh, and added as Decima looked puzzled, 'the goddess of war.'

'Good Heavens, but why?'

'My grandfather brought a statue back from the Grand Tour. Nobody quite knew what to do with her — a fierce female brandishing a sword in one hand and a severed head in the other. Hardly suitable for a rose garden.'

'Ugh!' This from Catherine.

'You could have said that she was Judith with the head of Holofernes,' said Decima. 'Then she would have had a proper Biblical reference.'

Hugh laughed. 'She has wings.'

'Knock them off.'

'My dear Miss Wells, deface a Roman statue? What barbarism!'

'The Romans did it all the time,' Decima pointed out. 'Didn't they put . . . ' She caught sight of Catherine's agonized look and hastily amended her sentence. 'Didn't some emperor depose his predecessor, knock the heads off all his statues and put his own head on instead?' She shot Catherine an apologetic glance.

Catherine gave a sigh of relief. For one awful moment, she thought Decima was going to make some reference to fig leaves.

Alexander thought so too. He would have bet anything that only the look on Catherine's face had stopped her. She'd covered her tracks remarkably well. He leaned towards her.

'Well done,' he whispered. 'Very quick-witted.'

Decima blushed.

As it was a family party, the gentlemen joined the ladies in the drawing-room after no

188

more than one glass of port. Sir George did not accompany them; these days he was easily tired and he retired to bed.

They found Decima seated at the piano. Her playing was competent rather than brilliant, but she could certainly trip through a sonata without too much trouble. Hugh immediately came across and asked her to play again.

'I shall turn the pages for you.'

Decima allowed herself to be persuaded, played a short piece and then said that she was tired.

'Do you turn the pages for Mrs Peverell, sir,' she said. 'Her playing is vastly superior to mine.'

'Yes do, Hugh,' said Alethea. 'Alex is hopeless and Freddy always loses the place.'

Decima moved away and studied a potted plant.

Alexander had been awaiting his moment and now came forward. 'Some coffee, Miss Wells? Very neat,' he murmured as they sat down. Nobody was within earshot.

'Wasn't it,' said Decima, pleased. 'Perhaps I have an aptitude for deceit, after all. My brothers seem to think so, at any rate.'

'They are not worthy of a moment's consideration. Come, we are private enough. What is it that I should know?'

Decima had decided that, little though she relished the office of tale-bearer, she would have to mention overhearing Bob and Hugh, and Georgie letting Bob into the house, as well as about seeing Hugh's sketch book. The whole took some telling and she didn't notice Frederick giving them curious glances as she talked. Alethea won't like this, Freddy was thinking. He knew she feared a growing understanding between Alex and his young guest. She had several young ladies of impeccable birth and breeding in mind for Alex . . .

'I cannot help wondering if this Springer who Bob mentioned is the same person as the second man I saw in that room,' Decima ended.

'Hm.'

'I don't want to pry into your family business,' she went on mendaciously, for she was naturally dying of curiosity, 'but is Mr Hugh badly dipped!'

'I should imagine so. How far do you think that Georgie is mixed up in this? Is she a willing accomplice?'

'I cannot be sure,' said Decima wretchedly, for she was fond of Georgie. 'She's certainly sweet on Bob.'

'I'll have to think about this.' Alexander took Decima's coffee cup and rose. 'Thank you. You've confirmed something I've feared.'

'You will tell me what is going on, won't you?' pleaded Decima.

'When I know myself.'

Alexander left.

★ ★ ★

Later than evening, in his room, Alexander was holding out his arm and Wilmot was removing the tiny gold and ruby cufflinks and placing them carefully in a small box on the dressing-table. There had been one awful day when one had fallen through a small gap in the floorboards and neither wanted it to happen again.

'There's trouble, Wilmot,' said Alexander, once the cufflinks were safely removed. He told Wilmot what Decima had said.

Wilmot shook his head. 'Ooh, that Mr Hugh! A bad penny, sir.'

'Poor devil,' said Alexander. 'He did not look comfortable tonight. I wish I knew what he is planning.'

'Mr Timson's your weak point, sir,' said Wilmot. 'He's getting as deaf as a post and, ooh, how he snores. Bob could use gunpowder to open the safe and he wouldn't hear a thing. He likes a drop too much, too.'

'This Springer must be the accomplice,'

said Alexander. 'If they're after the silver, there's a lot of it. Bob won't be able to manage it on his own and my brother will surely not get directly involved. Where can Springer be staying?'

'Guildford, probably,' said Wilmot. 'There are some very unsavoury places down behind the castle. It'll be a sort of hedge tavern which hires out vehicles on the quiet.'

'Smuggling?' mused Alexander. 'It's more than thirty miles from the coast, surely?'

'People want their cheap tea and brandy in Guildford as much as they do anywhere else,' said Wilmot dryly.

Alexander laughed. 'You may well be right. I'm committed to this temple trip tomorrow, I shan't need you with me, so . . . '

'Quite like old times,' remarked Wilmot. He'd been in one or two sticky places with Alexander in India. 'I'll see what I can find out. Do you want me to come over to the island if I learn anything interesting?'

'Yes, please. You could bring my telescope over for Master James, if you feel you need an excuse.'

'Very well, sir. And what about Georgie? Shall I ask Mrs Wimborne to keep an eye on her?'

'Difficult. I suspect that Mrs Wimborne doesn't altogether approve of Georgie. She knows that she's not really a lady's maid.' He didn't want Georgie harried.

'I could say that Georgie sometimes sleep-walks,' suggested Wilmot. She'd never believe him of course, but it might serve as an excuse for extra vigilance.

Alexander laughed. 'Why did you never think of the Foreign Office, Wilmot? Intrigue is your natural *forte*.'

'I know about covering up, sir,' said Wilmot quietly.

Alexander put his hand on Wilmot's shoulder and patted it.

* * *

Bob was feeling uneasy, an unusual state with him, and he put it down to being out of London. It didn't suit him. He liked to have buildings around him, lots of people and noise. The countryside unnerved him. It was too damn quiet, and when there was noise it was unexpected, like the ruddy owl which had kept him awake half the night.

He didn't care for Collins either. He was a twitchy sort of fellow, which Bob distrusted, with a habit of laughing silently to himself. Simmonds said that he was a bit touched in the upper works, but Bob didn't think that was it — he'd been sharp enough to offer

Springer help, and to take five quid for it, too. If Collins was thinking of double-crossing them, then he, Bob, would see that he got a knife between the ribs double-quick. He'd keep an eye on Collins.

Mr Hugh was yet another problem. He'd come down to the stables that morning.

'No news yet, sir,' said Bob. Mr Hugh was like a cat on hot bricks. He'd betray everything if they weren't careful. 'Springer only went up to town yesterday, I daresay he'll be back this evening. I'll go to this . . . place where 'e's staying and see. You tell Mr Simmonds you sent me out on an errand, if 'e asks.'

'Why the devil should I send you out at night?' enquired Hugh irritably.

Gawd give me patience, thought Bob. 'That ain't none of Mr Simmonds's business, sir.'

'Let me know when Springer's back,' said Hugh after a moment. He had stumped around the stable, fiddled with a bridle bit and eventually taken himself off.

This wasn't turning out as easy as he'd imagined, thought Bob that night, as he sat in the Old Grey Mare in Guildford, his jar of stout on a rickety table in front of him. He hadn't realized just how many servants there would be in a house like Peverell Park; maybe twenty inside and nearly as many in the stables and gardens. It wasn't easy to go about unnoticed.

The only consolation was that Georgie was proving more willing than she'd been in London. Last night, she'd only been wearing a nightrobe — and Bob was expert at undoing buttons. She was plump and soft in just the right places. If it hadn't been for that curst bowl toppling, he might have got what he wanted. There would be another opportunity — he'd make sure of that.

The Old Grey Mare was a hedge tavern in the back streets behind the castle. It was a building of undoubted antiquity, jutting out crazily over a cobbled courtyard, with various carts and a couple of ancient carriages in what had once been an old mews. Several surprisingly strong-looking horses poked their heads out of the looseboxes. At one time, the inn must have seen better days, but those times had long gone.

An outsider might have wondered where the money came from to keep such horses, and why a hedge tavern needed them in the first place, but Bob knew better than to ask. Doubtless, the local officers of the law had their palms well greased to turn a blind eye.

'Wotcha, cock!'

'Springer! When you get back?'

Springer slid on to the bench beside him. '’Bout an hour ago.'

'You got it?'

Springer nodded.

'We do it tonight?'

'Better tomorrow. We need to prime Collins. You'd best sweet-talk that dolly-mop o' yours into lettin' you in. How safe is she?'

Bob shrugged. 'I ain't trusting 'er not to squawk. Don't worry about Georgie. She won't cause no trouble.'

After twenty minutes or so, Bob drained his tankard and got up. 'I'd best be gettin' back.' He grinned. 'Tomorrow looks like bein' a busy day!'

★   ★   ★

Breakfast the following morning was a lively affair. Most of the talk was about the forthcoming trip to the temple, but there was one other item of news which interested Decima very much.

Alexander looked up from his pile of post and said, 'Miss Wells, Upshawe writes that Liza has had her baby safely — a little boy. I asked him to go and see them and he reports that both are well and Joey and his sister are flourishing.'

'Oh, I'm so pleased!' cried Decima.

196

'Catherine, isn't that good news? Thank you, Mr Peverell.' He had taken some trouble over it, she realized with amazement.

Alethea exchanged a sharp look with her husband.

Since Hugh's first mention of a visit to the temple on the island, interest had grown, and the final tally of visitors far exceeded the original boatload. An hour or so after breakfast, two boats set out from the jetty by the boathouse. One carried Hugh, James and Catherine, and the second, Alexander, Decima, Janey and Clara.

Earlier, Collins and William, one of the footmen, had rowed across, together with two of the maids, the picnic basket and a canvas bag containing the struts, guy ropes, tent pegs and silk covering of an Indian pavilion. Its red silk embroidered with gold stars and the gold tassels gave the impression that some strange bird of paradise had landed on the island, with its willow trees and daisies in the grass.

There was a small store-room inside the temple, which contained a couple of trestle tables, two benches, some folding chairs and a large worn piece of jute matting. There was also a tripod, a kettle, a pile of logs and some kindling.

Collins made a fire on the beach and erected the tripod to boil the kettle. Cold drinks stood in their boxes in the lake to keep cool.

Little Frederica had wailed pathetically on being told that she was too young to go and had to be consoled by being offered a special tea downstairs with her parents.

Decima, who had promised to look after Janey and Clara whilst Alexander rowed, soon realized that it was no sinecure.

'Clara! Sit down.'

Clara was bouncing up and down, scarcely able to contain her excitement. Before Decima could stop her, she had crawled underneath the bench and was perched on the gunwales. Janey was leaning precariously over the side, trailing her hand in the water.

'Clara!' shouted Alexander. 'Get down at once.'

Clara giggled. Decima turned round, grabbed Clara's sash and pulled. 'If you and Janey don't sit still,' she said firmly, 'you will both go back with William. A boat is no place for bad behaviour.' She took hold of Janey's sash with the other hand as she spoke.

'Now listen to me, you two,' said Alexander, as they neared the jetty, 'any silliness and you both go straight home. Miss Wells wants to enjoy herself, not spend her time worrying about what you are up to.'

'Yes, Uncle Alex,' chorused two small voices.

'I'll get William to keep an eye on them,' said Alexander. 'If they fall in, it will be his job to haul them out.'

'They will keep him busy, I daresay,' said Decima smiling.

'I'm glad to see that you do not agree with Rousseau's idea of allowing children to become over-indulged.'

'No, indeed!' cried Decima, thinking of Anna-Maria and her siblings. 'To allow a child to be ill-mannered and out of control does it no favours, in my opinion. We all have to live in society and the sooner a child, of either sex, learns consideration for others, the better. Any children of mine will be properly brought up.'

'I thought you were never going to get married,' observed Alexander, with a smile. 'I see you've changed your mind.'

'Changed my mind?' echoed Decima crossly. 'No, of course I haven't.'

7

Catherine enjoyed the boat-trip far more than she expected. Hugh rowed smoothly and it was peaceful being able to sit next to James and dabble her fingers in the water. She smiled at Hugh and said, 'This is really very good of you.'

'Not at all. It's not every day that I acquire a sister and a nephew.' He liked Catherine, he decided. She was so restful.

'My mother never spoke about Peverell Park, though she knew it, of course. She grew up on the estate. I had no idea that it was such a beautiful place. Look, James, see how the house is reflected in the water.'

James turned round. The house, on a small eminence, sloped gently down to the lake. To the right was the park with its fallow deer and clumps of elms and to the left a small hill topped by a wood.

'It would be something to design a place like that,' cried James. He looked at it critically. 'It's a bit too short, though. What do you think, Uncle Hugh?'

Hugh looked up and rested his oars for a moment. 'Yes, perhaps you're right. Another yard or so on either side would do it.' He smiled at James.

Then he caught sight of Alexander, whose boat was twenty yards behind him. Damn him. Why did he have to invite himself on this trip and turn the whole thing into a family picnic? He, Hugh, would have been perfectly happy rowing James over, with Miss Wells to provide the female interest. If there was one thing Hugh detested it was a family party. He could see Clara bouncing about and making the boat rock. It would serve them all right if the boat tipped over. For two pins, he'd push Alex in himself.

★ ★ ★

The jetty was underneath a weeping willow. Alexander's boat slid under the hanging, leafy fronds and instantly they were in a green world.

'A waterfall of green!' cried Clara, trying to jump up and catch a handful of leaves.

Decima grabbed her.

William came down to the boat. Alexander threw him the painter and William tied it to an iron ring. Hugh's boat had already arrived.

'Here, William, take Miss Clara before she falls in.' He picked her up and handed her to William. 'Now you, Janey.'

Decima made to climb out. Suddenly, Alexander's hands were on her waist. He picked her up and put her safely on the jetty before jumping ashore himself.

Decima felt herself colouring — she seemed to do nothing else these days. 'Was that really necessary?' she asked indignantly. 'I could have climbed out by myself, you know.'

'I daresay, but you'd have risked me seeing your ankles and I'm sure you wouldn't want that.'

Decima looked uncertainly at him. He was laughing at her, she was sure, but she didn't know what to do about it. Somehow, his picking her up was far more shocking than his seeing her ankles, but how could she possibly say so?

She could see Hugh standing with Catherine and James in front of the temple. Hugh was obviously explaining its points to James, and Decima hurried towards them away from Alexander's disturbing presence.

'I congratulate you, Mr Peverell,' she said to Hugh as she came up. 'It is most impressive. I suppose that's Bellona?' She gestured towards the statue of a goddess inside the pediment of the projecting portico.

'Yes, Miss Wells. She's safely out of the way up there.'

'It's a miniature Pantheon!' exclaimed James, looking critically at the temple.

'I've always rather admired the domed roof,' said Alexander, sauntering up. 'You're a clever fellow. Hugh.'

Hugh grunted.

'Why does it have Ionic capitals, Uncle Hugh? Shouldn't they be Corinthian?'

'True. But Ionic capitals are more soldierly. I bent the rules.'

'Can we go inside, Uncle Hugh?' demanded Janey.

Inside, the plaster roundels decorating the walls echoed the martial theme with shields and crossed spears and a helmet over the door.

Alexander remembered Decima's description of Hugh's drawing of the room she'd been held in. Hugh had a trained eye, he obviously knew exactly what that room had looked like. Could he have been responsible for kidnapping Miss Wells? And, if so, why? There had been no ransom note, which was odd, since her clothes must have indicated that she came from a wealthy family.

It certainly looked as though Hugh were involved in planning a robbery, but would he really sanction kidnapping? Alexander could see that under the friendly chat, Hugh was not at ease. He did his duty as a host, but he often fell silent.

When Alexander was little, his mother had told him stories of what Hugh and Freddy had got up to as children, and he had come to England looking forward to meeting them for the first time. 'I'm going to see Hugh and Freddy,' he'd told Sikander, proudly. He had wanted to love his big brothers.

Freddy had been kind and welcoming, but, from the very first, Hugh had made his aversion very clear. Alexander still remembered his bewilderment and hurt. Time had made no difference to Hugh, if anything, his hatred and resentment had increased. Alexander wished it were otherwise, but he had learned to live with it.

★ ★ ★

The Indian pavilion was much admired by Catherine and Decima and lunch was served there. After luncheon, Janey and Clara rushed round the island, jumping and squealing and William and one of the maids ran after them. When they'd tired themselves out, Catherine took them both inside the pavilion, gave them lemonade and sat them down.

'I'll tell you both a story,' she said, 'of a naughty little girl who got lost in the woods . . . '

When Catherine married, she had hoped for a large family. Three sons and two daughters had died in their infancy before James was born. She found Freddy and Alethea's little girls just what she'd have wanted. Her own daughters had died too young for stories, but she'd sung to them and Janey's rosy cheeks reminded her poignantly of her long lost little Katie.

'Once upon a time . . . ' she began.

Decima found that she was anxious to keep out of Alexander's way. She wandered over to where Hugh was sketching. He looked up and closed his book.

'I'm sorry,' she said, 'I didn't mean to interrupt you.'

Hugh smiled. At least Miss Wells preferred to talk to him rather than his brother. He could see Alexander out of the corner of his eye demonstrating ducks and drakes to James. Every now and then Alexander glanced in their direction. Good, thought Hugh, he will see that Miss Wells is ve content with my company. He opened sketch book to show her.

'I was drawing an imaginary house. Something I'd like to be able to design properly.'

Decima studied it. 'It's very grand.'

Hugh laughed. 'I have grand ideas.'

'I hope the kitchen isn't half a mile from the dining-room,' observed Decima. 'I visited a stately home when I was staying with one of my brothers and I couldn't help thinking that one's dinner would be cold by the time it reached the dining-room.'

'Ah, but the compensation would be no smells of boiled cabbage.'

'I'm not convinced that that's worth a cold dinner.'

'Any other criticisms?'

'Oh, please don't take offence!' cried Decima. 'I didn't mean to insult you. I'm interested. After all, where one lives is important, and how it's designed says a lot about how people think, don't you agree?'

'Perhaps.'

'It's house as metaphor,' continued Decima eagerly. 'For example, look at the prominence given to public space in a great house. Huge reception rooms, halls, staircases even, and so on. They are not built for privacy. Surely that ʏs something about the priorities of the ʏople who live in them?'

Hugh shut his book again. What an extraordinary girl, he thought.

'I'm sorry.' Decima stared out across the lake to where a fish jumped. 'I'm always being told off at home for my flights of fancy.' Why could nobody understand that she liked to speculate about life? Except Alexander, a small voice added treacherously.

'You have nine brothers, haven't you?' said Hugh. 'I daresay you can't help questioning things.'

'Like a man, you mean,' said Decima drily. Hugh was nicer about it, but he was just as bad as her brothers. She smiled at James who had just come up. 'Enough of ducks and drakes?'

James indicated his crutch: 'I can't do them as well as Uncle Alex. His skim across for ages. He's really accurate, too. He can throw a stone and hit whichever lily pad he wants.'

'Showing off,' muttered Hugh, but *sotto voce* because he liked James.

Decima left them and James sat down, easing his bad leg.

'The ground's uneven over there,' remarked Hugh. 'I noticed it myself.'

James hunched a shoulder.

'You know, James, I think you should be an architect when you grow up, if you want to. Mind you, I daresay your grandfather would disapprove, as he did with me — 'not a gentleman's profession'.'

'Uncle Alex has said I can be what I want,' replied James. He didn't notice Hugh's grimace. 'It isn't up to Grandpapa. In any case, I'm hardly a gentleman, thank God.

What will I need, Uncle Hugh? Drawing, of course, but what else?'

'Mathematics, Latin. Italian would be useful.'

'Italian?'

'The best architects have come from Italy. There are books in Italian that aren't translated into English. Besides, you should try and go there one day.'

'I . . . I wish you'd go with me,' said James. He didn't say so, but he didn't like the thought of negotiating an Alpine pass on his own. He tried to ignore his disability, but being a cripple in a strange land was a frightening thought.

'If only the dibs were in tune.' Hugh tried to turn it into a joke. He'd like to show his nephew round Italy, he realized.

James looked up at him. 'Are you in debt?' he asked curiously. There was a pause. 'I'm sorry, I shouldn't have asked, I suppose.'

'I'm a fool, James. Yes, I'm in debt, though God knows there are many in far worse case than I am.'

James thought for a moment. 'Mama was always terrified of being in debt,' he confided. 'Before Uncle Alex came, things were sometimes very bad. She took in lodgers and they weren't always very nice.'

'I admire your mother,' said Hugh sincerely.

'So do I, but she doesn't really understand me at all. Perhaps that's just women. It's all very puzzling.'

'Females are,' agreed Hugh, thinking of Decima.

James sighed and leaned back against Hugh's knee. Hugh patted him on the shoulder. They both stared out at the lake and pondered on the oddities of women.

★ ★ ★

Wilmot was having a busy day. As soon as the boating expedition had set off, he went down to the stables. This was going to need careful handling. Alexander wanted to keep Hugh's name out of it, but he needed to know a bit more about Bob's activities, especially any movements which might be suspicious.

He wandered slowly past the row of looseboxes and put up with several derisive catcalls from the stable lads.

'Want anything, Mr Wilmot?' called out one of the stable lads cheekily.

'Nothing you're offering,' retorted Wilmot.

Bob was nowhere to be seen, but Simmonds was in the tack-room. After a moment's hesitation, Wilmot went in. Simmonds knew how to hold his tongue, he was sure.

Simmonds looked up and put down the saddle soap, 'Yes, Mr Wilmot?'

Wilmot shut the door carefully. 'Just looking round. On behalf of Mr Alexander, you understand.'

Simmonds looked at him steadily for a moment and then said, 'Something worrying him, perhaps?'

'You might say that.'

'Would it be anything to do with our friend from London?'

'It would indeed.' Wilmot relaxed. 'Is he here now?'

Simmonds shook his head. 'He comes and goes at mysterious hours you might say.'

'Ah, now where to, Mr Simmonds? And who does he see — he who is supposed to know nobody from this part of the world.'

'I don't know who he sees, but he's been going to Guildford. A mate of mine at the White Hart saw him in town.'

Wilmot nodded. He'd thought as much. 'Mr Simmonds, strictly between you and me, if you wanted to hire a cart or a carriage maybe, on the quiet, where would you go — in Guildford?'

'Try the Old Grey Mare. But you're never

going dressed like that!' Simmonds looked at Wilmot's impeccable black suit and patent leather shoes.

Wilmot grinned. 'I shall look most disreputable, take my word for it.'

Simmonds looked sceptical, but said, 'Ask Tom Watts at the White Hart for directions — and tell him I sent you.'

Wilmot rose to go. 'Thank you. One more thing. Where does our friend sleep?'

'Shares with Collins.'

'Mm, isn't he with the island party today?'

Simmonds nodded. 'He's all right, is Collins. My brother-in-law's nephew. A good lad.'

★ ★ ★

Nobody in England knew, but the Wilmot whom Alexander had rescued from drudgery in a small indigo business, was a very different creature. There, he had been a shabby backroom boy with a straggly moustache and hair which crept down over his collar. He had learnt early the value of being invisible.

When he left Peverell Park half an hour or so after talking to Simmonds, he had on shabby trousers, a frayed shirt with a twisted handkerchief which did duty for a cravat, and

211

a threadbare jacket. He wore a battered old hat and his shiny pumps were replaced by scruffy boots. He had carried these clothes in a linen bag to the old gamekeeper's hut in the back wood and changed there.

He did not go to the White Hart — he was hardly respectable in his present garb. Instead, he found his way down to the narrow crowded streets behind the castle and asked directions.

The Old Grey Mare proved to be a dirty hedge tavern with a weatherbeaten inn sign creaking above the door. To the left were the stables and half-a-dozen surprisingly well-cared-for horses poked their heads over the loosebox doors. There was an open coach-house door opposite and in it were two carriages, both old and shabby, but certainly fit for use. Wilmot noticed that the wheels were freshly oiled and the shaft of one had recently been replaced.

He could hear noises from the taproom at the bottom of the yard. He must go carefully, Bob might be there. He peered into the tack room.

'Oi!' A voice came from behind him. 'What you want?'

Wilmot turned. A large coarse man in an open-necked shirt exposing a doormat of ginger chest hair, stood on the cobblestones.

'My mate wants to know if there's a carriage available for this evening.'

'Where to?'

'London.'

'Nah, mate.' The ostler indicated one of the carriages and said, 'This one's already been taken — going to Lunnon. T'other ain't suitable for long journeys.'

Wilmot glanced round the tack-room. Bridles, halters and saddles hung on the walls, together with harnesses, spare girths and back and neck straps. A scrubbed wooden table and a battered chest of drawers for brushes, rags and saddle soap stood next to an old desk with an open, stained leather-covered book on it.

'What a neat hand!' Wilmot exclaimed.

' 'T'ain't mine, can't write.' The ostler spat on the cobblestones.

'I can't read very well,' said Wilmot, leaning over the desk and scanning the open page. 'I left school too early.' His eye had found what he was looking for. The carriage was hired by a D. Springer.

'Me neither,' said the ostler. 'Waste o' time, if you asks me. A young lad wants to be out working, not sitting in school.'

Wilmot excused himself and made his way to the taproom. It was dark, malodorous and filled with pipe smoke. So much the better.

He crossed over to the bar and ordered a pint of porter. A couple of men glanced at him curiously, but no one accosted him; the Old Grey Mare was well used to shady characters who slunk in and out. Wilmot chose himself a corner seat, hunched over his drink and peered about him.

He gradually became aware of a voice he recognized. It was coming from behind him, from a small ante-room, half hidden by a frayed curtain.

'Mr Hugh gettin' the wind up, is 'e?' said an unknown voice.

' 'E's as jumpy as a kitten,' replied Bob.

'And Collins?'

' 'E's all right, 'E don't have much to do; get the cob and trap into position; wait for us to load the goods; 'elp load the carriage and then return the cob and trap. 'E's made sure the cob's stall is to 'and and 'e's put new straw down to deaden the noise. If 'e's caught when we've gone, that's 'is look-out.'

'That's it then. Two o'clock it is. You'd best be off, Bob.'

There was the noise of scraping chairs, the sudden draught from a back door and there was silence. Wilmot waited ten minutes and then left.

★ ★ ★

214

Decima peeped into the pavilion. Catherine was still telling stories and the children were listening eagerly. Clara, her thumb in her mouth, was sitting on Catherine's knee and Janey sat on a cushion at her feet. They looked contented and absorbed. Decima crept away.

She would try to find a spot where she could be by herself for a while and avoid Alexander, who made her feel awkward. She didn't want to bump into him. She walked slowly round the island looking for him — in order to avoid him. When she couldn't find him she was perversely disappointed. Eventually she wandered past a large weeping willow hanging over the water.

She parted the fronds and stepped inside Clara's waterfall of green. The branches were almost horizontal. Decima considered them. She would climb up. There was one place where two branches crossed which would make a good perch. Nobody would ever think to find her here.

The branch she wanted was about seven feet off the ground. The willow trunk was rough, but still too smooth for an easy purchase. She jumped, but it was just too high. Then she noticed a small block of masonry, probably left over from the temple, half-hidden by a clump of grass. If she stood on that?

After several efforts, she managed to grab the branch she wanted. Clutching it with both hands, she swung herself towards the trunk and walked up it. By the time she had clambered up she had shown far more of her legs than her ankles, but she sat triumphantly on her perch and tried to shake bits of bark and leaf off her skirts. There was a green stain on one of her stockings, but she ignored it.

There was a sound of clapping and Alexander, who had been watching, strolled forward.

'Well done, Miss Wells. I'd have offered to lift you up, but I know how much you'd have disliked that.'

Decima, suddenly conscious of swinging ankles, tried to pull up her legs and nearly lost her balance.

'Move over,' said Alexander. He jumped, caught the branch and a moment later was up.

Decima edged along the branch as far as she dared. There was nothing she could do. He was between her and the trunk and the ground suddenly seemed a long way off.

'There's a much better place further round,' said Alexander. He pointed to a large branch going out over the water with a smaller one underneath for feet and another in front to lean on and peer down safely.

'It's quite safe. I used to come here a lot. If we're lucky, we might see a pike.' He stood up, climbed over and turned to hold out his hand.

Decima hesitated and then pulled herself up. Alexander seemed to think it perfectly commonplace for her to be up a tree and she couldn't help responding to that. There were no reproaches or expressions of shock.

'I can manage, thank you,' she said, primly.

The first steps were easy, but there was a longer stride out over the water to the branch Alexander was on. She looked down nervously.

'Don't look down,' advised Alexander. 'Here, take my hand.'

Decima did so. His grip was firm and secure and very soon she was sitting on the branch beside him. In front of them, the falling fronds were thinner and Decima could see the pink and yellow of the water lilies on the lake.

'It's lovely up here,' she said. 'So peaceful. Did you discover it yourself?'

'Oh yes, I used to come up here to be alone. There's something about it which reminded me of a lake I used to know in the foothills of the Himalayas. That, too, had waterlilies.'

'How old were you when you first came to England?'

'Fifteen — and I hated it at first. It was cold, wet, grey and unfriendly.'

'It must have been a change indeed,' said Decima, trying to picture it. 'Different plants, different animals, different people. I think the thing I would find most difficult would be understanding — I'm not putting this very well — what lies underneath what people think. The assumptions.'

Alexander looked at her. 'That's very acute of you, Miss Wells. I remember thinking when I first came to England that although I could speak English, I really had to learn it all over again. There was a sort of code to which I had no key.'

'What did you speak in India?'

'Punjabi or Hindi, though I spoke English with my mother. But for much of my childhood she was ill and I was mainly left to my own devices. I ran about the hills with two Punjabi boys I knew.'

He stared out across the lake. Decima had the feeling that she had just been told something significant.

'What sort of things did you do with them?'

'The usual things boys do. Swam, rode, fished.'

'You must have missed them as well, when you came to England.'

'I did.' And the worst thing was, he thought, that the new world he was in was one they could never understand. How could he explain England and Peverell Park to Kamal and Kumar? It was an immense distance away, and not only geographically.

'I think communication can sometimes be very difficult,' said Decima, unconsciously echoing his thoughts, 'when one's inner landscape does not match the world outside. It can be lonely.'

'Yes.'

'If you are the only one who notices that there are two worlds and not just one. I've often thought about this.'

Alexander turned to look at her. 'Have you?'

'Oh yes. Bloomsbury Square is a very male world with men's standards. Inside me, I knew that there were other ways of thinking, other standards. Later on, of course, I realized that I was not alone — the servants, for example, must have known that there were different ways of seeing the world to which Papa and my brothers were quite blind.'

'True. I hadn't considered that.' Wilmot, he thought. Wilmot must have this feeling of living in an alien world. Perhaps that was why he liked him.

'It used to worry me,' Decima continued. 'Now, it doesn't so much. I'd rather know that there are other ways of thinking than be in a sort of straitjacket and believe that the way I see things is the only way.'

'Giraffes again?' smiled Alexander.

Decima laughed. 'Oh yes, they gave me hope, those giraffes. I shan't forget them.'

Behind them came sounds of Janey and Clara laughing. Catherine was talking to James. There were clashes of china as maids carried plates into the pavilion. Alexander consulted his pocket watch.

'Tea-time. We'd better get down from our eyrie.'

He rose, climbed back onto the original branch and turned to help Decima. Once she was safely there, Alexander jumped down.

'Now, you.'

'I shall be all right,' said Decima firmly. She would turn round and edge herself over until she could lower herself and then drop. She just hoped that she wouldn't rick her ankle.

'Don't be silly, I'll catch you.'

Decima thought of protesting, but in the end she tucked her skirts firmly round her legs, took a deep breath and slid down into his arms. For a moment he held her tightly and she could feel his heart thudding against her own and the next he released her, put her gently on the ground and stood back.

'There. Safely on *terra firma*.'

Safe? thought Decima. She wasn't at all sure that she felt safe. She busied herself patting her skirts into shape and tidying her hair.

'There isn't only spoken language,' Alexander observed. 'There are other ways of communicating. They, too, are important and have their own laws.'

Decima found that her heart was beating erratically. She swallowed but didn't reply. Alexander held the hanging fronds apart and they stepped back into the world outside.

★   ★   ★

Wilmot returned to Peverell Park by the back road, pondering on the possible sequence of events. Springer would drive the carriage from Guildford and park it somewhere near. In fact, the grassy verge he was passing would be a good place, it was hidden from the house by trees. It would be risky to bring the carriage much nearer. Then what?

Collins was involved somehow. There was a

small dog cart in the stable which would be ideal. The back let down to allow the dogs to jump in and out — and it would be convenient for loading. It was small enough to negotiate the narrow path between the kitchen-yard wall and the drying area. For example, it would be easy enough to reach from the butler's pantry. The stolen goods could be loaded in relative safety and Collins could then lead the cob to the hidden carriage for the goods to be transferred.

Wilmot had now reached the old hut where he had stored his clothes and ten minutes later, he was once more in the proper garb of a gentleman's gentleman. He turned down the back drive which crossed a paddock and led to the stable and kitchen yards. He was encouraged to find that the gates at each end of the paddock had had their hinges newly oiled. Good, he thought, he couldn't be too far out in his suppositions.

He arrived back at Peverell Park in time to catch Mrs Wimborne in her parlour. Mrs Wimborne had a soft spot for Wilmot. She was well aware that some of the servants mimicked his speech and finicky ways, but she admired his loyalty to Mr Alexander and she knew that Mrs Peverell and Céline had great respect for his taste. His private life was no concern of hers. At least he would never be caught with his hands up a maid's skirts.

Accordingly, she smiled at him and rang the bell for one of the kitchen maids to make a fresh pot of tea.

'Mr Alexander is a trifle concerned about Georgie,' he said, when he'd complimented her on the plum cake and taken the cat onto his lap.

'Oh?' Mrs Wimborne would commit herself no further.

'She's a good girl, but she's in love with Mr Hugh's groom.'

Mrs Wimborne had seen Bob making eyes at Georgie, but she'd also caught him stealing a kiss from Dorothy. 'He's not serious, Mr Wilmot.'

'No, but Mr Alexander thinks that Georgie may be — and Bob's an opportunist if ever there was one.'

Mrs Wimborne looked at him. There was something behind this. Once or twice she'd found Bob inside the house where he had no business to be. He'd excused it as getting lost, but she'd sent him on his way pretty sharp.

'What would Mr Alexander like me to do?'

'Keep an eye on her, Mrs Wimborne, especially at night. She's a good girl, but even good girls can be foolish.'

'I'm a light sleeper, Mr Wilmot. No girl creeps past my room without I hear her.'

Wilmot smiled and rose to his feet. He had promised to tell Mr Alexander if he discovered anything.

★ ★ ★

Georgie had had great hopes of her visit to Peverell Park. She would be able to see more of Bob; she would have the temporary status of a lady's maid, and maybe she would be able to pick up some tips on how to do hair elegantly, or special ways to starch a lace collar. Georgie had ambitions for herself and she saw the visit as a step up.

Reality was sadly disappointing. Céline, Alethea's French lady's maid, sneered at her; the other maids ignored her, and the footmen made jokes about her appearance. Worst of all, there were few opportunities to see Bob alone. She hadn't realized that, although the outside staff ate in the servants' hall, Bob would be at another table and surrounded by far too many pretty maids.

After the fiasco of their midnight meeting in the kitchen, Bob seemed to be avoiding her. When she managed to speak to him the following day, he was short with her. 'I have a job to do, Georgie.'

'Are you going on this trip to the island?' asked Georgie, despairingly.

'I ain't had my orders yet.' He gave her a brief peck on the cheek and left, whistling as he went.

At breakfast on Tuesday, Georgie learned that Collins and William and two of the maids were to go over to the island. Mrs Wimborne was busy chivvying the kitchen maids and supervising cook and the picnic hamper. Perhaps this would be an opportunity to see Bob. She hovered round after breakfast, trying to catch his eye. Eventually he came in her direction.

'Shall you be up near the house today?' she whispered.

'Not till later. Maybe after tea. I have some business for Mr Hugh.'

Georgie looked suspiciously at him. Whatever could Mr Hugh want him to do that would take all day? If he was looking to spend time with Dorothy, she'd scratch her eyes out, the little bitch.

She would spend the afternoon in the laundry room. There were collars and cuffs to be washed in milk starch and dried carefully. Decima's silk chemises and petticoats, which Mrs Alfred had sent on, needed her particular attention. The laundry had access to the outside for drying — and even Mrs Wimborne, who kept a strict eye on what the maids were up to, had to acknowledge that clothes must be dried in the fresh air. Laundry maids could flit in and out with impunity and Georgie had envied them their freedom.

Bob was not there at lunch-time and Georgie started her washing with a heavy heart. The laundry maids were unhelpful and it was late afternoon by the time she was ready to hang out the washing. The laundry had a door which led directly to the kitchen yard, which itself led out through a narrow arched doorway in the yard wall to the secluded drying area. No wonder the laundry maids liked to come here, thought Georgie. Any gardener's boy or stable lad, who kept his eyes and ears open, would know when the laundry maids were outside and come up for a quick chat or kiss.

She was in the middle of hanging out Decima's petticoats, when she saw Bob and waved. He vaulted over the fence, came up and gave her a squeeze.

' 'Ello, beautiful. Want any 'elp?'

Georgie put her hands on her hips and surveyed him. 'Your hands are dirty, I'll be bound.' She picked up a petticoat and shook it in his face.

Bob eyed it and whistled. 'Cor, plenty of lace!' Nell wouldn't half like to get her hands on it.

Georgie pegged up the petticoat, allowing Bob to admire her swaying hips and straining bodice. When he reached round to fondle a breast, she did no more than giggle and say, 'Give over, Bob. Supposing someone should see.'

'Georgie, 'ow about you and me having a quiet cuddle tonight, eh?'

'I don't want no repeat of last time,' scolded Georgie. 'Your hands were everywhere.'

'Honest, Georgie, you can trust me.' He set about cajoling. 'After the old cat's gone up, eh, Georgie? Let me in, eh? I shan't stay long.'

Fifteen minutes later a flushed and breathless Georgie agreed. 'All right, Bob. About one o'clock. Mrs Wimborne doesn't settle until after midnight and she always checks up on the maids.'

'I'll come up at one and tap gently on the kitchen window.'

'I'll do what I can,' said Georgie, suddenly nervous.

'I'll wait all night for you,' promised Bob. She'd better come, he thought. He didn't want to force the back door unless he had to.

★   ★   ★

227

Hugh and James talked for some time, mainly about James's hopes for the future, but also about the problems during the building of the temple. Eventually, James left to wander round and Hugh went up to the pavilion. He was feeling curiously unsettled. Talking to James had brought back all his old longing for the career that had been denied him and, on top of that, the awful realization that he was now committed to a burglary that had become increasingly abhorrent.

Catherine was in the pavilion helping the maids to organize the tea things.

'Come for a stroll with me, Catherine,' called Hugh, trying to push aside his feeling of walking in a nightmare. 'James is all right. He's gone to look at the back of the temple. Do you want me to take you to find him?'

Catherine shook her head, 'I like him to do things on his own. He'll come when tea is ready, I'm sure.'

'Come and look at the water lilies, then.' Hugh offered her his arm. 'Were you never tempted to send James away to school? I'm sure Papa would have supported him, if you'd asked.'

'Send him away to school?' echoed Catherine. 'Certainly not!'

'My brother and I came back to England for our education when I was eight.'

'I can understand that the climate in India may be unhealthy for English children,' said Catherine hesitantly. 'I know your mother was sickly and might not have survived the voyage home, but surely it can't be a right thing to do, though I don't mean to blame Sir George, of course.'

Hugh picked up a stone and hurled it at the water lilies. It tore through a lily pad and the impact set all the water lilies rippling.

'I survived. I soon forgot. Small boys do, of course.'

'I cannot believe that,' said Catherine quietly. 'I only have the experience of James to go by, but I would never separate an eight-year-old boy from his mother.'

Hugh picked up another stone and threw it. 'She soon had Alex.' The stone ripped through another lily pad.

'That is not the point. She didn't have you and your brother. Alex is Alex, I'm sure he was welcome, but that doesn't mean that you were not missed dreadfully.' There was a pause, Catherine stared out across the water with blinded eyes before adding, 'I lost five children before James. I love him dearly, but I have never forgotten my other babies. One doesn't.'

Hugh leaned over and kissed her cheek. 'I'm sorry,' he said. He suddenly had the feeling that somewhere underneath him, a well of tears was waiting to drown him. He pushed the thought away. 'I really meant to talk to you about James. You'll let him study architecture, if that is what he wants, I hope?'

'Oh yes. Meeting you has given a great boost to his ambitions. I do hope you will come and see us when we are back in London. James wouldn't like to lose touch now he's met you.'

'I don't visit at Golden Square,' said Hugh curtly.

'I am sorry.'

'I may leave London, I don't know.' Hugh's boot heel was busy grinding a daisy into the grass.

'Leave London?' Something is very wrong, she thought.

'Possibly.' When he got that money, thought Hugh, with a sickening lurch of the heart, he'd have to go away. How could he bear the guilt of staying? Oh God that he'd never met Springer or Bob.

'James and I would miss you, Hugh,' said Catherine, putting her hand timidly on his arm and then removing it.

Hugh sighed, picked up another stone and then dropped it. Across the lake a boat was coming towards them. He stared. 'Oh God, here comes that Mollyish valet of Alex's. I'm damned if I want to talk to him.' He turned and with a muttered apology left her.

Catherine, dismayed and concerned, made her way to the pavilion. She turned for one last look at the lake and saw Decima and Alexander emerging from underneath a willow tree. They were walking a yard apart, almost as if they'd quarrelled, but Alexander was smiling to himself and every now and then Decima glanced towards him when she thought he wasn't looking. Something was going on there, too, she thought — and she was not the only one to notice it. She had overheard Frederick and Alethea whispering to each other about it the previous evening.

The moment they reached the pavilion, Decima went across to supervise Janey and Clara. Catherine, after a moment's hesitation, went over to Alexander and said quietly, 'Have you a moment?'

He turned at once. 'Is anything the matter?'

'I'm worried about Hugh.' She related the conversation.

'I've always known that he resented me,' said Alexander. 'He's never liked me.' As for the rest, he thought, Hugh was obviously suffering from the pangs of an uneasy conscience. Poor devil.

Catherine sighed. 'I like him, and I think

he's unhappy. Can't you talk to him?'

'It takes two. I can't talk to a brick wall.' He looked up and saw Wilmot nearing the island. Good, he must have some news. 'Excuse me, Catherine.' He turned and went down to the jetty and a few moments later was seen in earnest conversation with his valet.

Hugh and James were watching Wilmot's boat arrive. 'I'm surprised Wilmot can row,' muttered Hugh sourly.

'Don't you like him, Uncle Hugh?' asked James, surprised.

Hugh didn't answer. A moment later Alexander came up and handed James his telescope. 'I forgot this this morning,' he said. 'I thought you might like to use it. Wilmot kindly brought it over.'

James turned to thank him.

Hugh's mood communicated itself to the rest of the party. James began to look worried and even Janey and Clara became unwontedly quiet. By common consent, the moment tea was over, the parties made to return to Peverell Park.

'Goodbye, temple!' called Clara, as their boat pulled away from the jetty. She was tired from all the fresh air and running about and soon her head was on Decima's lap where she fell asleep. Janey gave her sister a pitying look, but it wasn't long before she, too, closed her eyes.

Alexander had taken off his jacket and rolled up his sleeves. Decima watched his strongly muscled arms pulling at the oars and felt her cheeks flush. Alexander's words came back to her: 'There isn't only spoken language.' She shivered.

'Cold, Miss Wells?'

'A little.'

'Are those two asleep?'

Decima bent over them. Clara's thumb was firmly in her mouth and Janey's breathing was soft and even.

'Yes.'

'It is as I suspected and you confirmed, Miss Wells, there is a robbery planned for tonight. Your room is near the back stairs, so you may hear noises, and I'd rather you didn't come down and get yourself into danger. Lock your door if you're at all frightened. Please try not to worry; so far as Wilmot can gather, only three people are involved and Wilmot and I are prepared.'

'But . . . they may be armed!'

'Possibly,' said Alexander unmoved. The hill tribes he'd grown up among were a war-like lot. He had known ambushes and sudden raids. He didn't think he had much to fear from Bob and his ilk. 'Don't forget that the first shot would bring the indoor servants downstairs and the men from the stables up to the house. The robbers will want to avoid that.' He looked at her concerned face and added, 'Don't look so worried, Miss Wells, I assure you there is no need. They must know very well that to be caught is a hanging matter. They will escape rather than fight it out.'

Decima gulped. 'You . . . you will tell me when it's over, won't you?' she pleaded. 'I shan't sleep a wink until I know.'

'My dear Miss Wells,' said Alexander smiling, 'if I start knocking at your bedroom door in the small hours, there'll be more than your brothers demanding our instant attendance at the altar!'

Decima blushed and was silent.

8

The moment his boat was secure and he'd seen Catherine and James safely ashore, Hugh stumped off to the stables to find Bob. He had, he realized, only the slightest notion of how the robbery was planned. Springer would be involved, he knew, but how were they going to transport the stuff?

Bob came out of a loosebox, took one look at Hugh's face, and pulled him back inside.

'I've seen Springer,' he told Hugh. 'There ain't nuffin' to worry about. It'll all go like clockwork.' Hugh was shaking and Bob set himself to reassure. Hugh was in it up to his neck. There was no way he could betray them without betraying himself. All the same, Bob was worried. 'I'll report to you first fing tomorrow, sir. I'll spike Timson's drink tonight and he'll go to sleep like a babby. Nobody'll notice the stuff's gone. We stay a day or so, go back to London and Springer'll have it fixed.

'You've no cause to worrit. You'll get your money all right and tight.'

Hugh rubbed his hand over his face. 'I wish it were well over.'

'Yes, sir. It's always like this. I likes the excitement meself, but I knows some doesn't.'

Hugh grunted. He felt defeated. 'I'd best be getting back to the house then.'

As he stumbled back, he thought, what was to stop Bob scarpering along with Springer and the booty? Hugh couldn't possibly go to the police with the tale. He'd be immediately suspect. His financial affairs would be under scrutiny and the size of his debts uncovered, maybe even his loan of £250 and the exorbitant interest. He would never be able to get away with it.

How could he have been such a fool?

Somehow the thought of James's shock when he learned that his uncle was a thief, was worse than anything. He couldn't go on with it.

But how could he stop them? Springer was a dangerous man. Even if Hugh found out where he was staying and told him it was off, he doubted whether Springer would turn back with such sums at stake. He'd be more likely to cosh Hugh over the head, to ensure his silence.

Bob watched Hugh walking back to the house and felt a prickle of unease. Then he thought, come on Bob, you'll be out of all this in a few hours' time. Tomorrow morning,

Mr Hugh would find that his groom had scarpered, along with the family silver and he would realize that he'd been duped. Not at once, maybe. Perhaps he would still hope for a day or so that he'd get his share. There would be nothing he could do. Poor mug.

★ ★ ★

The family party broke up shortly after ten o'clock that evening. Those who had been on the island declared themselves tired after a day in the fresh air. Hugh was looking strained. Decima was struggling to behave normally. Alexander was his usual self, but he confessed to being tired. 'All that exercise,' he said smiling, and, after he had helped Sir George upstairs, he said good night to the company, nodded reassuringly to Decima and went to his own room.

The house slowly settled for the night. Mrs Wimborne chivvied the maids upstairs. The menservants had their own corridor on the other side of the house.

★ ★ ★

Georgie usually enjoyed the moment when she went upstairs with the other maids. She liked to lie in bed and enjoy the feeling of being in her very own room — the first time in her life she'd had a room of her own. At home she'd been one of six children and had to share her room with her three sisters; in Golden Square she shared with Meg, but here, as befitted her new status, she had a little room to herself. There were pretty flowered curtains at the window, a mat by her bedside and even her own chest of drawers. Before going to sleep, she enjoyed imagining all she'd have to tell Meg when she got back to London.

That afternoon, it had seemed so easy. Bob was loving and persuasive. The sun was shining, it was broad daylight and her promise to creep downstairs in the dark to let him into the house, seemed perfectly possible. Now, as the grandfather clock downstairs in the hall chimed midnight, a sound echoed faintly by the stable clock, things felt very different.

She didn't want to do it.

She would tell him she overslept, she told herself. But, a little voice whispered, he'll be so disappointed. Remember what happened last time? said her conscience sternly; it was only that bowl crashing which stopped him from going too far. What about Dorothy? came the small voice. You don't want her to get her claws into him, do you? And don't think she isn't interested.

Georgie twisted and turned in her bed. Sleep, her virtuous ally, refused to come. There was a noise on the landing outside. Georgie closed her eyes. Mrs Wimborne opened the door gently and peered in. After a moment, the door closed.

Time moved on.

★　★　★

The clock struck midnight. Wilmot quietly tapped at Alexander's door.

'Everything quiet?' asked Alexander as he opened it.

Wilmot nodded. 'Except for Mr Timson's snores.' Timson slept in a small room off the butler's pantry — ostensibly to guard the silver.

'He's too old for this sort of thing,' said Alexander. 'Let's hope he doesn't wake.' He was worried about Timson, but could think of no satisfactory excuse for removing him from his post. He had toyed with the idea of confiding in Frederick, but dismissed it. Freddy had made his abhorrence of Alexander's suspicions perfectly clear. Timson would have to take his chance.

Alexander ran through their options. 'I don't think we need worry too much about

Collins. He's unlikely to be armed.'

'He could raise the alarm.'

'He'll have to be watched,' agreed Alexander. 'He's a damn fool. The lure of easy money, I suppose.'

He opened the chest of drawers and took out a leather case containing a brace of pistols, then sat down to prime and load them ready for use.

Wilmot was laying out a pair of dark trousers, a dark jacket and a grey scarf. Alexander shrugged himself out of his evening clothes and flung his cravat over a chair. 'Here, Wilmot, help me with these cufflinks.'

'Not much will happen until Springer gets here with the carriage, I daresay,' said Wilmot, putting the cufflinks carefully on the dressing-table. 'Whatever Bob does with the safe, he can't get the stuff away until Springer's arrival.'

'I wonder if I should tackle Springer first?' pondered Alexander. With Springer out of the way, the plot would inevitably fail. But what if Hugh decided to go it alone with Bob? He had his carriage in the stable; Springer's sudden removal might make him desperate. He didn't want to face his brother at the other end of a gun barrel.

'I think I'd best deal with Springer, sir,'

said Wilmot. He, too, was thinking of Hugh. If anybody were capable of restraining him, it would be his brother. 'All it needs is for me to un-pole the horses. They'll make their own way back to Guildford, I daresay. Springer can't do much with a carriage with no horses.'

'Are you sure he'll come down the back road?'

'The paddock gates are both oiled,' Wilmot pointed out.

'Very well. Make sure Springer's out of the way before you do anything. He may well be armed. Do you want one of my pistols?'

Wilmot shook his head. 'I'm not a shooting man, sir.'

'I want the whole thing hushed up as far as possible. If that means Springer and Bob escaping, so be it. My father's peace of mind is more important.'

'I'll deal with the carriage horses and then I'll come back to the house. Where shall I meet you, sir?'

'Try and get to the pump in the kitchen yard. It's secluded and there's some cover from the rainwater butt. But you'll have to play it by ear, Wilmot. I can't tell what the situation will be.'

He slid his pistols into the holster and opened a wooden box on the dressing-table.

Inside was a small, wickedly sharp throwing knife in a leather sheath. He pulled on his boots and thrust the knife down the side.

'What's the time?'

'Nearly a quarter to one, sir.'

'Too early. Let's just run through it again.'

★ ★ ★

The stable clock struck the three-quarters. A snore from Mrs Wimborne's room showed that she was asleep.

Nearly one o'clock. She couldn't let Bob wait, thought Georgie, she just couldn't. She must at least go down and tell him that she couldn't let him in, it would be only fair. She got up quietly, put on her dressing-gown, opened the door and tiptoed out. She had to go past Mrs Wimborne's room and noticed, to her alarm, that her door was ajar.

Her heart was thumping so loudly that it seemed it must be heard. Mrs Wimborne stopped snoring and turned in her bed. Georgie held her breath.

Eventually, Mrs Wimborne started snoring again and Georgie crept downstairs, avoiding the tread which creaked, and made her way to the kitchen. All was quiet there. The cat, sitting on the chair by the side of the range, opened its yellow eyes and stared at her reproachfully. The trays for the morning's hot chocolate were already laid and set out neatly on the sideboard.

Shivering with excitement and fright, Georgie crept along the passage to the back door. The stable clock struck one. Outside, there was a gentle scratch at the little window beside the back door. Georgie saw Bob's face, pale in the moonlight. He pressed his lips to the glass, Georgie put hers to the other side, smiled and went to open the door.

'Now, where can we be private?' whispered Bob, after the first kisses were exchanged. He didn't want to risk Timson waking up just now — later, he could deal with him. Springer was not due for another hour and Bob didn't see why he shouldn't enjoy himself before the real work of the night began.

Georgie gave a stifled giggle and led him towards the laundry at the end of the opposite corridor. They wouldn't be heard there. Don't do it, whispered the small voice, but it was now so faint as to be almost inaudible. In the laundry was a pile of carpets waiting to be beaten and cleaned.

'Hm, nice and cosy,' said Bob. He led Georgie to the carpets and pulled her down beside him.

'I thought you didn't like me no more,'

whispered Georgie. 'You ain't hardly been near me.'

'I ain't used to grand places like this,' Bob confessed. 'You've gone up in the world, Georgie. I thought you'd be too good for the likes o' me now.' The usual old line, he thought.

This time, though, there would be no interruptions and, softly, softly, he'd get what he wanted. One hand began, very gently, to stroke her neck. Georgie pressed herself against him. Hold your horses, he told himself. He could afford to take it slowly.

★   ★   ★

One-fifteen. Wilmot and Alexander came quietly down the front stairs and made ready to go to their separate destinations. Wilmot was setting out for his rendezvous with Springer's carriage.

'We don't know what time Bob and Collins will come up,' he whispered, as they reached the front hall. 'I'd best avoid the back door. Don't want to meet our friends.'

Alexander nodded, pulled back the front-door curtain and turned the key. 'I'll leave it unlocked,' he said. 'We'll try and meet as planned. Just keep out of any danger. Good luck.'

Wilmot avoided the gravel path that bordered the house, and made his way along the edge of the front lawn and turned down towards the back paddock. The stable block was in front of him, hidden by a wall and a small apple orchard. All the same, he was dangerously exposed to view if Bob or Collins came past. He moved cautiously in the shade of the apple trees and kept his ears open for any sound from the stables.

As he edged out from the shelter of the orchard, he saw a faint glimmer of candlelight from the small carriage-house window. The carriage-house doors were shut and Wilmot took his chance and hastened past.

He reached the top gate to the back paddock, it opened noiselessly — somebody, Collins probably, had done their work well. There was silence. He skirted round the edge of the paddock in the shadow of the hawthorns along the hedge, reached the bottom gate and climbed over. He was now standing in the moonlight on the grass verge of the back road which led to Guildford. His shadow, long and blue, lengthened on the grass. Then, in the distance, he heard the noise of hooves. Springer was early.

Ooh, Wilmot, we are in a pickle, he thought. He was all too exposed. There was no time to get into the shelter of the bushes.

The carriage was coming down the hill towards him — Springer, if he looked, would have a clear view.

Wilmot crouched down as close as he could to the hawthorns bordering the fence and waited. He remembered Alexander telling him once never to look at an enemy who was too close. 'Stare at their feet, the ground, anywhere but at them. It's far less dangerous.' He hoped to God that Alexander was right.

★ ★ ★

The stable clock struck half past one. Downstairs in the laundry, Bob was stroking the insides of Georgie's thighs and edging his way upwards. He had unbuttoned himself and was ready. Georgie, eyes shut, was moaning. Gently does it, thought Bob, we're nearly there.

The stable clock moved on.

Upstairs, Mrs Wimborne stirred. She often slept lightly and the shaft of moonlight coming in between the curtains had woken her. She sat up, straightened her night cap and got out of bed to straighten the curtain. That done to her satisfaction, she was just about to get back into bed when a creak stopped her. She opened her door and peered out. Georgie's door was ajar and moving slightly in the draught. She padded across and edged it open. The bed was empty, the sheet thrown back.

Suddenly awake, Mrs Wimborne went back to her room, put on her slippers, tied her dressing-gown cord firmly, lit her oil lamp with the tinder box she kept by her bedside and went downstairs with righteous tread to do battle for Georgie's honour.

Georgie was lying, hands and ankles bound with rope and a soiled table napkin tied round her mouth to gag her. Bob, feeling pleased with himself, was in the butler's pantry opening the safe. Timson, eyes goggling in terror, was trussed up in his cubby hole.

It had all been too easy, thought Bob, smiling reminiscently, Georgie had been eager and afterwards, if she'd cried a little, well, that's what girls usually did. They'd go on about how wicked they were, but it didn't stop them doing it again, he noticed. He'd reassured her, petted her some more and then gagged and bound her quickly. He'd pulled down her nightdress and tidied her up — he had his moments of chivalry — buttoned up his trousers and left.

The duplicate key was in his pocket. He checked his watch. Springer should be here soon and in the meantime he had work to do. He'd left some packing baskets filled with straw tucked away in a corner outside the kitchen door. He went to get them.

Gagging Timson had been easy. The old man was no match at all and in a trice he, too, was gagged and bound and dumped back on his bed in the cubby-hole where he'd bleated in terror.

'You ain't going to get hurt, so stop whining,' Bob said impatiently. He lit the table lamp with quick efficiency, closed the door and got down to work. He knew precisely what he had to do. Clear the safe as fast as possible and sort out what they'd take. Jewellery, of course, was portable. Silver, if it were sellable; cutlery and smallish bowls were the best. Gold plates, if they were real gold and not a figment of Collins's imagination. They could be melted down.

The key fitted. Nice piece of work there, though he doubted whether Peverell would appreciate it — the man was lily-livered in Bob's opinion. With a final click, the safe door swung open. Bob emptied it fast, putting the items on the pantry table and sorting them rapidly. Through the closed cubby-hole door, he could hear Timson weeping. He ignored him.

Serve him right, he thought. He was a

boring old codger, always going on about the splendours of the past and the titled guests he'd known. Now he'd have another fund of stories to bore them with.

⋆　⋆　⋆

Mrs Wimborne walked into the kitchen and knew immediately that something was wrong. There was a draught as from a door left open.

⋆　⋆　⋆

Alexander gave Wilmot five minutes. It would be better if they operated separately. He went back upstairs to check on Hugh. God forbid that Hugh should join in the burglary. If he'd been Springer or Bob, he'd have squashed that possibility firmly. He went upstairs to the end of the corridor where Hugh's bedroom was and listened. The poor devil was awake. Alexander could hear him shifting about and the bed creaking, but, thank God, he seemed to be staying put.

Alexander went back downstairs, let himself quietly out of the front door, and went round to the stables. He had been in far more dangerous places than this on the North-west Frontier and he was alert for any tell-tale noise. Once he stopped to listen.

There were rustles in the leaves, mice probably; a fox crossed his line of vision as it trotted over the lawn going down towards the lake.

As he neared the stables he could hear somebody moving about. Bob or Collins? The end stable had a line of stalls, most of which were empty, but the old pony was there and the cob. The door was open.

Alexander entered silently and stepped into the shadows of one of the empty stalls. The cob was rustling in its stall and a voice was saying, 'Quiet now, girl. There, there.'

Cautiously, Alexander raised his head. Collins was bent over, tying leather shoes round the cob's hooves. Then he led the cob out towards the stable yard. There, in a corner, was the dog cart, its wheels bound with sacking. He worked swiftly and as soon as the cob was harnessed, he led it up the path to the right of the kitchen yard and alongside the drying area.

He was plainly nervous, for he kept glancing round and Alexander could hear his indrawn breath. If this were India, he thought, Collins would be dead meat by now. When the cob reached the drying area, Collins turned it round to face the back paddock.

Alexander had seen all he wanted. Collins

was in position. Wilmot, he hoped, was still waiting for Springer, and Bob should already be in the house and at work in the butler's pantry.

He hesitated. He could go and check on Bob but something told him that he should get back to the house. Alexander always followed his hunches. Hugh was awake and stirring. If he should decide to come downstairs, he could spoil everything.

He entered the front door just in time to hear a muffled scream from Mrs Wimborne, followed by a thump and then the sound of a body falling to the floor.

At the same time, Hugh, fully dressed, came running down the stairs. He did not see Alexander. He burst into the kitchen.

'You devil!' he cried. 'What have you done?'

Bob had silenced Mrs Wimborne by hitting her on the back of the head with the rolling pin. She lay slumped on the floor.

'Get back to your room, you fool,' hissed Bob. 'Just get out.' He reached into his pocket and brought out his knife. 'I'm warning you.'

Standing in the shadow of the grandfather clock, Alexander pulled out one of his pistols and cocked it, but Hugh was in the way.

'Oh God, Dorrie!' cried Hugh. 'What have I done?'

'Move!'

Hugh stepped back. Bob bent over Mrs Wimborne for a moment and said, 'She's alive, ain't she? Now go, afore I loses my temper. I ain't got time to deal with your quibbles. You should 'ave thought of them afore.'

Hugh hesitated.

'Do you want I cut her throat?'

Hugh turned and stumbled back into the hall. Bob closed the door on him. Hugh sank down on the stairs and buried his face in his hands. He thought wildly of borrowing his father's old duelling pistols and putting an end to it all then and there. At least the noise would bring Freddy and Alex down and put a stop to this miserable business. He wished he were dead anyway. His whole life had been a mess, what would it matter if he shot himself? Who would care — apart from James? Yes, perhaps James would care a little.

It wasn't until Alexander sat down next to him and put his arm round his shoulders that Hugh realized that anybody else was there. He jumped, saw who it was and desperately tried to pull himself together. That Alex, of all people, should see him like this seemed the ultimate humiliation.

'Come to triumph?' he said acidly.

But Alexander was not triumphing.

Instead, he tightened his arm and said quietly, 'Hugh, it'll be all right. I promise you. I'll sort it out. Don't worry.'

Hugh's bravado collapsed. 'Oh God, Alex, you don't know . . . '

'Shh, yes I do. You are in debt and you called in Bob and Springer.'

'I wish I'd never met them, but I was desperate, Alex. And mad.' Hugh began to shake, 'Oh God. Dorrie! When I first came to England — she was only a housemaid then — she was so good to me.' I'll never forgive myself for this, never.'

'Shh! It's all right.' Alexander patted his back. 'Listen, are you up to helping me sort this out? Wilmot and I know roughly what the plan of action is, but we could do with another hand.'

Hugh looked bewildered. 'You know? But how? What can you do? Bob has a knife and Dorrie is in there, and poor old Timson. Springer will be armed.'

'Hugh, either go up to bed and leave it to me, or come along and do as I say. For God's sake, for once in your life, just trust me.'

Hugh drew a deep breath and said shakily, 'Tell me what to do.'

Alexander handed him his second pistol. 'Careful, it's loaded. Come with me and I'll explain as we go along. Hurry, we haven't much time to lose.'

Hugh rose slowly. He looked down at the pistol in his hand and then he looked at Alexander as he went to open the front door.

★ ★ ★

Springer was taking his time. He pulled up scarcely ten yards from where Wilmot was crouched down by the hedge and jumped down to manoeuvre the carriage and horses so that they turned to face back towards the main road. That done to his satisfaction, he went to check them, running his hands down their legs — all right there — and loosened the girths a fraction. He was early; the road from Guildford had been quicker than he thought. He didn't like sitting here in the moonlight at half past one in the morning, where anybody could see him and demand his business, but there was no help for it. He got his pipe and tinder box out of his pocket and lit up.

Wilmot was excruciatingly uncomfortable. A nettle had found a bare bit of skin and stung him. His knees were damp and he was kneeling in something which stank. But Springer was now facing away from him, even though he was still uncomfortably close; Wilmot could smell the tobacco and hear

Springer clearing his throat and spitting into the hedge.

The stable clock struck the three-quarter hour and Springer tapped out his pipe and tethered the horses to an ash. He took out his pistol, cocked it and walked purposefully towards Wilmot.

Wilmot held his breath, froze and stared carefully at the ground. Springer passed so close that he was within inches of Wilmot's hand. Wilmot could have jumped him, but he held back; Springer was a big man, and armed.

Springer passed the crouching man and reached the back gate of the paddock, fastening it open as he went through. Wilmot raised himself cautiously and watched as Springer crossed the back paddock, opened the far gate, secured that and disappeared in the direction of the house.

Wilmot counted out a couple of minutes and rose, heart pounding. He had work to do. The original plan was to un-pole the horses, point them in the right direction, smack their rumps and let them find their own way back to the Old Grey Mare. On the other hand, they might stay by the carriage and an expert could pole them up again within minutes.

After a moment's thought, Wilmot un-poled them, took the reins and led them towards the back paddock. They'd be safe there and would provide him with cover if Springer came back unexpectedly.

Once inside the paddock, he closed the gate, led the docile horses to the top gate, removed their harness, dropped it by the hedge and let them go. Then he quietly closed the top gate and, keeping to the cover of the bushes on the north side of the path, made his way up towards the drying ground. The wind had freshened and he was upwind. Good. Springer and Collins would be less likely to hear him.

He could now hear voices; Springer and Collins were standing on the path behind the kitchen-yard wall, conferring in low voices — they were evidently waiting for some signal from the house. Collins was soothing the cob, which was getting restless and shifting its feet. Every now and then Springer took a quiet step through the arched doorway into the yard and listened. Somehow, Wilmot had to cross their line of vision to get to his rendezvous with Alexander.

He was just wondering what to do, when several things happened at once. There was a noise from the kitchen yard as of something falling.

Springer motioned to Collins to be silent and moved to the arched doorway. Wilmot crept closer behind the cover of the hedge. Collins was crouched down by the cob, shaking. His teeth were chattering so loudly that Wilmot could hear them.

'Shut up, you fool!' hissed Springer over his shoulder. He then stepped into the yard and disappeared from sight.

Wilmot seized the moment and jumped on Collins, silencing his cry with one hand. The other was on his windpipe. Wilmot might look insubstantial but he was wiry — and Collins was terrified. He pulled Collins back through a gap in the hedge and into the shelter of the wood behind the drying area.

'Now listen, Collins,' he whispered. 'It's over! Whatever happens now, the robbery's not going to happen, understand?' He gave Collins's throat a squeeze to gain his attention. Collins nodded.

'Right. I have no quarrel with you, but Bob and Springer are for the drop. Now, if I let you go, you get over that back stile and away. I don't care where you go — to Hell for all I care, but if you're ever seen around here again, you'll swing.' He loosened his hand slightly.

'They made me do it, Mr Wilmot,' whispered Collins. 'Honest, they did.'

'And I suppose you couldn't tell Mr Simmonds?' said Wilmot contemptuously.

'Get away, if you value your life. One squeak from you and you're a goner. We've had our eye on you for some time.' He gave Collins a push.

Collins fled, dodging through the trees. One down, thought Wilmot.

★ ★ ★

Springer entered the back yard, pistol at the ready. Nothing. The silence was absolute. But some sixth sense told him that something wasn't quite right. The back door was ajar — Bob had got in then. But the noise hadn't come from the house.

He stood irresolutely for a moment, then made as if to enter the house. Behind him a shadowy figure began to cross the yard. Springer, glancing at the kitchen window, saw something reflected in the glass, spun round and shot. There was a stifled cry.

It's that damned darky brother, thought Springer. He cocked the second barrel. As he did so, Hugh stepped out from behind the rainwater butt.

'Go on, then,' said Springer, grinning. 'It's your turn. I've 'eard as 'ow you've always 'ated the bastard.'

Hugh turned towards Alexander, who was clutching his right arm. There was a pause of

258

perhaps five seconds. Alexander looked down at the cobblestones. I have misjudged, he thought, and I shall pay the price. Then, poor Hugh.

Suddenly, Hugh's arm jerked up. He fired. There was a horrible gargling sound and, as if in slow motion, Springer's pistol dropped, he spun round, collapsed and lay spreadeagled on the cobblestones.

Alexander took several deep breaths and pulled himself up slowly.

Hugh came forward. 'Alex! Are you all right?'

Alexander pulled him back into the shelter of the wall with his good hand. 'For God's sake, Hugh! Bob's still in the house and we don't know whether he's armed. Quiet!'

'But your arm!'

Alexander gave it a cursory inspection. 'A flesh wound. Nothing serious. My fault. I was careless.' His eyes were sparkling. He tossed his hair out of his eyes and laughed, 'Shh! Here he comes.'

Bob had heard the noise and came running, pulling on his jacket as he did so. He pulled his knife from his belt and tested the edge. Razor sharp.

One glance at Springer's body told him that he was dead. His throat had been shot through and in the moonlight Bob could see the dark blood staining the cobblestones. It's that bastard Collins, he thought. Decided he could take over, did he? He ran through the arch just as Wilmot came through.

Wilmot shouted. Hugh ran. As he came through the arch, Bob grabbed Wilmot and held him as a shield, the knife to his throat.

'Right,' snarled Bob, 'I cuts 'is throat if you moves a finger. Drop that gun.'

Hugh hesitated and Bob ran the blade lightly round Wilmot's neck. Wilmot gave a whimper. He could feel drops of blood trickling down his neck. Hugh dropped the gun. Bob edged forward, still using Wilmot as a shield and kicked the gun out of reach. 'Now, I wants you to — ' He got no further.

Alexander had somehow climbed up on to the yard wall, taken his throwing knife in his left hand and hurled it with deadly accuracy.

Bob gave a small surprised groan, twisted and crumpled. Wilmot fell back against the wall, panting. Hugh picked up Bob's knife and the pistol.

'You all right, Wilmot?'

Wilmot felt his throat warily. 'I think so.'

Alexander jumped down and came over. 'I thought I told you to keep out of trouble?' he said. He looked at Wilmot's neck. 'Messy, but it's only a surface cut. You'll live. Here,' — he pulled off his scarf — 'take this.'

Hugh, stunned by the speed of events, was staring down at Bob. 'Is he dead?'

Alexander bent to pull out his knife and wiped it an the grass. 'Oh, yes.' Bob had jerked once as the knife came out and now lay still. Alexander looked down at him for a moment. Sikander had taught him that throw and insisted that he learn to do it with either hand.

Hugh laughed a little shakily and looked at his brother. 'Now what?' He was vaguely surprised that the gunshots hadn't woken the entire household. 'How are we going to explain the shooting?'

Alexander smiled grimly. 'We're not — or as little as possible. The wind's coming from the south, thank God. The sound would be blown away from the house.'

Wilmot bound his neck and told Alexander about Collins.

'You let him go!' exclaimed Hugh.

'Yes, sir, Mr Alexander's orders.'

'Come on, Hugh. Have your wits gone begging? This must not get out. Only think of the effect on Papa. Right, Wilmot, we have work to do. Are you up to it?'

'Yes, sir.'

The bodies were carried to the cart. As they moved Bob, there was a tinkle and half a dozen spoons fell out of a jacket pocket.

Hugh went to check the other pockets and removed rings, bracelets and a couple of gold chains.

'We could put the bodies into the hired carriage,' suggested Wilmot. 'The horses are in the back paddock and can be poled up again. If Mr Hugh drives it up to the main road and points it in the direction of Guildford, the horses will in all likelihood take the bodies back to the Old Grey Mare. What happens to them after that is not our problem.'

Alexander nodded. 'Very neat.'

Wilmot went to the cob's head. Alexander turned to Hugh.

'Why didn't you shoot me while you had the chance?' he asked in a low voice.

'I found I couldn't,' replied Hugh. 'You're my brother.'

'Am I?'

They looked at each other.

'Go and get that wound attended to,' said Hugh.

9

Decima had not slept at all. It was all very well being told to keep out of the way, she thought crossly, but she was worried. She managed to doze for an hour or so until she heard stealthy footsteps creep past her room. The guest wing was near the back stairs, which was normally used only by servants. The footsteps could be Georgie's or, possibly, Alexander's. She sat up and chewed her nails in an agony of indecision. She didn't want to interfere with whatever plan Alexander had in mind, but nor did she want Georgie to get into trouble.

Then, much later it seemed, she heard heavier footsteps and the characteristic wheeze of Mrs Wimborne.

She gave a sigh and tried to settle down again. Mrs Wimborne would surely stop Georgie from doing anything foolish. She closed her eyes. Half an hour later she heard faint gunshots and sat up abruptly.

Whatever had gone wrong? She pulled on her slippers and dressing-gown and opened the door. As she came out into the corridor, she saw Catherine, her hand still clutching her nightcap, coming out of the room opposite.

'What was that?' whispered Catherine.

'Gunshots,' said Decima, more calmly than she felt. 'There was a robbery planned for tonight. Your brother told me. He was going to stop it.'

'Is it anything to do with Hugh?' asked Catherine with surprising calm.

'Sort of. At least with Bob and an accomplice.'

'I did wonder. I couldn't think why Alex was so keen on coming here when we did. When I knew that Mr Hugh was to be a guest, I suspected that something was up.'

'You had an invitation from Sir George,' Decima pointed out.

'Yes, dear, but I knew that couldn't be the whole story. Sir George has known of my existence for over forty years.'

Decima smiled. Alexander had been more devious that she had realized. There was also her own position, which she was almost sure had played its part in the invitation.

She moved over to the small window on the landing. By squinting down she could see most of the back yard and over the wall towards the stable block. All was quiet. Then a movement caught her eye. The pony cart was being led down to the back paddock.

Somebody, could it be Hugh? was opening the paddock gate and, as the cart trundled through, Decima was sure that the other figure was Wilmot. As the moon came out from behind a cloud she could see that thin, elegant silhouette.

What had happened? And where was Alexander?

Then she saw him coming into the yard and walking slowly towards the back door. His left hand was holding his right arm.

'Oh God,' whispered Decima. 'Alex . . . I mean, Mr Peverell, has been shot!'

Decima and Catherine reached the kitchen a few moments before Alexander came in. Mrs Wimborne was trying to pull herself up. A small oil lamp was lit on the kitchen table and Decima could see the rolling pin, covered with blood, lying on the floor.

Catherine fell to her knees beside her.

'Oh, poor Mrs Wimborne! Come, let me help you up. Oh dear, I wonder what . . . ? Decima, some warm water in a bowl and a clean cloth, please.' Catherine put an arm gently round her and helped her onto a kitchen chair.

Decima went across to the dresser, found a bowl and took it to the kettle on the hob. Thank goodness it had been filled for the morning and the water was warm. She filled the bowl, took a clean tea towel and brought them back to Catherine. At that moment, there were footsteps and Alexander came in, took the situation in at a glance and bent over to pick up the rolling pin, holding it up to the light of the oil lamp.

'Mrs Thompson will make you feel more comfortable directly,' he said reassuringly. It could have been worse, he thought. He'd once seen an appalling injury inflicted by an ordinary domestic flat iron — and there were several at the back of the kitchen range.

'You are hurt, Mr Peverell!' Decima's voice quavered. She wanted to run over and hold him and was so horrified by this revelation that she had to clutch onto the back of a kitchen chair to stop herself.

'Grazed by a bullet. I've had worse. I'll deal with it in a moment. Catherine, can you deal with Mrs Wimborne?'

'Yes, of course,' said Catherine quietly. Somehow, since arriving at Peverell Park, Catherine had acquired more self-confidence.

'Shout if you need help. I have work to do before Wilmot and Hugh come back. Miss Wells, is there a sharp kitchen knife handy?' He didn't think she'd want to use his and his right arm was useless at the moment.

Decima pulled herself together and went to the kitchen drawer. 'Large or small?' Her voice had steadied.

'Small, I think. Is it sharp?'

Decima tested it. 'Yes.'

'Good. Come along.' He left the room and turned down the back corridor towards the butler's pantry.

Bob had left an oil lamp lit on a side table. Piles of silverware, gold plates and tumbled jewellery gleamed on the table. Decima blinked. It was like something out of the Arabian Nights; there were silver vegetable dishes with elegantly carved finials, coffee and milk jugs, teapots, sugar bowls and an array of cutlery. The gold plates shone like a pile of yellow moons. A couple of strong boxes stood forced open. Inside, jewellery cases lay open, their contents tumbled all over.

Behind them came a faint groan. Alexander crossed over and opened the door to Timson's cubby-hole. Timson, gagged and bound, was lying trussed up on his bed. Alexander went to fetch the lamp, holding it carefully in his left hand.

'Come, Miss Wells, can you set the poor fellow free?'

Decima knelt down and cut carefully at the gag. The knot was far too tight to be undone. 'I'm sorry,' she whispered, 'I'll be as gentle as I can.'

Alexander watched her. 'We need some

brandy and some laudanum,' he said after a moment. He took a candle from the mantelpiece, lit it and left the room.

Decima cut the string which tied Timson's arms and feet and then helped him under the bedclothes. The poor old man was shivering and shaking and seemed incapable of speech. Decima sat beside him and massaged his hands gently.

Alexander came back with the brandy, tipped a generous measure into a silver goblet and held it to Timson's lips.

'Sorry, Mr Alexander,' quavered Timson. 'I could do nothing. He was on me before I knew.'

'Don't worry. Nothing's been taken. He and his accomplice are dead.'

'Dead?' echoed Decima. 'Bob's dead?' Georgie will be upset, she thought.

'He threatened to cut Wilmot's throat. I killed him.'

Decima gulped.

'Quite right, Mr Alexander,' said Timson approvingly in a stronger voice.

'Forget I said it! Mr Hugh and I have decided to keep the whole thing quiet. We don't want to upset Sir George.' He reached into his jacket pocket and took out a bottle of laudanum. 'Here, Miss Wells, give Timson a spoonful.'

Decima did as she was told, taking a silver

teaspoon from the pile on the table. She then settled the pillow more comfortably under his head and pulled up the blankets.

'Now, Timson, we'll come back and see how you are in due course. Miss Wells, we'd better see how Catherine is doing. Leave the lamp.

'Poor old boy,' Alexander continued, as they went back towards the kitchen. 'He looks badly shaken. Still, he should go off to sleep now, which will be the best thing.'

Back in the kitchen, Mrs Wimborne was looking more herself. There was a neat bandage round her head and she was sitting sipping a cup of tea. Catherine was sitting next to her.

'Mrs Wimborne came downstairs after Georgie,' Catherine told Alexander, worriedly.

'Where is Georgie?' asked Decima. She should have got up when she heard Georgie creeping down, she thought. Maybe she could have stopped all this happening. She looked across at Alexander. He was leaning heavily on the kitchen dresser.

'She doesn't know. She was attacked almost as soon as she got downstairs. But Georgie wasn't in her bed.'

'I'll go and look for her,' said Alexander, picking up the candle. He was swaying slightly.

'No, you won't,' said Decima suddenly. 'For heaven's sake, Mr Peverell, sit down, unless you'd rather fall down.'

Mrs Wimborne blinked at hearing Alexander bossed about. Even Catherine looked startled.

Alexander smiled and sat down. Just then voices were heard outside, then footsteps. Wilmot and Hugh came in. Hugh's gaze went straight to Mrs Wimborne and his expression lightened. He crossed over and kissed her cheek. 'Dorrie, I wouldn't have had such a thing happen for the world. Catherine, how is she?'

'A nasty bang and she may be slightly concussed. She should see a doctor.'

'I shall be all right, Mr Hugh. I don't need a doctor,' put in Mrs Wimborne.

'We'll see,' said Hugh. He turned to his brother. 'Alex, are you all right?'

'No, he's not,' said Decima. 'His arm should be looked at. And he wants to go and look for Georgie.'

Hugh shot her a startled look, but all he said was, 'Give me the candle. I'll find Georgie. Wilmot, you sit and let Mrs Thompson look at your neck.'

Catherine rose, emptied the bowl of reddened water and went to pour some more from the kettle. Wilmot unwound the cravat and shrugged off his jacket.

Decima turned to Alexander. 'I think you'd better let me look at you,' she said. 'Blood is dripping down your sleeve.' A small pool of it was forming on the floor.

'All right. You'll have to help me out of my jacket and shirt.' Now he'd sat down, he realized that his upper arm hurt abominably. He was curious as to what Decima would do. She was wary of men, he knew. How would she cope with undressing him? He saw Wilmot make as if to come over and shook his head slightly.

Hugh returned. 'Catherine,' he said urgently, 'leave Wilmot for the moment; I think you'd better come.'

Catherine left the room. Wilmot picked up the clean rag, dipped it in the bowl of warm water and cleaned himself in front of the small mirror which the parlour maids used to check their appearance before they served in the dining-room. There was a faint line of blood where the blade had touched his neck, but it was merely a scratch. It had barely broken the skin.

He'd have nightmares for weeks, doubtless, but it would soon heal.

Hugh came back again. Alexander looked at him over Decima's head — she was easing off his jacket — and raised an enquiring eyebrow. Hugh looked grim and nodded.

'Dorrie,' said Hugh. 'I believe you'd be best on the sofa in the housekeeper's room. You can't go upstairs in your present state. One of the maids shall make you up a bed down here and stay with you. Who would you like?'

'Aggie,' whispered Mrs Wimborne. 'Aggie's sensible.'

'Wilmot, do you feel up to fetching Aggie?'

'Of course, sir.' Wilmot gave his neck a last pat with the cloth and put his jacket back on. Miss Wells was quite absorbed in her task of undressing Alexander and he was looking down at her bent head. Well, thought Wilmot, best leave them to it.

Alexander looked up briefly. 'Take some laudanum, Wilmot, otherwise you won't sleep.'

Hugh lifted up Mrs Wimborne. 'Wilmot, bring the candle, would you, and light me to the housekeeper's room before you go upstairs.'

They left.

Decima dropped the torn and bloodied jacket on to the floor and went to undo Alexander's shirt. 'Your jacket's ruined,' she said.

She pulled the oil lamp nearer. The right shirt sleeve was bloodstained and the force of the bullet had pushed bits of linen into the wound. Alexander shrugged himself out of the left sleeve, wincing as he did so.

'It will be less painful if I cut your shirt off,' said Decima.

'Go ahead.'

She stood for a moment, biting her lip and looking down at the wound, then went to the kitchen drawer for a pair of scissors. She cut around the top of the right sleeve, freeing it from the rest of the shirt, cut from the neck down the shoulder seam and gently pulled the shirt off. Then she stopped.

'I've never dealt with a bullet wound before,' she said, looking at his torso, 'you'll have to tell me what to do. I can see that you've had some experience.'

There was the puckered scar of a bullet on Alexander's side. She touched it lightly. There was another thin scar line going up his rib cage which she traced with her finger.

Alexander drew in his breath. He was watching her as she touched him. Did she know how it made him feel? Probably not. Perhaps she should learn.

Ignoring his wound, he reached up with his good arm, brought her face down to his and gently kissed her. Decima put a hand on his bare shoulder to steady herself. For a moment their lips met and then she pulled back to look at him with shocked eyes.

'Why did you do that?' she whispered.

'Don't you know?' Alexander smiled at her consternation.

Decima shook her head.

'Maybe you should find out.' He pulled her back to him and kissed her again.

There was the sound of footsteps. Alexander released her just as Hugh came in.

'I've woken William. I've told him to saddle the chestnut and go for the doctor. How's the wound?' He crossed over to look at the remains of the sleeve still stuck around the wound. Decima stood back. 'Hm, warm water, I think. We'll have to get it clean.'

'The doctor should certainly look at Mrs Wimborne.'

'You, too.'

Decima moved over to the range. The kettle was on the hob and, with a bit of luck, should still hold some warm water. She felt it. Good. She filled the bowl Catherine had used with clean, warm water, brought it over and handed Hugh a clean tea towel. She didn't trust herself to touch Alexander. She didn't trust *anything*.

'Where is Georgie?' she asked in a voice that was not quite steady.

'In the laundry. Catherine's with her.'

'I'll go and help,' said Decima and left.

Hugh looked at Alexander. 'She seems upset.'

'Maybe she doesn't like the sight of blood,' suggested Alexander.

He watched while Hugh began to clean the wound, pulling gently to release the material which had been driven into the broken flesh. He winced. 'Tell me how you and Wilmot got on. It takes my mind off it.'

'We put the bodies in the carriage, poled up the horses again and I took them up to the top of the hill and pointed them on their way. They seemed to know where they were going.'

'And then?'

'Then Wilmot and I put away the dog cart, put the cob back in the stall, removed the cob's leather shoes and the sacking tied round the wheels. Everything is now back as it was, so far as we could see. One of us will have to have a word with Simmonds tomorrow — Collins's disappearance will need explaining, and I daresay rumours will fly, but we should avoid the worst.'

Alexander nodded. 'Collins will be the obvious culprit. He and Bob will be assumed to have fled.' He winced as Hugh eased a piece of material out of the wound.

'Sorry. I'm being as gentle as I can.'

'I've had worse.'

'So I see.' Hugh glanced down at the other scars. 'Things can get lively on the North-west Frontier, then?'

Alexander laughed. 'Just a skirmish or two.' He watched as Hugh carefully cleaned the wound and then bound it with strips of Alexander's shirt. 'Hugh, when you've finished, we'd better get that stuff back in the safe.'

'With one arm?'

'I'll hand you things. Come on, we haven't much time to lose. And somebody ought to throw a bucket of water over the blood on the cobblestones.' He got up, ignoring his brother's expostulations and went through to the butler's pantry. He peered in at Timson.

'Good. Fast asleep.' He closed the door to Timson's cubby hole.

Hugh picked up the lamp which was still burning on the side table and brought it over, whistling as he saw the stuff spread out on the table. 'I'd no idea there was so much.' He gestured towards the gold plates. 'Where on earth did they come from? I don't believe I've ever seen them.'

'Papa was given them by some maharajah or other.'

They worked swiftly. Hugh felt in his pockets and put back the jewellery and spoons that had fallen out of Bob's jacket.

'Alethea should check these,' he said.

Alexander picked up a key, looked at it and quietly handed it to Hugh. 'You'd better get rid of this.'

Hugh put it in his pocket. After a moment he said, 'I wanted to kill myself yesterday. The only thing that stopped me was the thought that the shock might kill Papa.' He gave a harsh laugh and added, 'I daresay it'd have been a relief, too.'

'When I was little,' replied Alexander, 'Mama used to tell me stories of what you and Freddy used to get up to. Mostly you. Perhaps you don't remember, but there was the story of you and the mongoose that I made her tell me over and over again. She loved you, Hugh. Sometimes she would cry when she talked about you.'

There was a pause, then Hugh said, 'Why are you telling me this?'

'I thought you needed to know.'

Another pause. 'You must hate me, Alex.'

Alexander shook his head. 'I know that I had Mama when you didn't, but I never replaced you in her heart — nor would I have wanted to.'

Hugh turned to put the remaining things back in the safe and spent some time carefully locking it. Once, he wiped his eyes on his sleeve. When he turned round he said,

'You'd better go to bed. Wilmot insisted on waiting up for you. I'll bring the doctor up when he comes. Go on, Alex. I can deal with the cobblestones.'

'Very well.' Alexander left the room, pausing only to pat Hugh briefly on the shoulder.

Up in his room, Wilmot was waiting.

'There's not much point in putting on my nightshirt when the doctor's coming,' said Alexander. 'Still, you can help me off with my boots and fetch me my dressing-gown.' He considered Wilmot. He was pale, much paler than usual. 'There's some brandy on the tray over there, you look as though you could do with it. The cut will heal, but you may well have nightmares.'

Wilmot shuddered eloquently. 'I was quaking like a blancmange. Ooh, I was terrified.'

Alexander smiled. 'You'd be mad not to be frightened.'

'How did you do it, sir? Kill Bob. I mean, with your right arm useless.'

'I threw the knife with my left. I used to practise with both hands just for fun as a boy. Frankly, I was surprised that I still had the skill.'

'Do you mind having killed him?' asked Wilmot curiously.

'Your life is worth more than his, I shan't

278

lose too much sleep over it.' Alexander stretched out his other leg so that Wilmot could pull off the other boot. 'There, that's better. Pour us both a drink, Wilmot. You did very well this evening and I owe you my thanks. I trust my brother acknowledged your help?'

'He told me I wasn't such a muff after all,' said Wilmot drily.

★　★　★

From the moment Decima realized that Alexander was wounded, all thoughts of Georgie vanished, she was concerned only with Alexander. Now, when she reached the laundry, she realized that something serious had happened. Catherine was sitting on a laundry basket with her arm around the weeping girl.

Georgie was sobbing into Catherine's shoulder, every now and then pausing to mop her eyes or nose with a sodden towel.

'Has she . . . ?' Decima asked in a low voice. Catherine nodded.

'I thought we was going to get married!' wailed Georgie.

'Did he ask you?' Decima was surprised.

Another wail from Georgie. Catherine mouthed a 'No'.

'Does she know he's dead?' Decima mouthed back.

Catherine shook her head.

Georgie's sobs gradually quietened. She hiccuped once or twice and blew her nose more firmly. 'I wanted him so bad, but now I feel dirty,' she whispered. 'After, he said it was just a bit of fun and then he gagged me and tied me up. But it wasn't just a bit of fun for me. It was my first time and I thought he was serious.'

Catherine patted her.

'I know that now I'm ruined and I'll lose my job and where will I go?'

Catherine soothed her. 'Whatever happens, I'm sure Mr Peverell will see that you're all right. Now I'll get you some laudanum and then take you up to bed.'

'I can't go back up there,' Georgie pleaded. She didn't want to be the butt of speculation by the other maids. They were unkind enough as it was.

'No, dear, of course not. There's a truckle bed in my room. You can sleep there and I can keep an eye on you.' She turned to Decima. 'Stay with her a minute while I sort things out.'

Catherine left the room and Decima took her place on the laundry basket. Georgie began to cry again.

'I thought he loved me, Miss. He could be ever so nice and he said he didn't mind about my birthmark. Only, all the time . . . all he wanted was just one thing and when it was over, he didn't want to know.' She twisted the towel in her hands. 'I'll never trust men again. Never.'

Decima sighed.

'You've always said as you never wanted to get married, Miss, and you was right. Men just lie and deceive you. They don't care what happens to you afterwards. They've had their fun and that's it. My mum used to say that falling in love always brought heartbreak — and I didn't believe her. You're lucky, Miss. You haven't made that mistake.'

Decima said nothing. She was beginning to suspect that Georgie's warning was already too late.

★ ★ ★

It was an understood thing that Sir George never appeared at the breakfast-table. His valet brought him his breakfast on a tray and, on the Wednesday morning, he was big with news. There had been an attempted robbery the previous night, Sir George was told. Nothing had been stolen, but Mr Alexander had taken a shot in the arm. Georgie and

Timson were badly shaken and Mrs Wimborne was hurt.

'Is my son all right?' demanded Sir George, pushing away the tray.

'Yes, sir. It was only a flesh wound and Dr Lane has already seen it.'

'And Mrs Wimborne?'

'A nasty bang on the head, Sir George, but she should recover in a week or so.'

'Do you know what happened?'

'No, sir. Mr Alexander says you're not to worry. Everything is sorted out.'

Sir George grunted. 'He would.'

'It seems that Mrs Thompson, Miss Wells and Mr Hugh were all woken last night — they're at the back of the house, if you remember. They went down to help.'

Sir George was slightly reassured; he was ashamed of his first thought, which was that Hugh had been involved in the robbery.

'Any idea who did it?'

'It seems that Collins and that Bob were involved, sir. They've both vanished.'

When Sir George came down for luncheon, the situation in the dining-room was intriguing. Alexander had his arm bandaged and in a sling. Hugh sat next to him and cut up his food so that he could manage it. Sir George watched this development in some amazement. The two brothers usually sat as far apart an possible and Hugh rarely lost an opportunity to make some gibe at Alexander's expense. Whatever else had happened last night, things had plainly improved there.

Catherine and Decima were looking tired. Decima had lost her appetite as well. She had taken only the smallest portion of the food on the side table and was picking at it. She scarcely spoke. When questioned, she said that her part had been only a minor one, not worth mentioning. She didn't look at Alexander.

Frederick and Alethea were indignant at not being woken up.

'I run this house,' declared Alethea. 'I should have been woken. It should not have been left to our guests to deal with things.'

'I am sorry,' said Hugh, with unwonted consideration. 'It is my fault. You mustn't blame the others.'

'I have seen Mrs Wimborne this morning,' went on Alethea, still seriously put out and determined to take back the household reins. 'She is recovering as well as can be expected. Poor Timson is more shaken than he likes to admit. I've told him to rest quietly today. I think he should go and stay with his sister for a few days, if she's free to have him.'

Timson's sister was married to a corn chandler and lived in Guildford.

'An excellent idea,' said Hugh placatingly. 'Would you like me to go and see her?'

'No, thank you, Hugh. Freddy will go.'

Hugh glanced at Alexander, who raised an eyebrow as if to say, what did you expect?

'How is Wilmot, Alex?' asked Catherine.

'Fine. Just a graze,' said Alexander shortly. He and Wilmot had discussed it last night and decided that the exact nature of his injury should remain a secret.

Sir George's attention swung back to Alexander. He was leaning over and saying something to Hugh, who laughed. Sir George's anxiety lightened. He had long been worried by Hugh's animosity towards his younger brother. Perhaps it was worth a shot in the arm to have them on better terms.

But there was something else. From time to time Alexander glanced at Decima. Once she caught his eye, flushed and looked away.

Hm, thought Sir George. Interesting.

★ ★ ★

As the luncheon party broke up, Hugh said quietly, 'Alex, I haven't had a chance yet to clean your pistols. I left them locked up in the gun-room. I didn't want the housemaids getting the wrong idea.'

'No, indeed. There will be enough speculation as it is. Shall we go there? We need to make sure that our stories tally, in any case.'

They discussed things while Hugh cleaned the pistols.

'It seems a pity,' remarked Alexander, 'but I think your fine shot had better remain between us. You'll have to be content with my grateful thanks.'

'Naturally, I had to save my little brother,' said Hugh. He cleared his throat and added, 'Pass that oil, would you?'

Alexander grinned and passed the oil. In some ways he found the English incomprehensible. Whenever he parted from Sikander, Kamal and Kumar, they embraced and kissed each other soundly on both cheeks. Hugh's reticence amused him.

'Hugh, how badly are you dipped?'

Hugh wiped his fingers carefully on a rag before saying, 'About five thousand pounds. Just over half of that is gaming debts.'

'Do you enjoy gambling?' He remembered seeing Hugh's white face as he stumbled out of the Great Subscription Room at White's.

'Sometimes I hate it,' Hugh confessed, 'but when I'm blue devilled, that's what I find myself doing. When I lose I hate myself, so I go back to the gaming table and so it goes on.'

'Have you ever thought of going to Italy?' Alexander asked next. He saw Hugh's eyes flash and added, 'I don't mean escaping from your creditors. Just for a visit. Plenty of wonderful old buildings. I have an Italian friend I met in Madras, Claudio Sottile, I could give you an introduction. You'd like him, I think. He's interested in architecture, like you, and he lives in Rome.'

'What would I do in Italy?' asked Hugh, holding the pistol up and squinting down the barrel.

'Enjoy yourself, draw, meet people who are interested in the same things as you . . . '

Hugh said nothing. He seemed absorbed in checking the barrel of the pistol.

'I can't,' he said at last.

'Why not?'

'If I leave the country without settling up, particularly my gaming debts, I'll be drummed out of White's. I could never show my face in London again. You should know that.'

'I'll settle your confounded debts.'

Hugh put down the pistol. 'I don't want your damned charity.'

'For God's sake, Hugh! You saved my life last night. That's worth a few thousand to me, even if it isn't to you. I'm fed up with your hostility. I want a proper brother.'

'You've got Freddy.'

'I want both my brothers.'

Hugh fiddled with the pistol for a moment or two longer then, reluctantly, he looked at Alexander. 'God knows if I'm worth it, but thank you.' He held out his hand.

Alexander grasped it in his left one. 'Good. That's settled then. Now, about last night, we'd better discuss what we're going to say to Papa. He's bound to ask for a full account.'

⋆   ⋆   ⋆

Decima was reminded over the next day or so of Alexander saying that there were other ways of communicating apart from language — and it seemed that, suddenly, she was aware of all of them. The more she thought about that episode in the kitchen, the less she understood herself. She must have given him the idea that she was quite without modesty. Why on earth had she touched him like that? God knows she'd had it dinned into her that no lady ever behaved in such a way. Whatever must he think of her?

Secondly, she noticed that Alethea was watching her. She didn't think that Alethea knew about Edmund and Peter's visit, but she suspected something and she was a lady who felt it her right to know exactly what was going on in her household.

She had suggested several times that Decima might like to accompany her to the nursery to see her daughters. 'They do so enjoy playing with you, Miss Wells,' she'd said.

Decima had been happy to oblige. Now she wondered whether it wasn't to keep her away from Alexander. When she overheard Alethea saying to her husband, 'A charming girl, Miss Wells, but hardly out of the top drawer,' she was sure of it. Alethea did not want her for a sister-in-law.

Now Decima thought about it, Alethea must have been concerned for some time and she, Decima, had been blind to it. How had Alethea got the idea that something might be going on when Decima herself had been completely ignorant?

Then she realized that Hugh might be trying to fix his interest with her. The idea seemed preposterous, but he often came over to engage her in conversation and the questions he asked her now seemed more significant than she'd previously thought. For example, how did she feel about the prospect of living on a smaller income than she had been used to?

At the time, Decima had not read anything particular into it. She had responded in all innocence that she looked forward to the challenge of living on a reduced income.

Hugh had smiled and said, 'You're a splendid woman, Miss Wells. I really admire you.'

She had laughed and thought no more about it.

Now she was worried. The last thing she wanted was to have encouraged Mr Hugh. Perhaps she was mistaken? But he continued to come over and talk to her and she couldn't help thinking that she might be right.

Time was running out for her. In less than two weeks' time, she would be twenty-one and in control of her little fortune. She would have to find that honeysuckle-covered cottage and have a cat for company, even though it was no longer what she wanted. Alexander was not for her. His family would not approve and how could he be interested in herself, with her round face and shorn-off hair? What he needed was a girl of impeccable breeding and a marriage which would squash any rumours surrounding his birth. To marry a girl of little beauty, with an unfeminine interest in metaphysical speculation, an uncertain portion and parvenu into the bargain would be social disaster.

She discovered that, whilst she could still do without most men, there was one and only one in the whole world for whom she would happily give up everything. And she had turned him down.

What else could she have done? She must have been right to block her brothers' attempts at blackmail. Such a marriage would be doomed to failure. Whatever happened in the future, and Decima held out very little hope for herself, Alexander must be free to walk out of her life without feeling any regret at his action in saving her.

★   ★   ★

Sir George had cross-questioned his two younger sons about the attempted robbery and both their stories sounded suspiciously well-rehearsed. He hadn't believed a word of them, but it was obvious that neither son had any intention of saying more. The contents of the safe were intact. Alexander and Hugh remained on good terms. Perhaps he should stop worrying.

'Papa, could you lend me the travelling carriage for a few days?' asked Alexander on Wednesday afternoon.

'You're not going to take Catherine and the boy away, are you?'

'No. I hope you'll look after them while I'm away. Hugh and I have business in London and I need to see about Miss Wells's money. Her birthday is soon, and I want it all sorted out.'

'Very well. You're to take the under-coachman, mind. Hugh can be reckless and I don't want you driving with that arm.'

'I thought we'd go up tomorrow. We expect to be back by Monday. You'll make sure Miss Wells is all right, won't you? Alethea can be bossy.'

'I've nothing against Miss Wells,' replied Sir George. 'She is very pretty-behaved, but I agree with Alethea that she's hardly out of the top drawer and her family are a distinct disadvantage.'

Alexander's lips tightened. He said nothing.

'All right, my boy. I see I'm not to interfere,' said Sir George wryly. He was well aware that Alexander trod his own path. He always had. And he was financially independent of his father. 'May I ask how you and Hugh have come to this new understanding? Was it he who shot you, by any chance?'

'Good God, no!'

'Perhaps I should have let him study his damned buildings. Now it looks as though the boy wants to go the same way. God knows where they get it from.'

'You should be grateful, Papa. My friend Bertie Camborne's cousin was forbidden to study art and is now involved in smuggling! Architecture might not be your cup of tea, but at least it's respectable — and legal.'

Sir George grunted. If Alexander was not the son of his loins, he was certainly a son after his own heart. Best not interfere.

'I must thank you for bringing Catherine and the boy,' he said next. 'I like Catherine. She's not at all like her mother, but she's a sensible woman and young James is an engaging child. I'm thinking of asking them to stay permanently. Catherine's a good soul and I'd like the boy under my eye.'

Alexander frowned. 'You won't always be here, Papa. What will happen to Catherine then? She's had enough of being the poor relation. For God's sake, discuss it with Freddy and Alethea first.'

Sir George raised his eyebrows at the preposterous idea of discussing any arrangements he chose to make. He didn't say so to his son, but if Catherine stayed at Peverell Park, then Miss Wells would have no option but to return to her family. Maybe that would be no bad thing.

* * *

It was Alethea who mentioned to Decima that Alexander and Hugh were going up to

London. Decima realized that she was being closely watched and managed to say that of course Mr Peverell must have business affairs which could not be kept waiting. Privately, she greeted the news with dismay. The party at Peverell Park was breaking up, and what would become of her? Where would she go?

'I'm sorry you heard the news from my sister-in-law,' said Alexander in the drawing-room, after dinner, 'I had hoped to tell you myself.'

Decima, acutely aware of Alethea's eagle eye, said brightly, 'Shall you be gone long?'

'Only till Monday. Apart from various bits of business which need my attention, I hope to go and see Liza.'

Decima forgot her caution. She turned to him impulsively, 'I have been wondering how they were all getting on. You will ask about Joey won't you? He promised that he'd work hard at school.'

'I shall. I'm not sure that I should mention Bob, however.'

'Poor Bob,' said Decima with a sigh, 'I cannot help feeling that in other circumstances he might have made something of himself.'

'You're magnanimous.'

Decima shook her head. 'Maybe I am wrong. It was not my throat he threatened to cut, after all.' She glanced round. Alethea was talking to Catherine on the other side of the room, but she was looking across from time to time.

'And Georgie,' continued Alexander. 'What should I do about her? Should I pack her off to the nearest magdalen or point her in the direction of the Foundling Hospital if she finds herself in a certain condition?'

Decima looked up sharply, 'You can't do that!' she cried. It would be too cruel.'

'Mrs Peverell would say, if she knew, that an unchaste maid is a danger to the virtue of the entire household.'

'Humbug!' retorted Decima. 'Georgie was deceived in Bob. She is not the first girl to be bamboozled by a man and she won't be the last. She's a good girl, Mr Peverell. She needs compassion, not moral outrage.'

'I thought you'd say that.'

'Then why ask me?'

'For the pleasure of talking to you.'

Decima looked at him uncertainly.

'I'm sorry if I embarrassed you by my behaviour in the kitchen. I enjoyed it myself and I hoped that you would too.' He moved his hand along the sofa and took hold of hers. 'I wasn't mistaken; you did, didn't you?'

'Mr Peverell, remember where we are! It's really . . . I cannot . . . oh dear . . . '

Alexander was amused by her confusion. 'Never mind, I shall be back by Monday at the latest. We can have this conversation again — in a more private place.'

'It would be most improper in any place!' declared Decima virtuously.

Alexander laughed, gave her hand a squeeze and let it go.

★ ★ ★

That night, as Decima was preparing for bed, there was a tap at the door and an agitated Catherine came in. Her nightcap was tied askew underneath her ear and her dressing-gown awkwardly thrown on.

'Catherine, is anything wrong? Come and sit down.' She patted the bed invitingly.

'Oh, my dear Decima, I hardly know whether I am on my head or my heels. Sir George has asked me, and James, of course, to live here!'

'You mean at Peverell Park?'

'Yes, as a permanent guest. I hope I expressed my sense of obligation but all the same . . . ' Her voice trailed away.

'I would be seriously worried about Mrs Peverell's bossiness!'

'She has been most kind. But to be always a guest . . . '

'What does Alex . . . I mean, Mr Peverell, say?'

'I haven't had a chance to talk to him.' Catherine's finger traced the pattern on the eiderdown. 'It is rather awkward. Alex has hinted that he is thinking of getting married. Of course, at his age, it is right and proper and I wouldn't wish to stand in his way and, naturally, his bride will want to run her own household, so how can I possibly discuss it with him, when I know he will say that we may always command a home with him?'

'I didn't realize that Mr Peverell was about to get married,' said Decima in a voice which sounded most unlike her own. She cleared her throat firmly and added, 'All the same. I think you should talk to him. Do you really want to stay here, Catherine?'

'It's not a question of what I want!' cried Catherine, wringing her hands. 'I have my duty towards Sir George to think of.'

'Humbug! What about his duty towards you, pray?'

It took time to calm Catherine down but, in the end, she acknowledged that she was entitled to think about it. 'Wouldn't you be more comfortable in a cottage on the estate?' Decima asked. 'You must say what you want.'

Catherine shuddered, 'I shouldn't dare.'

Long after Catherine had gone back to her

room, Decima sat in the dark, her knees drawn up, and contemplated a straitened future. She had a stark choice: either she returned to her father — if he would have her — or to one of her brothers; or she found her cottage, with or without the honeysuckle and cat.

A few weeks ago, the cottage was the height of her ambition, now it seemed like a dead end, a closed future.

Decima did not think that Alexander was set on seduction, like Bob, but nor did she think that he had more in mind than a summer flirtation. She had seen her brothers in action before their prudent marriages. She had overheard discussions that females were not normally meant to hear: bets about women and their degrees of availability. Alexander was an extremely attractive man, none knew it better than herself. She did not want to be on a list of his conquests.

10

Hugh and Alexander left the following morning and Janey, Clara and Frederica stood on the steps outside the house to wave them off. Decima watched the carriage disappear down the drive from an upstairs window and tried not to feel as if all the light had gone out of her life.

She stood there for some time. The little girls came back inside and scampered past her going up to their nursery. A gardener's boy came round to rake the gravel. He had barely started before he stopped, touched his cap and stood to one side. Alethea's landaulet came round from the stables and Alethea ·herself, in a smart carriage dress and carrying a small fringed parasol, climbed up and was driven off.

It was all perfectly innocent. Mrs Peverell often went out to pay calls, Decima reminded herself. Then she thought; but calls are always paid in the afternoon. Why is she going out now, it is not yet eleven o'clock? Somewhere, at the back of her mind, a warning flickered.

It wasn't until luncheon that she learned the reason for the call.

'We are expecting guests to dinner this evening,' Alethea announced. 'I have invited Mr and Mrs Wells.' She turned to Decima. 'I felt it was only courteous as you are our guest. They are so anxious to see you.'

'Isn't that a little hasty, my dear?' asked Frederick. 'Why not wait until Hugh and Alex are back?'

Sir George understood all too well what Alethea was doing. She had seen the danger of Alex becoming too interested in Miss Wells and was determined to scotch it. She might well succeed, too. Sir George had made his own views perfectly plain to his son, but, looking at Miss Wells's suddenly pale face, he rather regretted it. Dammit, she was a plucky wench. If Alex turned out to want her, he wouldn't interfere — and Alethea should not either. Not that that would stop her, of course.

'You are very silent, Miss Wells,' observed Alethea. 'Are you not delighted?'

'I do not like my brother and sister-in-law,' said Decima frankly.

Catherine closed her eyes for one agonized moment.

'Come, come, Miss Wells,' put in Frederick. 'My wife has your best interests at heart.' He saw, with alarm, that Alethea was looking furious.

Decima stared stonily at him.

Sir George raised an eyebrow at Decima's alarming capacity for speaking the truth. 'Your life will be more comfortable if you are on speaking terms with your family,' he informed her. Still, he couldn't blame her. He hadn't cared for Mr and Mrs Wells himself.

'I always treat them with civility,' declared Decima. She put up her chin and surveyed the company defiantly. Mrs Peverell was planning something, she was sure of it. She would fight for her liberty if she had to. But what could she do if Sir George turned her out? She had nowhere to go but her brother's.

Alethea decided that she had seen enough of Miss Wells's free manners for one day and turned the conversation.

Catherine sat quietly throughout the meal. This was how it would be if she lived here with just Sir George and Mr and Mrs Peverell, she thought. It was civil, certainly, but without Hugh and Alex it was not comfortable. Whatever else could be said about Hugh, he didn't tolerate pomposity in his elder brother, nor did he object to arguing with his father. Alexander, of course, had always welcomed her entering into the conversation.

This lunch-time seemed to be nothing but statements from Frederick supporting his wife, Alethea being bossy and Sir George barking out his opinions.

Catherine was normally timid and the very idea of going against Sir George's wishes made her quake in her shoes, but her mind was suddenly made up.

As the company rose after grace, she touched Sir George lightly on the arm and said, 'Might I have a word with you, if it is convenient, Sir George?'

'Of course, my dear. Give me your arm into the library.'

They moved through and Catherine settled him in his chair, fetched his footstool and placed his medicine within reach and then said, 'I have been thinking of your kind offer of a home, Sir George. I do not think that I can accept.'

The bushy eyebrows shot up. 'And why not?'

'I am devoted to my new-found family,' Catherine went on earnestly, twisting her hands in her lap, 'but to live here, as a guest . . . I do not expect you to understand, but James and I need a home of our own.'

'I daresay it's Alethea putting you all on edge. I shall tell her that you are to be treated as my daughter.'

What good would that do? thought Catherine, despairingly. Daughters could be mere family drudges — witness poor Decima.

'I want James brought up under my eye,' stated Sir George. 'I like the boy and will do what I can for him. No, I want you both here.'

'We could have a cottage on the estate,' Catherine suggested. That way, she thought, as well as being mistress of her own home, she could at least offer Decima a refuge if she needed it.

'If you're thinking of asking Miss Wells to stay, no,' said Sir George, reading her mind. 'I like the girl, but I am concerned that Alex may be becoming too attached to her. Frankly, my dear, she's not out of the top drawer.'

'Nor am I,' said Catherine quietly. She had never been able to stand up for herself, but she could fight for others. Decima was being most unfairly treated. If she, Catherine, could offer her a home, she would.

Sir George considered her more in amazement than in anger. Whatever had happened to the dull mouse-like creature who had arrived not two weeks ago? He was well aware that if she turned down his offer, then she could return to Golden Square — and Miss Wells with her. Damn her.

'Oh, go away, woman,' he said testily. 'I shall think about it.'

Catherine rose, curtseyed and left the room.

★ ★ ★

Georgie was subdued since the events of Tuesday night. She was still sleeping on a truckle bed in Catherine's room and each night Catherine heard her sobbing. Only time would tell whether there were any unpleasant consequences of her escapade and, in the meantime, she had to endure the curiosity of the servants.

On Thursday evening she came in to do Decima's hair and to help her dress.

'How was Mrs Wimborne?' asked Decima. She knew that Georgie had been dreading seeing her.

'She gave me a real scold, Miss. I said how sorry I was, though she doesn't know that . . . but she's forgiven me. Said I was a foolish chit and should be ashamed of myself.'

Decima smiled. It sounded as though things were not too bad there, thank goodness. Poor Georgie had enough to cope with without the housekeeper's enmity.

'I wish we was back in Golden Square, Miss,' confided Georgie. 'This house is ever so grand, I know, but I don't feel comfortable here. They're so stiff downstairs — and as for that Mamzelle Céline . . . ' She raised her eyes to Heaven expressively.

'I'm sure you'll be going home soon,' said Decima. Why should they stay longer?

'What about you, Miss?'

'I don't know about me,' sighed Decima.

What was Edmund after, she asked herself for the twentieth time? Surely he wasn't planning to take her back to Little Haldon Hall? Mrs Wells would certainly not want her and she was long past the age when she could be confined to the nursery.

Or should she be asking, what did Mrs Peverell want?

Georgie arranged her hair carefully and helped her on with her sage-green evening dress.

'Lovely, Miss. It brings out the colour of your eyes. It's a good colour for you. Wilmot's ever so clever about that.'

Outside the stable clock faintly struck the quarter-hour.

'Quarter past six.' Decima found that her throat was dry and butterflies in her stomach were making her feel sick with nerves. 'Where is my fan? I must go. Thank you, Georgie.'

As she went downstairs, she decided that she must be a model of propriety. No unfeminine phrases must pass her lips.

304

However provoking Edmund and her sister-in-law were — and she expected the worst — she must not retaliate.

The family was assembled in the drawing-room and Decima took her place beside Catherine and prepared to be submissive. She suddenly remembered how playing goody-two-shoes used to annoy Timothy; she was oppressively well-behaved in inverted commas, as it were, and, whilst it never failed to infuriate him, there was nothing he could complain about.

A carriage was heard on the gravel outside. She could hear William opening the door and then voices. In a few moments, William announced, 'Mr and Mrs Wells.' Alethea surged forward.

Decima saw at once that her brother and sister-in-law were on their best behaviour. Plainly, some bargain had been struck with Mrs Peverell: the Wellses would be accepted socially by the Peverells — at a price. What that price was, Decima didn't know, but for the moment all was affability.

'Decima,' Mrs Wells offered a cheek.

'Mrs Wells! How delightful this is!' Decima kissed it enthusiastically enough to remove some of her sister-in-law's *papier poudré*. 'Edmund! I've been *so* looking forward to this.' She offered her own cheek, then turned and gave Alethea a brilliant smile.

Sir George, watching appreciatively, thought, *the little baggage*.

Mrs Wells was disconcerted. She had prepared a few phrases of reproof if Decima should utter something which required censure. She did not know how to counter girlish eagerness.

Then Sir George said, 'You may not have met my daughter, Mrs Thompson.' He introduced Catherine.

Mrs Wells barely touched Catherine's fingers before withdrawing her own. Whatever was Sir George about? Surely his love-child should be kept out of the way? There was no mention of this Mrs Thompson being part of the bargain when she had spoken with Mrs Peverell that morning. She had no intention of being fobbed off with any second-class acquaintance.

The gong sounded and the company prepared to go down to the dining-room. Sir George offered Mrs Wells his arm and Edmund gallantly escorted Alethea. The shortage of men meant that Decima was sitting between Catherine and Edmund who was, naturally, on Alethea's right. She was grateful for Catherine's supportive presence.

Decima was largely silent during the first course. Edmund was talking to his hostess and Sir George, who was sitting on Catherine's other side, was occupied with Mrs Wells. Catherine and Decima occasionally exchanged small smiles, but said little.

When the first course was removed, Edmund turned to his sister.

'I trust you have been enjoying your little sojourn here, Decima?'

'Everybody has been most kind,' returned Decima. 'Mrs Peverell kindly lent me a riding habit and I have been learning to ride.' Edmund did not approve of females riding, she knew.

Edmund compressed his lips.

'How are my nephews and nieces?' asked Decima brightly. 'Anna-Maria must be quite grown-up by now.'

'Seventeen. She will be coming out next year.'

'How delightful. Shall you be taking a house in London for the Season?'

The conversation continued, if not exactly flowing, then at least moving. Decima thought she was doing rather well.

Then Edmund said, 'You do not ask after Papa. Have you no interest in his health?'

Decima put down her knife and fork and clasped her hands together. 'Papa! How is the dear man?'

Things were rapidly turning sour.

Across the table, Mrs Wells was saying, 'I shall be bringing my elder daughter out next season. Did you come out, Mrs Thompson?' She knew perfectly well that she had not and was determined to put Catherine in her place. Mrs Peverell should see that she would not tolerate being forced to be civil to Sir George's by-blow.

'No, Mrs Wells,' said Catherine quietly. 'I married young and have led a very retired life.'

'Do you have daughters?'

'No, just the one son.'

'Ah yes, I have seen him in church,' said Mrs Wells dismissively. 'A poor crippled boy.'

Decima was outraged. 'Mrs Thompson's son is turning out to be a real scholar,' she informed Edmund in a clear voice. 'The governess, Miss Price, is most impressed by him.'

Catherine smiled at her gratefully.

Sir George, listening, admired the way she defended Catherine and James. He thought, I like her. Her family are appalling, but she's a spirited filly. He would have a word with Alethea, tell her not to interfere. She'd been left in his charge and here she'd stay.

'My dear Decima! A twopenny-ha'penny governess can hardly be a judge of intelligence!' said Edmund good-humouredly. 'Though I am sure that she must be a most respectable female,' he added, bowing towards Alethea.

Alethea exchanged a glance with her husband. These people were quite impossible! The sooner Miss Wells went back to them the better. She would fulfil her side of the bargain and invite them to a couple of evening receptions and then quietly drop the acquaintance.

When the ladies retired to the drawing-room, Catherine whispered to Decima, 'You know, my dear, I don't think you need worry about being posted off to your brother and sister-in-law before your birthday. I could see that Sir George was pleased with you. I do not think he will turn you out before you attain your majority.'

Decima felt better, but not for long. Mrs Wells finished a whispered conversation with Alethea and came over.

'Come, Decima, you and I must have a comfortable *coze*.' She drew Decima towards a sofa and they sat down. 'Now, we have discussed things with Mrs Peverell, and it has all been decided. You will come to us and next year I shall take you to London when I bring out Anna-Maria. If you manage to find yourself an eligible *parti*, I daresay you will not find your Papa unreasonable.

'Edmund and I have decided to let bygones be bygones.'

'May I ask what is Mrs Peverell's part of the bargain?' Decima tried in vain to control the quaver in her voice. Her stomach seemed to be doing the most unpleasant things and she wanted either to scream or to burst into tears.

Mrs Wells shot Decima a frosty look and said, 'We understand each other.'

Decima could see it. In return for removing a guest whose presence had become embarrassing, Mrs Peverell would support Mrs Wells's social pretensions. Doubtless, she could count on being able to display Mrs Peverell's calling card and an invitation or two.

The only question in Decima's mind was how soon would Edmund claim her? Once she was in his house she doubted whether he would allow her to go. The little cottage seemed to be receding fast. If only she could leave it until after her birthday then legally she would be a free woman. Before that she was under her father's control and she was sure he had liaised with Edmund about this.

Her only hope was to appeal to Sir George. If he would allow her to stay the few days until her birthday, then she had a chance. She would speak to him in the morning.

'We shall come for you on Saturday,' said Mrs Wells.

Alexander and Hugh reached London in good time. The carriage dropped Hugh off at his lodgings and Alexander arranged to meet him there later. The groom then drove Alexander and Wilmot to Golden Square before making his way to the stables.

Nobody had been expecting them and there was a chorus of exclamations. Mrs Salter reeled up from the kitchen, smelling heavily of gin.

'There'sh not a morshel in the housh!' she informed him.

'I shall be dining out,' said Alexander, noting that now Decima was no longer there, the cook had reverted to type. 'Meg, see that the beds are made up, please. Is Upshawe here?'

Alexander went into his study to catch up with various outstanding bits of business. They then discussed how best to settle his brother's debts.

'I don't want to sell my railway shares! What about the Bernstein account?'

'He will owe you just over three thousand at the end of this month, sir.'

'I have a thousand or so with Coutts and about fifteen hundred with N.M. Rothschild.

That should do it. I shall know more by tomorrow.'

Having sorted out what he could, he left the house and took a cab to Hugh's rooms in Piccadilly. Hugh was going through his desk when Alexander was shown up by Mrs Hart. Piles of bills lay on the table.

'You don't have to go through them with me if you'd rather not,' said Alexander, seeing his brother's shame-faced look. 'I brought a case with me, just throw the lot in, I'll deal with it with Upshawe. For God's sake, Hugh, don't look at me like that! I'm not here to humiliate you.'

Hugh dropped his eyes. 'I feel like I did when Papa raked me over the coals for getting into debt at Oxford.'

'Who am I to tell you how to run your life?'

'You're the first member of the family not to do so, then,' retorted Hugh. 'Oh, sit down, Alex, we might as well go through them. I suppose I should know exactly how I stand.'

Interesting what a man will spend his money on, thought Alexander. Apart from his gaming debts, Hugh owed money to his tailor, his bootmaker, the local stables and a staggering amount to his wine merchant. The only bills that were paid promptly were to his bookseller.

'Books on architecture,' said Hugh, following his gaze. 'If I can't pay I don't buy. It would be wrong, somehow. My bookseller has to live. Anyway, I enjoy my conversations with him.'

Alexander made no comment. Hugh's debts seemed a result of frustration with his life. Where something was important to him, he was scrupulous about paying.

At last they had finished.

'Four thousand eight hundred and forty-seven pounds, sixteen shillings and ninepence,' said Alexander, who had been making notes in shorthand. 'Are you sure that's it?'

'Oh yes. I never paid the blasted things, but I always kept the bills.'

'That's an advance on Bertie Camborne, who always throws his on the fire,' remarked Alexander. 'Right, Upshawe and I will deal with these so that nobody will know that it isn't you who pays them. That's that, then.' He put the neat piles of bills in the leather case and locked it. 'Come and have dinner with me at the club. I'd ask you home, but Mrs Salter's cooking isn't all it might be.'

There were a number of eyebrows raised in White's at the sight of the two Peverells dining together. Hugh was feeling both buoyant and guilty. His hatred had vanished. It had disappeared the moment he had decided to shoot down Springer rather than his brother.

They didn't discuss either Hugh's debts or how he should reform his life. Instead, they discussed Catherine and James.

'Papa wants Catherine and James to stay at Peverell,' said Alexander.

'Good God! Poor Catherine!' exclaimed Hugh. 'She'd never be allowed to call her life her own.'

'I know. I must talk to her about it when I get back. I'm worried she might accept out of a sense of duty. The problem is that she's really most unsuited to acting as my housekeeper, though James, bless him, is happy at Golden Square.'

'I really like Catherine,' said Hugh. 'I didn't think I would, but I do. Perhaps I should offer them both a home. What do you think? I could help James, and Catherine could keep an eye on me.'

'I don't know what you get up to, Hugh, but you couldn't bring back any bits of muslin if Catherine and James were with you!'

'I can't bring any bits of muslin back with Mrs Hart as landlady!' retorted Hugh. 'If I want anything of that sort I go to a place I know in King Street. Is Catherine very straight-laced?'

'You should have heard her scolding Miss Wells for mentioning the word 'petticoats' in my hearing! But she turns a blind eye where necessary.'

'You mean that if you're out all night, she doesn't scold you?'

'Something like that.'

'I need a woman to keep me on the straight and narrow,' continued Hugh. 'Perhaps I'll ask the delectable Decima to marry me.' He shot Alexander a mischievous glance.

'Don't you dare!'

'Ah!' said Hugh. 'It's like that, is it? I did wonder.' He tilted back his chair and regarded his brother with satisfaction.

Alexander, his colour heightened, poured himself another glass of wine and drank it without replying.

Oh well, thought Hugh, I'm too old for her and I daresay I'm too set in my ways. I should probably make a damnable husband. But there was something that Alex ought to know.

'Did you realize that Alethea was planning to visit Mr and Mrs Wells this morning? I overheard her ordering the landaulet to be brought round just before we left.'

Alexander looked up, suddenly alert.

★   ★   ★

315

On Friday morning, the day after the dinner party, Georgie appeared with Decima's morning chocolate, looking grave. Decima had not slept well and she yawned as she sat up and tugged at her pillow so that she could lean against it.

'What is it, Georgie?'

'Oh, Miss, it's Sir George! He had a turn in the night and the doctor's come and there's such a to-do, you can't think!'

'W . . . will he live?' Decima's heart sank. She knew it was selfish of her, but she couldn't help thinking of her own hopes of appealing to him. She could not possibly trouble a sick, possibly dying, man with her request. In the circumstances, the only thing a guest could do was leave as quickly as possible.

'His valet says that he's rallying, but it's early days.'

'Have Mr Hugh and Mr Alexander been sent for?' asked Decima, clutching at straws.

'No, Miss. Mrs Peverell says not to. She hopes Sir George will be better in a day or so.' Georgie looked at Decima's pale face and added, 'Though I think she should have told them no matter what. It ain't her business to keep them in the dark.'

Decima thought that Alethea probably wanted to keep them out of the way until *she* was safely gone.

'I'm surprised that Mr Peverell agrees,' she couldn't help observing. 'Surely his brothers have a right to decide for themselves whether they will return or not.'

'He wouldn't dare do otherwise, Miss,' said Georgie, and giggled. 'He's one as lives under the cat's paw, as the saying is.'

Decima smiled, but it was with an effort.

The household at Peverell Park was subdued that day. Sir George kept to his room. Georgie busied herself with Decima's packing and Catherine hovered about miserably; she, too, did not know where she would be living. Eventually she urged Decima to come outside for a short walk and they wandered down to the lake-side.

'I can't stay here,' whispered Catherine, though there was nobody else within ear-shot. 'Mrs Peverell is very kind, I'm sure, but she is so very sure of herself. I feel quite *crushed*.'

'Mr Alexander will be back on Monday,' Decima reminded her with a sigh. She herself would be in Little Haldon House, scarcely five miles away, yet it might as well be in another country. She gazed out across the lake to the island where they had sat up in the willow tree and talked. It seemed like the land of lost content.

'I shan't forget you, Decima,' promised

Catherine. 'If I can offer you a home, I will.'

Decima kissed her cheek. 'Thank you.' It was the only hope she had to cling to.

Luncheon was a quiet affair. Catherine and Decima said very little. Alethea spoke with determined affability, but every now and then she threw out a little reminder to Decima.

'We shall miss you, Miss Wells, but in Sir George's present state of health, I do not know when we shall see you again.'

Decima felt too dispirited to reply. She excused herself and said that she had packing to do.

When she had left the room, Frederick said, 'I do not like this getting rid of Miss Wells, Alethea. My father will not be pleased, nor, I am sure, will Alex when he returns.'

Alethea glanced at Catherine, who was studying her plate, and said, 'Miss Wells can hardly stay here with your father so ill. She is a pretty-behaved girl, but she is no relation of ours. It is all for the best that she goes. I'm sure Mrs Thompson agrees with me.'

'No I don't.' Catherine spoke quietly. 'Alex trusted Sir George to look after her here. He knows what she has put up with from her family.'

'Sir George may not be with us for much longer. How awkward would her position be then! She could hardly stay in a house of mourning!'

'I agree with Catherine,' said Frederick unexpectedly. 'It's going to look as though Miss Wells is hustled out of the house the moment Alex's back is turned.'

Two spots of colour flew in Alethea's cheeks. 'Frederick! Are your wits gone begging? If Miss Wells stays, Alex will end up by offering for her! Now do you see why she must go?'

'Why shouldn't he offer for her? Charming girl.'

'I only want what is best for the family!' cried Alethea. 'I am very fond of Alex, but thanks to your odious brother Hugh, he has to contend with the most wounding aspersions on his legitimacy. The last thing he needs is a wife without background, connections or fortune. It would be a disaster for him!'

* * *

By mutual consent, Hugh and Alexander left the club after dinner on Thursday night and went back to Hugh's rooms. They talked into the small hours. They had, as Hugh observed, a lot of ground to cover, some of it difficult. At last, as his brother talked painfully and jerkily, Alexander began to understand Hugh's misery at being parted so cruelly from his mother and the depths of his hatred for himself, the usurper.

They shared a bottle of brandy and sat by the light of a single candle and, if there were tears as well as talk, the darkness hid them. There was much to say and many years of estrangement to undo.

'You know, Alex, there must be at least a sporting chance that you're a Peverell, after all,' said Hugh at one point.

Alexander shrugged. 'I asked Sikander when I was about thirteen and he told me. 'The *memsahib* needed comforting' was how he put it.' He stared down into his brandy glass and added, 'I think the worst moment was after he died last year. I knew he was failing and went to see him a month or so before. The next time I went, his sons, Kamal and Kumar, came down from the village to tell me he had died. They wouldn't let me see his wife, Meera, who was almost like another mother to me. I'd played with Kamal and Kumar all my life, Hugh. I loved them. They were my brothers and suddenly they treated me like a stranger.

'We sat on a rock just outside the village and they were very polite, but I knew it was the end. I could never go again.' Alexander couldn't go on. He sunk his face in his hands and muttered, 'Oh, hell.'

Hugh sighed, 'I wish we'd talked years ago, I've made a lot of trouble for you. I'm sorry.'

'It doesn't matter. Frankly, I don't care what people think. I decided long ago that I was who I was. If I live up to my own standards of what an honourable man should be, then the rest of the world can go hang.'

'Maybe you're right.' Hugh stood up, wandered over to the window and peered down into the gas-lit street outside. A lonely horse and cab stood in the cab stand near the Egyptian Hall. He yawned suddenly. 'All this emotion is exhausting.'

Alexander rose. 'I ought to be getting back. Wilmot insists on waiting up for me.' He picked up the leather case with the bills. 'I'm seeing Upshawe at ten. Come round at about midday — if you can rise at so ungodly an hour — and you can sign things where necessary.'

'Here,' said Hugh, 'your arm. Let me carry that.' He took the case and motioned Alexander to go down the stairs. A lamp was burning on the landing.

Alexander hailed the cab, gave his brother a brief hug, took the case and climbed in.

Hugh waved him off and went back to his rooms. He felt both extraordinarily tired and yet strangely exhilarated, as if he were emerging from a chrysalis. Eventually, he pinched out his candle, went to bed and slept deeply and dreamlessly.

★ ★ ★

Alexander woke early the following morning. He lay in bed and thought about the events of the previous evening. He couldn't wave some magic wand and put Hugh's life right, only Hugh could do that, but he hoped that his brother would now be happier. Perhaps if Catherine and James went to live with him, they would give his life the ballast it sorely needed.

At ten o'clock Upshawe came and they dealt with Hugh's affairs. When Hugh arrived there were letters for him to sign and then it was done. Alexander gave his brother lunch — Mrs Salter having sobered up — and then Hugh went off and Alexander spent the rest of the day out of the house. He met his brother again in the evening for dinner at White's.

'You're looking worn out,' said Hugh with concern. 'Your arm troubling you?'

'It's all right. I'm worried about Miss Wells. I can't help feeling that something's wrong.'

'Why don't we go back to Peverell

322

tomorrow?' said Hugh reasonably. 'My carriage is there in any case, and I want to talk to Catherine and James. I'm serious about offering them a home: I know they live with you, but if you're going to marry . . .'

'She may not have me.' She'd already turned him down once.

★ ★ ★

Decima went to bed on Friday night feeling utterly dejected. Her fighting spirit seemed to have vanished. She even burst into tears all over Catherine when she popped in to say goodnight.

'At least I've had one month of happiness,' she sobbed. 'Oh, Catherine, it's like going back into prison. It would be easier to bear if I'd never known what life could be like outside!' What price the giraffes, she thought bitterly.

Catherine tried to soothe her. 'James and I will come and see you,' she promised.

Decima shook her head. 'Mrs Peverell will never lend you her landaulet and how else could you get there?'

'I shall ask Sir George,' said Catherine bravely, but she thought that Decima might well be right. She hadn't mentioned Alethea's angry words in the dining-room, but if Mrs

Peverell wanted the connection dropped, it would be very difficult to sustain it. And having met Mr and Mrs Wells, she doubted whether Decima would ever get her cottage.

Her future looked bleak indeed.

* * *

Alexander and Hugh's journey back to Peverell Park on Saturday was uneventful.

'I feel as if I've been away for weeks,' remarked Hugh. A whole lifetime seemed to have passed since he left.

'I know the feeling.'

They turned into the Peverell drive immediately after two other vehicles. The first was a smart black barouche with a lot of gold leaf decoration and the other a gig. Hugh leaned out of the window to look.

'I don't recognize the barouche,' he said, pulling his head back in, 'but the gig is Dr Lane's.'

They looked at each other.

'Papa?' said Alexander.

Hugh leaned out again and shouted to the coachman, 'I want a word with the gig!'

The carriage gathered speed and soon the gig was alongside.

'Lane, what's up? Is it my father?'

'He had a turn on Thursday night, Mr

Hugh. He's holding his own and may well rally.'

'Why the devil wasn't I told?'

'Mrs Peverell didn't want to bother you or Mr Alexander, sir.'

Hugh pulled his head inside. 'Did you hear that?' Alexander nodded. 'Oh God, it's all my fault. All this anxiety over the robbery . . . '

'There *was* no robbery, Hugh. He told me, before we left, that our better understanding had lifted a load of worry from his mind, so don't blame yourself. He's an ill man in any case.'

Hugh said cynically, 'I dare say Alethea has taken the opportunity to get rid of Miss Wells. If that's not the Wells's barouche in front, I'm a Dutchman.'

Alexander pulled down his window sash and leaned out in his turn. 'You're right. I recognize it. This could get interesting.'

'If you can squash Alethea's insufferable organizing of everybody's life, you'll have my full support. It's intolerable.'

Their carriage drew to a halt just as Edmund and his wife were being greeted at the door by Alethea and Frederick. Hugh ignored Frederick's start at seeing him, pushed past and ran up the stairs towards his father's bedroom. Alexander climbed out more slowly.

'Alex!' exclaimed Alethea, trying to hide her confusion. 'We weren't expecting — '

'So I see,' said Alexander coldly. 'Where is Miss Wells?'

Edmund strutted forward. 'Miss Wells will shortly be where she ought to be . . . '

Alexander ignored him. His eye moved past Edmund to the stairs. Catherine and Decima were coming down, Decima with her pelisse and bonnet already on. She looked pale and drawn and did not at first see Alexander in the group clustered around the front door.

Alexander pushed Frederick to one side, strode across the hall, grabbed hold of Decima's wrist with his good hand and propelled her towards the library.

'Mr Peverell!' exclaimed Edmund. 'Unhand my sister!'

Alexander took no notice. He elbowed open the library door, pulled Decima inside, shut it and they heard the click as the lock turned.

'Decima, take off that bonnet and pelisse. You're not going anywhere.'

Decima meekly did as she was told.

There was a hammering on the door. 'Open the door at once!'

'He is *furious*!' said Decima, awed.

'Good. Ignore him. Decima, my sweetest girl, if I'd thought for one minute that this would have happened, I'd never have left you.'

Decima looked at him. Happiness and relief flooded over her.

'Do you know what I want?'

Decima thought of Georgie alone with Bob. She shook her head, suddenly uncertain. Alexander reached inside his pocket, took out a folded piece of paper and handed it to her. She opened it.

'But . . . this is a marriage licence.'

'I want to marry you, Decima, as soon as possible. I know you've turned me down once, but . . . ?'

Decima looked up. 'Surely you didn't want me to accept you?' She was still feeling bemused at the speed of events.

'No, but the moment you turned me down I realized that it was the one thing I wanted.' He smiled and added ruefully, 'Such is the perversity of human nature.'

'Do you love me?' Decima asked anxiously. 'Or is this just chivalry?'

'I love you very much.'

Decima gave a sigh of relief. 'Oh, Alex, I'm *desperately* in love with you!'

The banging on the door reached a furious crescendo and then stopped. Alexander and Decima, locked in each other's arms, noticed neither the knocking nor its cessation.

Upstairs in Sir George's room, Hugh was sitting by his father's bed telling him of his reconciliation with Alexander.

'Are you sure all this hasn't tired you, Papa?' he asked eventually.

'Everything tires me nowadays,' said Sir George good-humouredly. 'You've been a damned fool about Alex, Hugh, but you've had a rough time of it. I hadn't realized and I suppose I should have. For what it's worth, I'm sorry.' Hugh looks different, he thought. Younger and more open. 'If you want to offer Catherine and James a home, I shan't stand in your way. I hoped they'd stay here, but Catherine isn't happy about it. Can't blame her. Alethea can be very trying.'

'And Miss Wells?' asked Hugh. 'Alex seems determined to marry her.'

'Let them be happy. Alex can cope with her appalling family, not I.'

'He has brought a licence with him,' added Hugh.

Sir George gave a crack of laughter which turned into a cough. Hugh held a glass of water to his lips.

'He doesn't waste time.' They both stopped to listen to the shouting and banging downstairs. 'Go and see what's going on, dear boy. And bring Alex and the girl up here. They can have my blessing.'

Hugh gave his father's hand a pat and left the room.

He came downstairs to find Frederick, Alethea and Mr and Mrs Wells exchanging icily civil platitudes in the hall. Every now and then Edmund cast a fulminating glance at the unresponsive library door. Catherine was sitting alone on one of the hall chairs. Hugh went across.

'Where are Alex and Miss Wells?'

Catherine nodded towards the library.

'Alex has a marriage licence with him. He loves her, he told me.'

'Oh, I'm so glad!'

'Things will be uncomfortable here, Catherine. I gather you don't want to stay. Not that I blame you.' He gestured towards Alethea.

'Oh, Hugh! If you'd seen how unhappy poor Decima has been — and all through Mrs Peverell's meddling.'

'Why don't you and James come to me?' continued Hugh. 'You can keep me in order and you know I like James. The only thing is, I'm nothing like as rich as Alex. You'll have to be content with a couple of maids. It would mean a lot more work for you.'

'I shouldn't mind that,' said Catherine gratefully. 'James will be so pleased. He has resented being kept up in the nursery, though he likes the girls.'

There was the sound of a key turning. The library door opened and Alex and Decima came out hand in hand.

'Congratulate me!' Alexander was smiling. 'Decima has promised to be my wife.'

Edmund stepped forward. 'I warn you, sir, that Decima will not have a penny beyond the miserable pittance her aunt left her.'

'I wouldn't take a penny from Mr Wells under any circumstances,' retorted Alexander. 'I have a licence in my pocket and I shall marry Decima on Monday. If you have any foolish intention of forbidding it, I shall marry her on her twenty-first birthday.'

Mrs Wells was thinking quickly. Edmund could be so mulish, but this match would surely help dear Anna-Maria's come-out? The Peverells would be connections of theirs! 'Pray do not be over-hasty, Mr Wells. Let us go home now and meet again, perhaps after church tomorrow. I am sure we shall all be better for a little rational reflection.' She shot him the sort of look that wives give their husbands when they have something particular to communicate.

Edmund, after a couple of harumphs, did as he was told.

When they had gone, Alexander turned to

330

Alethea and said, 'Alethea, you have some explaining to do. Your treatment of Decima has been outrageous.'

Alethea drew herself up. 'I meant it for the best,' she said indignantly. 'I only have your welfare in mind.'

'You had no right to hide father's condition from us,' added Hugh. 'It is not up to you to decide for us what we do. I agree with Alex about your treatment of Miss Wells. She is Papa's guest, not yours.'

'I did tell you, my dear,' put in Frederick, 'but you would insist.'

Alethea gave a wail and ran upstairs. Moments later they heard her bedroom door slam.

'Oh dear, should I go up to her?' worried Catherine.

'No,' said Hugh. 'Freddy, you're her husband, it's your job. Tell her to mind her own business.'

He watched while Frederick went slowly upstairs. When he was out of sight he turned round and said, 'That's cleared the decks.' He kissed Decima and wished her happy and clapped Alexander on the shoulder. 'I promised Papa I'd tell him what is going on. Why don't we all go up? He'll be waiting.'

MERMAID'S GROUND

Alice Marlow

It's been five years since Kate Williams' beloved husband died, leaving her with two young children to raise. Now she's built a good life in one of Wiltshire's prettiest villages, and she has her dream job, as gardener at Moxham Court. For the last year, Kate has had a lover, roguishly attractive Justin Spencer, but he won't commit to more than a night here and there. When she takes in a male lodger, Jem, Kate's secretly hoping his presence will provoke a jealous reaction in Justin. What she hasn't reckoned on is exactly how attractive Jem will turn out to be.

HOT POPPIES

Reggie Nadelson

A murder in New York's diamond district. A dead Chinese girl with a photograph in her pocket. A plastic bag of irradiated heroin in an empty apartment. A fire in a Chinatown sweatshop. The worst blizzard in New York's history. These events conspire to bring ex-cop Artie Cohen out of retirement and back into the obsessive world of murder and politics that nearly killed him. The terrifying plot uncoils first in New York — in Artie's own back yard — then in Hong Kong, where everything — and everyone — is for sale.

Elizabeth Hawksley has been writing since she was six: As a child she had free run of her grandfather's well-stocked nineteenth-century library and, as a result, has always felt at home in that century. She has a grown-up son and daughter and lives in London.